ALL THE LIES THEY TOLD
A NOVEL

ROBIN MAHLE

Published by HARP House Publishing
August 2025 (1st edition)

ISBN-13: 979-8-9869595-7-3 (paperback)

ISBN-13: 979-8-9869595-8-0 (hardcover)

AUTHOR'S NOTE

While this novel is entirely a work of fiction, the heart of it was inspired by the real and tragic loss of two young girls: Liberty German and Abigail Williams, of Delphi, Indiana, in 2017. Their story, and the strength shown by their families and community in the aftermath, stayed with me and ultimately became the emotional seed for the two fictional girls in this book.

This is not a retelling of their lives or the events surrounding their deaths. Rather, it is a story that explores the ripple effects of trauma, secrecy, and guilt.

Out of deep respect for Libby and Abby, and their loved ones, I want to be clear that the characters and events in this novel are entirely imagined. But the inspiration they sparked was very real.

TRIGGER WARNING

This novel contains brief, non-graphic references to sexual assault. Reader discretion is advised.

PROLOGUE

No one would ever find out. That was what we told ourselves. It echoed like a mantra, worn thin by repetition. I wanted to believe it. I needed to. No one *could* ever know. But we knew.

The secret lingered in the air between us, snaking its way into our stolen glances. And when we thought about saying too much, when the guilt became overwhelming, we turned away from each other. Avoidance became the norm.

We grew distant. No more barbeques. No more playdates. A passing wave of our hands as we were leaving our homes, and a polite nod when we'd drop off the kids at school—that's what we'd become. They felt it too—the girls, especially. They used to be best friends, but now only see each other out of necessity or circumstance.

Weeks, months, even years, passed. We all continued with our lives as if nothing had ever happened—as if we hadn't made a horrific mistake.

Time dulls the pain and erases the guilt. That's what I wanted to believe. It was a notion I'd clung to for dear life in my desperate search for absolution these past five years. That if I just kept moving forward, the past would loosen its grip on all of us. But I know now that we should have left this place. Because I've come to realize that time doesn't work that way. It doesn't heal all wounds; it only masks them. All the while, it waits for the opportune moment to rip off that mask, exposing the raw, gaping wound to the stinging air.

We're monsters. We're liars. We're everything we taught our children not to be. Would they forgive us if they knew what we'd done? How our selfish acts became central to our lives and dictated our every move? I could probably answer that question just by looking into my daughter's eyes—if she were here.

1

LEXI

She loves to make me wait. Skye Metcalf—former best friend, now popular cheerleader who's embarrassed to be seen with me. If it weren't for our parents, she wouldn't. But since we're next-door neighbors, and neither of us can drive yet, this is our sentence—walking home from school together. Safety in numbers and all that.

Skye's actions are always deliberate. In fact, everything she does is a performance, like right now. She's standing by the water fountain near the bleachers, her back turned to me as if I'm invisible. Her fingers twist a strand of her chestnut-brown hair, and she's laughing at something someone said—a laugh that sounds rehearsed. She knows I'm here. I know she knows. But still, she doesn't look my way. Not once.

The bleachers are empty, and I could sit down, but I don't want to be here longer than necessary. The metal seats glint in the afternoon sun, heat radiating off them in waves. There's a spot on the right side that looks shady enough, but I don't want to make myself comfortable. All I want is to leave.

Instead, I'll hang out here, near the field where her squad

practices, staring at her, waiting for her to see me. I cross my arms over my chest and lean back against the chain-link fence behind me. It rattles with a hollow metallic sound that barely registers over the hum of cicadas and the occasional thud of a basketball from the nearby court. My eyes stay locked on her, willing her to turn around.

I could be waiting a while. Skye never sees me, even when I'm right next to her. It's funny how someone can be so close yet feel so far away—like they exist on some other plane entirely. That's how it is with Skye—has been since the sixth grade when she got boobs, and I didn't. Even when we're standing side by side, her eyes seem to slide right past me as if I'm nothing more than background noise to whatever song is playing in her head.

The sun shines on me, its heat stinging my skin. Beads of sweat form at my temples and slide down the back of my neck, soaking the collar of my shirt. I swipe a hand across my forehead and glance at Skye again—still no acknowledgment, not even a flicker of recognition.

"Hey," I finally call out, my voice cutting through the sound of all the pretty girls' chatter. It's louder than I intended, and for a second, I think she might actually respond. Her head tilts slightly as if she heard something faintly interesting in the distance, but then she turns back to her conversation without so much as a second glance.

My jaw tightens, frustration bubbling beneath the surface. "Skye!" This time, my voice is sharper, more forceful. I'm done waiting.

She finally turns around, slow and deliberate, like she's annoyed at being interrupted mid-performance. Her eyes meet mine. Her expression is unreadable except for the smallest hint of enjoyment tugging at one corner of her mouth.

"Oh," she says, almost dismissively. "You're still here?"

Still here? "Yeah," I reply, forcing a casual shrug, my fists clenched. "I can't leave without you."

She smirks at that—a small, knowing curve of her lips that makes me feel both seen and unseen all at once—and turns back to her friends without another word.

And just like that, I'm invisible again.

We're in the same year, live on the same street. We had been as close as sisters once, but that was a long time ago. We're no longer friends, and neither are our parents.

I move closer to the football field, ready to yank Skye by her perfect hair, because if we don't leave soon, it'll be dark before we get home. Then we'll have to call one of our moms to pick us up, and it'll just get ugly from there because it'll almost certainly be my mom.

"Come on, Skye, let's go," I say. Finally, she rolls her eyes and picks up her gym bag. I scoff. Like I want to be here any more than she wants me to.

It takes another five minutes before she walks toward me, the tiny skirt of her cheerleading uniform swaying with each step. Her long, brown wavy hair shimmers in the sun. I don't want to admit that I'm jealous of her, so I pretend I'm not.

"We have to leave now, Skye," I insist. "I've been standing here for twenty minutes."

She rolls her eyes again. "Bruh, chill, would you? Don't you ever break the rules, Lexi?" She laughs—snorts more like. "I've known you most of my life, so I already know the answer to that."

Just as we're about to leave, I hear someone call her name.

"Skye?"

She stops and turns around. I walk ahead a few more steps, but then I'm forced to wait—again.

"Hey, Brendan," she says, wearing her perfect smile—the one she shows all the boys.

"Hey, the spring festival is next weekend," he says. "You want to go? A bunch of us are going on Friday night." Brendan pushes away his shoulder-length hair and then tucks his hands into the pockets of his baggy jeans.

"Yeah, of course," she replies.

"Skye, we have to go," I cut in.

An exaggerated sigh escapes her as if I'm the most annoying person on the planet. Whatever.

"I'd love to go." She places her hand on his broad chest.

"Great." He glances at me. "Hey, Lexi."

"Hey, Brendan." The fact that he knows my name should flatter me, but I recall him picking and eating a huge booger from his nose in fifth grade. So, I'm not flattered by anything that dork says. So what if he's hot now?

"I have to get home," Skye says to him. "See you tomorrow?"

"Yeah, see ya." He turns to leave.

"Can we go now?" I press.

"Fine. Whatever. Let's go," she replies. "I swear I can't wait to get my driver's license."

"That makes two of us," I say as we walk away from the school.

We're quiet for a while. Only the sound of our sneakers on the pavement and music coming from our AirPods fills the space between us. Sort of makes me miss the friendship we used to have.

Skye takes out her earbuds and glances up. "It's getting dark."

"Yeah, which is why I said we needed to go," I reply.

"We should cut through the woods. It'll save us time."

It's a route we've taken plenty of times before. We know those woods like the backs of our hands and used to play there as kids. All the kids played there. Swimming in the creek, building forts from fallen branches. That was back when none of us cared about the clothes we wore or what cars our parents drove.

"Yeah, I guess," I reply. "Do you have any bug spray? The mosquitoes will be bad."

"No, but we'll be fine." She turns to me. "Both our moms will be pissed if it's dark and we're not home."

"I know. We're almost at the cut-through, anyway."

Skye pats my shoulder. "See? It was meant to be, Lexi. You worry way too much."

I look at her, returning a half-smile. "Yeah, maybe." And in that moment, I'm reminded of how we used to be.

We reach the opening between the trees, where a footpath is carved into the forest floor. Years of people cutting through the woods to get to the other side of town left its mark. Right away, I hear the buzzing of mosquitoes as dusk arrives. It's not even summer yet, but it's been hot here lately. Combined with the April rains, the little vampires are out in full force at this time of day.

The tall white oaks that surround us nearly drown out what's left of the setting sun. The canopies loom overhead as we make our way down the path.

"I'm sorry for making you wait back at the field," Skye says.

I shrug, playing it off, but really, I'm happy to be acknowledged. "It's cool. I know you have competitions coming up and you need to practice."

"Yeah. So, what do you think of Brendan?" she presses. "He's super cute, right?"

"I guess."

She knits her brow. "You guess? Come on, Lexi, he's the hottest guy in school. And he's a senior. I mean, I should've asked him to drive us home tonight. I bet he would've."

"Maybe." I say nothing more because, somehow, we always talk about Skye and her friends, her cheerleading, and all the boys who fawn over her. She doesn't ask me what I'm doing. In fact, I can guarantee she won't ask me to go with them to the festival next Friday. No way will she want to be seen with me.

The deeper we get into the woods, the darker it becomes. "Oh, man. We need to hurry," I say.

"Yeah, okay," Skye replies, picking up her pace.

The snapping of a branch echoes behind us. I hesitate a moment and glance at Skye. From the look on her face, I know she heard it too. I peer over my shoulder but see nothing. "It's fine. Must've been a squirrel or something."

"Pretty loud for a squirrel." Skye holds her phone, scrolling through it as she walks. "What? Oh my God, I can't believe she posted this."

"Posted what?" I ask.

She clicks her tongue. "Nothing. Just Andrea being her usual self."

Another sound reaches us. Footsteps. My heart lurches, and I look at Skye. "Did you hear that?" I ask in a low tone.

"Yep." She's quiet. Worried. "Let's just hurry. We're almost home anyway."

I peer up, barely able to see the sky through the trees now. The footfalls continue, but I don't want to look back. I just want to get out of here. We say nothing more, we just walk faster.

The footsteps draw closer, louder. My heart is in my throat, and I look at Skye to see the fear in her gaze. Suddenly, nothing matters more than for us to get clear of these woods. Not school, not boys. Nothing.

"Girls?"

The word comes out throaty, spoken by a man. Skye and I trade glances, and we both know what we need to do.

Run.

2

MARA

She hasn't responded to my texts or returned my calls. I pull back the light floral curtain on our front window and peer out over the street again, expecting to see her walking up our driveway. Instead, all I see are blue shadows climbing higher, dimming the sun's final orange flare. Skye should've been home forty minutes ago. I swear, if she's with that Brendan again, I'll be giving her a piece of my mind.

It never fails. I rush home from work and start dinner before Garrett arrives. Meanwhile, Skye is hanging out with her friends or some boy instead of getting her little ass home when I tell her to. Honestly, I'm surprised Lexi hasn't gotten on her case. That girl is on time to a fault.

I turn off the stove and walk toward the living room. "Milo, honey, get off the games, would you?"

Milo is twelve, and his father and I refuse to let him sit in his room and play video games, so he has to come out to the living room to play. But as soon as Garrett gets home, it's time to turn them off.

"Why?" His whining gets pretty tiresome. "Dad's not here yet. Dinner's not even ready."

"Because I said so, all right?" I walk toward the front door. "I'm heading over to the Brewers. I'll be right back."

"Okay," he replies, still holding the gaming controller, shaking his too-long hair away from his eyes.

"Off, I said. You hear me? Turn it off."

He rolls his eyes. "Fine."

I press my lips together and walk out the door. The streetlights are already on. That kid better have a damn good reason for being this late, I swear to God.

I knock on the door to the Brewers' home. It opens, and Ashley Brewer stands on the other side. A ponytail holds back her red hair, making her slim facial features appear harsh. "Hey, Ashley. Is Lexi here by chance?"

"No. I just got home and texted her a little while ago. She hasn't replied." Ashley cocks her hip. "I'm guessing Skye isn't home yet either."

"Nope. Do you know if they had something going on after school today besides Skye's cheerleading practice?"

She shrugs. "Maybe practice ran late. Did you try the coach?"

"No, but that's a good idea," I say. "Still, I figured Lexi would've texted you or something."

"Come in. We'll figure this out." Ashley steps aside, closing the door behind me. The foyer stretches long. Family pictures, beaming with happiness, adorn the light gray walls. I don't enjoy seeing them happy. Ashley doesn't deserve to be happy.

We're not as close as we used to be—the four of us, Garrett and me, Ashley and Nate. When the girls were young, we did everything together. But that all changed a few years ago. Now, we hardly talk at all, we just offer the occasional wave when we catch each other outside.

"Smells great in here," I say as we walk into the kitchen. "What are you cooking?"

Ashley flicks off the gas stove, and I notice her figure. Slender, toned, freckles covering her arms. She's prettier than me. A little thinner, too. We're both in our thirties, but somehow, she just looks younger. Guess that's what happens when you get to stay home and focus on yourself all day. Not me. I don't get time for myself. I work and take care of two kids. Ashley? Who knows what the hell she does? Her husband owns a pharmacy, and her daughter is smart as a whip, never getting into trouble.

"Just pasta. Nothing special. It's Nate's favorite. Lexi—not so much."

I thumb back. "I just got dinner underway myself. Ran late with work and picked up a chicken. We'll see how well that goes over." I smile. "So, listen. Would you mind trying Lexi again? I can't get any response from Skye."

"Yeah, of course." Ashley picks up her phone and makes the call.

I can see she's waiting for an answer, and soon it becomes clear one isn't coming. I cross my arms. "Voicemail?"

She nods.

"Let me try again." I pull my phone from the pocket of my scrubs and press Skye's contact. It rings and rings before going to voicemail. "Damn it. She's still not answering either."

Ashley takes a deep breath. "Okay, now what? Should we go looking? Where's Milo? Is he home by himself?"

"He is. Garrett should be home in a few minutes. But I'll tell you, if Skye's not back by then, all hell's gonna break loose."

"I hear you." Ashley chuckles. "Well, look, how about I run out and see if I can track them down? They're probably still at the school. No point in both of us going. You have Milo to look after."

"Are you sure?" I ask, feeling somewhat guilty but grateful she acknowledged my circumstances.

"I'm sure." She places her hand on my shoulder. "Come on. I'll walk you out."

We head toward the door and step outside. Headlights capture my attention as Garrett pulls onto our driveway. "Shit. He's home."

"We'll walk over together and tell him I'm running out to pick up the girls, and that's why Skye isn't home yet," Ashley says. "I don't want her getting into any trouble. Not until we know for certain where she is."

"I hate lying to him," I reply, an intentional dig at our shared history. "But his work has been stressful lately. Maybe it's best not to set him off just yet."

I take the lead and walk back to my house with Ashley at my side. Garrett steps out of his Mercedes and regards us. He must've stopped at the gym after work, given his attire. Must be nice. "Hey, honey. Glad you're home," I say, moving in for a brief hug.

He gives me a peck on the cheek while keeping his gaze on our neighbor. "Hey, hon. "Hey, Ashley. What's going on?"

She glances at me, and I nod for her to continue.

"I was getting ready to pick up the girls. Seems they're running late this evening."

"Oh, I wish I'd known," he replies. "I could've swung by the school to get them."

Ashley swats her hand. "No problem. I don't mind. Nate won't be home for a little while longer, and I know Mara's making dinner for you guys now. Really, it's no problem."

He dons a smile. "Thanks, Ash. That's nice of you."

"Anytime."

"Okay, then," I interrupt. "We'd better let you get going. I appreciate it, Ashley. See you soon."

She walks across the yard and heads to her car. I look at Garrett as he keeps his sights fixed on her. "Let's go inside. I can feel myself getting eaten by the mosquitoes."

"Huh?" He looks at me. "Yeah, right. Better get inside."

3
ASHLEY

Nothing much happens here in Grant. Our small Idaho town has only one high school and two elementary schools. Both are on the other side of town. Lexi and Skye usually walk home together, refusing to take the bus that would drop them off only a block away from the house. They tell me it's embarrassing. That's all well and good until winter comes. I usually give in and take the girls to school while Mara picks them up.

Unless, of course, Mara is running late, which is often the case. I don't mind. Nurses work odd hours. Besides, I don't have a job—a fact Mara often holds over my head. There's more to it than that, so I let it slide, but it can only go so far.

I am irritated about neither girl picking up their phones, though. Lexi knows better. Skye's a bit of a wild child, but I stay out of it. She's not my daughter.

As I arrive at the high school, I notice the parking lot is almost empty. A few cars, likely belonging to janitorial staff or a teacher or two, are scattered around. I continue to drive toward the back of the school near the football field. I'm sure Lexi is sitting on the bleachers doing homework, while Skye practices her cheerleading. Although that doesn't explain why she's not answering her phone.

As I turn the corner, the field just ahead, I realize it's dark. The halogens—off. The staff wouldn't shut off the lights unless all the students were gone. Now I'm feeling less hopeful about finding them here. But I park and step out anyway, walking toward the bleachers. I hear no cheers, no music—only the sound of wind through the trees that line the back of the field.

"Lexi? Skye?" I call out. "Girls, are you here?"

There doesn't seem to be a soul around, and my nerves bundle in my gut. "Lexi? Skye?" I shout. Nevertheless, I get no answer. "All right. Where the hell are you two?" I snatch my phone from my purse and try Lexi again, my face growing hot with anger. "Girl, you better answer me."

The call goes to voicemail. I stare at my phone as if this was some mistake. Are the lines down? Do I have a signal out here? But the call went through. She just didn't pick up.

I scan the bleachers, walk around them, under them. I head to the concession stand. The bathrooms—they're already locked. "Okay. Okay," I assure myself. "Maybe they started walking home and their phone batteries died."

What are the odds that both of their phones are dead? Not good enough for me to take. I march back to my car, calling into the empty lot. "Lexi? Honey, are you here? Skye? Anyone?"

I'm answered by my own echo, and panic worms its way through me as I reach my car. My stomach clenches, my heart pounds. "Calm down. They're probably walking home."

I slip behind the wheel, taking a breath to relax. I turn the engine and head out of the school parking lot, toward the path they would take if they were walking home. For a moment, I consider calling Mara, but should I worry her now?

A text message arrives on my phone as I reach the school's

exit. "Lexi?" I say, praying it's from her. However, my optimism is short-lived when I swipe open the screen to see it's from Garrett.

All good? Do you have the girls yet?

I swear, he'll use any excuse to contact me. I saw the look in his eyes when I was with Mara earlier. But I type my reply anyway.

They aren't at the school. Gonna drive in the direction they would've walked. I'll keep you and Mara posted.

Okay, thanks.

That's all he replies. Never mind. Right now, I'm too busy to deal with him. My priority is finding the girls.

I'm out on the main road through town now. The local Albertson's grocery store is still open, but the hardware store next door to it is closed. It's coming up on 7 pm. The streetlights are on, and the sun has almost set. The few clouds in the sky absorb the remaining light, turning pink and purple.

With my windows rolled down, I call out to them again. "Lexi? Skye?" My car is crawling along, and I'm grateful no one is behind me. "Lexi?" As I peer down the road, the woods draw near. "Please don't tell me you girls took the shortcut."

It's a well-traveled path, but Lexi knows better than to go through the woods after dark. She wouldn't have made that decision, but Skye might have, knowing how pissed Mara would be if she wasn't home on time.

The turnout comes into view, so I pull over and roll to a stop. Pressing the button to lower my passenger window, I gaze out into the woods. It's too dark to see anything, so I shout out again, hoping for an answer this time. "Lexi? Skye?"

It's doubtful they'd hear me in there, so I'm left with only one choice—get out and check for myself. "Damn it." It's the last thing I want to do. Having grown up here, stories about these woods were plentiful. But they were just stories. Nothing has ever happened. Nevertheless, I'm reminded of how frightening these woods are at night.

With my phone in hand, its flashlight feature on, I step out of the car and head toward the footpath. For a moment, I stare at it. Narrow, only a couple of feet wide, surrounded by greenery. The ground is dry, and I see footprints. Several, in fact. Impossible to know who they belong to. But I stare at them, frozen, my feet refusing to move. It's the fear of not finding Lexi that cements me to this spot. She's the only thing that matters, but I will find her. And when I do, I'll ground that kid for years for putting me through this.

I eventually take a step. Then another. The air grows cooler the deeper I get. A light breeze rustles through the trees, and darkness settles around me. Mosquitoes whiz by my ears. I swat them away as if that alone will prevent them from leaving their mark on me.

"Lexi? Skye? Are you girls out here? It's Mom—Ashley. Lexi, honey, please answer me." That panic I'd felt when I left the school has tightened my gut to the point of inducing cramps. I'm feeling sick, but I press on.

I stop and try Lexi's phone again, but it goes straight to voicemail as if its power is off or the battery is dead. Either notion scares the hell out of me.

How much deeper do I go? Surely, they would've heard me by now if they were walking. Aiming my phone's light ahead, I see nothing but trees and the glowing eyes of a few woodland creatures. No sign of the houses on the other side yet. No lights anywhere else. It's just me out here.

My light sweeps down across the path, and a glint reflects off the ground. Is it a shard of glass or a piece of metal? Could be, but I investigate because whatever it is, it's out of place here.

Stepping toward the object, I squat low for a better look. "Oh my God." My breath hitches in my throat, and my head grows light. "Jesus." It's Lexi's phone. Do I pick it up, just to be sure it's hers? But I know it is. The cover is purple with pink hearts on it.

She'd spent hours picking it out at the mall a few months ago. It's hers.

Instinctively, or maybe because I'm terrified of what this could mean, I reach inside my purse for a tissue, then pick up the phone using it.

Standing again, my hand presses over my mouth, stifling the moans that threaten to claw from my throat. I try to stay calm, telling myself this could mean anything, knowing that's not true. Even going to lengths to preserve whatever evidence might be on her phone. Fingerprints. DNA. *Jesus.*

My gaze sweeps the area, scanning every inch around me. Where are they? I spin around once, twice, over and over, as if they might appear simply because I need them to.

But they don't.

They're not here.

They're gone.

4
NATE

I'm the last to leave the pharmacy, but that comes with the territory. I start by double-checking the safe. All the good drugs are in there, the ones addicts will kill for, which is why I make sure it's locked. I'm the only one with the code.

After closing out the register, I walk toward the front door to secure the deadbolts. The time is past 7 o'clock, and the other stores around here have already closed, except for the McDonald's on the corner.

As I'm locking the door, headlights draw near and shine in my eyes. "We're not open, pal. Sorry." But then the car parks out front, the lights turn off, and I recognize it immediately. "Ashley?"

She steps out of the car, and the look on her face sends my pulse racing. I hastily disengage the locks and open the door. "Ash, what's wrong? What are you doing here? I was just—"

"Lexi's gone," she says, cutting me off.

"What do you mean, she's gone?" You think you know how you'll react to hearing words like these. You might even think that people don't just blurt out that someone's gone. But they do. She did. And now, I'm not sure if I heard her at all.

Ashley grabs my arms, staring into my eyes. "Nate, she's gone. Skye, too. I can't find either of them. They didn't come home from school. I've been out driving, looking for them."

She's got a phone in her hand, holding it with a tissue. That's the first thing that scares me. Then I see that it's broken, and it takes only a moment to notice who it belongs to. My face drops, and I feel it draining of color. "Where did you find that?"

"In the woods. The cut-through the girls sometimes take." Ashley sets her worried gaze on me. "It's Lexi's phone, Nate. The girls—they're gone."

I rake my hand through my hair, feeling like I can't catch my breath. "Okay. Okay, just—just let me think for a minute." I pace a tight circle. "When was the last time you heard from Lexi?"

"Not since this morning when she left for school," Ashley replies. "Then, around six-thirty tonight, Mara came over to tell me Skye hadn't come home yet and asked if I knew anything. Of course, Lexi wasn't home either, so it wasn't hard to put it together. My God, what are we going to do? We have to tell them."

I nod, knowing that we need to tell the Metcalfs, but still believing there must be a logical answer. "And you're sure you checked the school? Everywhere?"

"Yes, of course I did," she replies. "Nate, I looked everywhere around the football field, the stands, the bathrooms." Tears run down her cheeks. Her lips tremble as she seems to search for words. "When I couldn't find them, I drove down their usual path home and something told me I'd better check the woods." She shrugs. "You know how they cut through all the time."

"Yeah, I know." I look at the phone again. "And that's when you found her phone. What about Skye's phone?"

Ashley shakes her head. "I didn't see it, but I also didn't walk all the way through. Nate, we have to tell them. We have to tell Mara and Garrett that we can't find Skye either. There's no time to waste. We need to get the cops out—everyone out looking for them before it gets too late."

I want to tell her to calm down, to not panic, but something tells me we're past that now. "Yeah, okay." I pull in a shaky breath. "I have to finish locking up. Go home. Go see the Metcalfs and tell them everything. I'll be five minutes behind you."

"What? No," she says. "We have to go now. Screw the store."

"Honey, I can't leave until I've secured everything. You know that. I could lose my license if I don't follow procedure."

"So you care more about your license than you do about our daughter?" she snaps back.

"That's not fair." I swallow my rising anger. "Look, this is getting us nowhere. Go. I'm almost finished, then I'll leave. If you want to wait until I get there—"

"Not a chance. I've wasted too much time already. We'll call the police." She turns away, hurrying to her car.

I watch her speed out of the parking lot. Reality sets in, pulling me down into a pool of despair. "I can't lose her. I can't lose my little girl."

Something finally launches me into action. Fear, I imagine. I hurry through the store, closing it down and shutting off the lights. Within minutes, I'm out the door and in my car.

My hands grip the steering wheel, worry coursing through me like nothing I've ever felt. Sometimes, I wish I was more like Ashley. God, how I wish I could summon even a fraction of her unwavering confidence, her ability to seize control when everything around us feels like it's falling apart. Her ability to take charge, to do the required things most people don't want or can't do...it's gotten us through past situations, and now she's already doing it again.

I press the ignition and roar out of the parking lot. Home is less than ten minutes away. Have the Metcalfs called any of Skye's friends? I didn't ask if Ashley called Lexi's friends, but then again, Lexi doesn't have many.

Our neighborhood is just ahead. I'm not sure how I got here, my mind going a million miles a minute, trying to think of where my daughter could be. When I pull onto our driveway, I see Ashley standing outside with Garrett and Mara. Even in the darkness, I can see the dread swirling around them. I jump out of my car, jogging toward them.

"Garrett, Mara, has anyone heard anything yet?" I ask, desperation tinging my voice.

Garrett shoves his hands into the pockets of his gym shorts. "No, nothing yet. We've all agreed we should contact the police."

"Will they do anything?" I ask. "They're only an hour or so late." I look at Ashley. "Have you tried getting into Lexi's phone?"

She scoffs. "As if she'd tell me the passcode."

I nod. "Well, then, maybe Garrett and I should take a drive around town. You two can make the call to the cops, and we can see if they're out there somewhere."

"Don't worry, Ash," Garrett says, grazing her upper arm with his fingers. "They're probably at a friend's house."

But even as the words leave his mouth, he doesn't believe them any more than any of us do. Our girls don't hang around in the same circles.

I put my arm around Ashley, pulling her close—an intentional gesture in present company.

"Let me run inside and get out of my gym clothes," Garrett says before turning to me. "Be ready in five?"

"Yeah."

I wonder for a moment if the other neighbors are peering through their windows, watching us. Do they see our panicked faces? Our concerned gazes? I look around, remembering when we all used to be friends. Then, new people started moving in. Old ones left. The kids got older, and there were fewer soccer games and volleyball matches. Everything began to change. Ashley changed, too.

5
SKYE

My head. *Jesus.* It feels like it's about to explode. I try opening my eyes, but that hurts too. All I feel is pain. "Hello?" I can't tell if I said that out loud. I manage to blink a little, and eventually, my eyes open, but everything's fuzzy. It's dark as shit, too.

I don't know where I am. I don't know what time it is. Where was I before this? The woods. Yeah. I remember now. We were walking home—me and Lexi.

Wait.

"Lexi?" I call out, but she doesn't answer. "Oh my God. Lexi, are you in here?" I reach out into the darkness, but something stops me. What the...? I'm chained to the wall, maybe the floor. I don't know, but I have to see if she's okay. "Lexi? Answer me. Where are you?"

"Here. I'm here."

Her voice sounds different. Gravelly, half-asleep. "Oh, thank God. Thank God. Are you okay?"

"I—I don't know. My head hurts. I can't see you, Skye. Where are you?"

"Over here." I yank my arms. "Holy shit. I'm chained up." Tears sting my dry eyes. "What's happening? Where are we?"

"I don't know. I'm scared," she replies, her voice cracking.

I hear her crying as the sound of more clinking echoes. "You're chained too, aren't you?"

"Yes," she whispers. "What is this place?"

"I wish I knew." I look around in the darkness, vague shapes forming, my mind trying to piece it all together. "It was that man. The man wearing the mask." My memories are all patchy. My head throbs harder and harder as I try to think. "We were taking the shortcut, right? Through the woods? And then, we heard that man."

"Who was he?" Lexi asks.

"I have no idea. That stupid mask he wore. Like a cheap Halloween costume. Did we try to run?"

"I think so," she says. "But he—I think he had that gun." She cries harder now.

"It's okay, Lexi. It's okay. We're going to get out of here, all right? Our parents must be out looking for us. They'll find us." I tell her this, but I can't even convince myself of it. "It's cold in here. There aren't any windows. It feels like I'm sitting on concrete. Where the hell are we?"

She doesn't answer. She just cries harder.

"Stop it, okay? Stop crying," I say, my voice raised. "Please, I can't take it. My head—my head is killing me. You have to stop, Lexi."

"I'm sorry," she breathes out. "I'm so scared."

"So am I, all right?" I lower my tone. "So am I."

A shaft of light cuts through the darkness. I squint at it as it lands on my face, practically blinding me. My heart races, making my brain feel like it's going to bust out of my skull at any moment.

"I thought I heard voices down here."

The light frames the man standing in it, casting his shadow across the floor. I can't make out his features, but he's tall.

"Who are you? Let us go," I say, trying to sound firm, but I don't think I'm succeeding.

He walks inside. His footfalls are heavy like he's wearing combat boots. And then a light flicks on. I blink hard, pain shooting through my head like an electric shock. But then I see Lexi. Oh my God. Do we both look that bad? *Jesus. Jesus.* God, if you're out there, you gotta help us, like, right now. "Lexi?" I breathe out.

She raises her gaze, and I'm certain the terror in her face matches mine. Like death is coming for us this very second and there isn't a damn thing we can do about it.

"Skye?" she says, her lips trembling. Cuts and scrapes. Dirt and grime. Blood covering her face, soaking her clothes. She's chained, just like me. Chained to a brick wall like this is some medieval prison.

"Let us go!" I yell, tugging on the chains. I look down and see myself. My skirt is torn and dirty. I'm missing a shoe. My legs are covered in blood, cuts and bruises, like we were dragged along the forest floor. I look at the man still disguised in shadow. "What do you want from us, you freak?"

He walks toward me, slow and deliberate, the heavy footfalls echoing in my ears. "What do I want from you?"

He squats down less than a foot in front of me, and it's the first time I've seen him this close. Only he's wearing that mask again. A creepy plastic doll's face with openings at the mouth and eyes. Bright yellow painted hair and pink circles of blush on the cheeks. It's too small for his face. His chin juts out from under it, and his cheeks bulge out of the sides. He's a big man, old, I think. Like at least thirty. I feel faint, sick to my stomach. I dart my gaze at Lexi, seeing tears stream down her face.

"Don't look at her. Look at me," he demands. "What I want is for you to keep your mouth shut and be quiet, or I'll put something in there to keep you quiet."

6

GARRETT

For most of my life, I've been the guy with the answers. The man who knew what he wanted out of life and demanded more from himself than anyone else. But I discovered who I truly was five years ago. And now, I feel impotent to do little more to find my daughter than to drive around town shouting her name, praying she answers.

Mara sees through me now. She has for a long time. She doesn't look at me the same as she used to. Tonight is proof of that. Instead of calling me on my way home from work to tell me about Skye, she goes to the Brewers' house—to Ashley—and tells her.

Maybe I'm making too much of it. After all, Mara thought she'd check with Ashley to see if she'd heard from her daughter.

And so here we are, the husbands, ready to head out, while the wives wait for the police to show up. I still don't know how much they'll do, but the girls are minors. And with Lexi's phone turning up, maybe they'll act quickly to search for them.

The pain of knowing my beautiful daughter is out there somewhere, hurt or worse, is unbearable. But I can't sit and do nothing, while the police do whatever it is they do in these situations. For Christ's sake, are they even equipped to handle this? It's not like we live in a big city with plenty of resources. This po-dunk town has, what, five cops?

I've changed out of my gym clothes. We're all inside our house now. Ashley and Nate. Mara and me. In our living room. Curtains closed. Lamps on. The TV muted. Our son is upstairs in his room, having no idea what's going on. It can't stay that way, but we're not ready to tell him what's happening when we aren't sure ourselves.

"We should head out, Nate," I say.

"I drove everywhere, Garrett," Ashley jumps in. "I walked halfway through the woods, which is where I found Lexi's phone. They were there, and now they're not. The police need to take this over."

I look at Nate. He's a mousy kind of guy. All right looking, I guess, but on the short side and thin, just like his hair. I shouldn't judge. Ashley loves him, or so she says. "Nate? What do you think, man? Shouldn't we do something? Our kids are out there."

"I know that, Garrett," he snaps back.

I watch as he looks at Ashley, checking to see if she's okay with this plan or if she wants him to stay put.

Pussy.

"I mean, it can't hurt, right?" Nate says to her. "The cops don't need all of us here. You were the one who found Lexi's phone."

Ashley sets her sights on me. Firm and unforgiving. Yeah, maybe I deserve it for egging Nate on. "No, it can't hurt," I say, keeping my eyes on her. "I have no idea how long it'll be before the police arrive, so it's better to do something rather than nothing."

Ashley turns to Mara. "What do you think?"

Mara's always been the type to defer to someone else. She

works, brings in decent money as a nurse at the local urgent care, but she's never been the take-charge type. Not like Ashley. I guess opposites really do attract. And I'll admit, I'm a little surprised Ash is even asking the question.

"Go," Mara insists. "Both of you. I can't stand this waiting either. At least you'll be out there trying to find them."

"Mara and I will start contacting the girls' friends," Ashley adds.

I nod and snatch my car keys from the side table. "Let's go, man. I'll drive." As I walk toward the door, I glance back at Mara. Her short brunette hair frames her soft features, highlighting brown eyes that can't hide how she really feels about me, despite her words. But one thing is certain, the look on her face right now tells me everything I need to know. *Find our daughter, or don't bother coming back.*

When we get in my car, I turn to Nate. "We should go to the woods where Ashley found the phone. There could be something else that points to where they went."

"Yeah, whatever you want to do," he replies, buckling his seat belt.

"Sure." I already see where this is going.

We head toward the cut-through—our side of it. It's pitch black out here. The streetlights are on the opposite side of the road, leaving the woods shrouded in night. I park alongside the footpath. "If we don't find anything here, I'm not sure where else to look."

"This is our best shot at figuring out what could've happened," Nate replies, stepping out of the car.

Easy for him to say when it was my idea. I join him as we stand outside the wooded clearing. It's a narrow path everyone in this town knows better than their own reflection. The weight of it all bears down on me. Like if I can't find my daughter in here, I won't find her anywhere. Then, what do I tell my wife?

"Come on. We can't just stand here." Nate steps in front of me.

He's the last one who'd ever take charge. I've experienced that first-hand. But none of us knows what we'd do when it comes to our kids. Maybe he'll surprise me. "Yeah, fine. Hang on. Let me get the flashlights."

I brought two MagLites, the type of flashlights police use. Bright enough to light up the whole goddam forest and better than any cell phone. As I open the rear passenger door, I grab them. "Here, take this. If anything is in there, we'll find it before the cops even get off their asses."

"I hope you're right," Nate replies, flicking on the light.

We walk into the woods, beams of light moving back and forth, taking cautious steps so we don't miss anything. I try to think of something other than the reason we're here. Other than the fact that our girls are missing.

"I'm still holding out hope that this is all just a misunderstanding," I say, as if I can somehow make this situation better.

Nate doesn't offer a reply. Instead, he keeps a steady pace through the darkness, through the trees, his flashlight aimed down, focused on finding his daughter. I look away, sensing the tension between us. We stopped being friends a long time ago. But now, we have to find a way to work together to get our kids back.

"Any luck?" I ask.

"No. You?"

I glance down in defeat. "No."

We walk in silence for several more moments before Nate presses his hand against a tree, leaning on it as if he's suddenly out of breath.

"Hey, man. You all right?"

He looks at me with eyes rimmed red. "No, I'm not all right. My daughter's gone. And so is yours." He laughs a sort of hollow, solemn laugh, looking up at the trees. "And yet all I can think about is how much I want to shove this goddam flashlight down your throat for fucking my wife."

I step back, feeling the color drain from my face. "Nate, man —that was—that was a long time ago, okay? We've got bigger problems right now, and we need to stay focused." I raise my hands in surrender. "Look, I can't change what happened—"

"Stop. Stop right there." He pulls back from the tree, returning his weight to his feet. "Forget it. Just forget it. I'm here for my daughter. And I'm not leaving until I find her."

We walk again, and I rest my hand on his shoulder.

"Get the hell off me, Garrett."

It's not my finest moment.

He pushes on, and I stay a couple of steps behind, not knowing what else to say. I didn't think I could feel worse than when we arrived, but I sure as hell do now. "Skye?" I call out. "Skye? Sweetheart, are you out here?"

"What the...?" Nate stops on a dime.

I almost slam into him. "What is it? What'd you find?"

He drops to his knees and breaks out into a sob. "Nate, what is it, man?" I ask, moving next to him. And as I look down, I see it too.

I can't breathe. I can't move. "Oh, God. Please, no."

Five feet in front of Nate lies a shattered phone.

"It's hers, isn't it?" he asks.

"Yeah," I whisper. "That's Skye's phone."

7

MARA

The police just arrived. They're sitting on my couch, talking to Ashley. I'm in the kitchen, getting everyone some water while Garrett and Nate are still out looking. We told the cops this, and they didn't seem happy about it. Screw them. It's not their kids, is it?

I have an ice bucket and place the bottles of water inside, carrying it back into the living room. "Help yourselves." After setting it down on the coffee table, I return to the side chair across from the sofa. Ashley is sitting on the chair next to me.

"Thank you, ma'am." Officer Dennis Blackwell grabs a bottle and drinks a quarter of it in one go. This doesn't appear to be new to him—talking to the parents of missing kids. His features appear hardened by age and experience. "So you've tried contacting the girls' friends, is that right?"

"Yes," Ashley replies. "I have. You called Skye's friends, right?"

Her question to me comes off like an accusation. She knows damn well I did. "Yeah, of course. The girls on her cheerleading squad saw her leave with Lexi at about six. They should've been home by six thirty. That was three hours ago."

Blackwell takes a few notes while his partner, Officer Rita Wiley, seems to look around for something. Her gaze finally lands on Lexi's phone on the coffee table.

"Did you charge this phone?" Her eyes shift between us. She's younger than Blackwell. More like my age. Athletic-looking, which I suppose in her line of work is a bonus.

"It's charged," Ashley replies. "I don't have Lexi's passcode, so it's not going to do you much good."

Wiley nods, making the bun in her hair pull her face taut. "We'll log it as evidence and see if Forensics can get into it."

"Yeah, okay," Ashley says.

Headlights flash in my front window, and I sit up tall to peer over the officers. "That's them. They're back." My heart jumps into my throat. I've never wanted anything more in my life than to see my girl right now. But if they'd found them, Garrett would've called. Still, I cling to hope.

The officers stand as I get up to open the front door. Ashley perches on the edge of the chair, her anticipation palpable. While I wait at the threshold, they step out of the car and walk toward me. Dread fills my chest when I see that they're alone. It's all I can do to keep my knees from buckling.

Garrett looks at me like he's just seen a dog get hit by a car, only this is far worse. And when I see the subtle shake of his head, tears fill my eyes. I grip the door handle to steady myself, then I feel a hand clutch around my waist to support me. It's Officer Blackwell.

"It's okay. I got you," he says. "Why don't I take you back to your chair?"

He glances at the two fathers before taking me back to have a seat. I feel Ashley's eyes on me, searching for answers, but I have none to give.

Garrett steps inside first, hands in his pockets, head down.

Then Nate enters, and I notice dirt on the knees of his pants like he'd been crawling around on the forest floor.

Blackwell returns to them, extending his hand. "I'm Officer Blackwell. Over there is my partner, Officer Wiley."

"Garrett Metcalf." He returns the greeting and then gestures to Nate.

Nate steps forward. "Nate Brewer."

Blackwell sighs loudly and plants his hands on his square hips, like he's done this plenty of times before. His eyes hold something dark. Maybe he's seen too much and already knows how this will end.

"I understand you two gentlemen were out searching for your daughters," he says.

Garrett looks down as though he's about to be reprimanded. "Yes, sir. As you probably guessed, we didn't find them." He retrieves something from his pocket. "Nate found Skye's phone not far from where Ashley mentioned she'd picked up Lexi's."

"What?" My voice falters, and I clamp my hand over my mouth. The room spins around me until Ashley grips my arm, anchoring me in place. I look at her, and for a moment, we're just mothers, not friends, not enemies, bound by our shared circumstance.

"We'll want to take that into Evidence if that's all right with you, Mr. Metcalf. We're doing the same with the other phone Mrs. Brewer located." Blackwell returns to the sofa. "Now that everyone's here, we can discuss next steps."

He talks as if our world hasn't just collapsed. Ashley's crying. Nate's lips are quivering. Garrett looks lost. That's when my emotions bubble over, and I rise from the chair. "Excuse me a moment." It's all I can do not to throw up as I rush into the bathroom, closing the door behind me. I perch on the edge of the tub, taking deep breaths to stave off the nausea. "Calm down. Calm down. She's still alive. She's out there." I repeat these words to convince myself that I can't give up. That we will find her.

A knock on the door momentarily distracts me. I clear my throat, and wipe away the tears. "Just a minute."

"Babe, it's me. Can I come in?"

I swallow hard, then stand and unlock the door, pulling it open. Garrett enters. "I just need a minute."

"I know." He pulls me into an embrace, and our other problems instantly dissolve from memory. At least, for now. All I can think about is making our family whole again and finding our daughter. "Where is she, Garrett? Where is Skye?" I step back. "Did you open her phone?"

"It's busted." He sighs. "The screen's smashed. Maybe the police can open it, I'm not sure."

"And you found nothing else?" I ask, as if he would willingly keep that information from me. We have our trust issues, but not about Skye. Never about her.

"No. Nothing."

His eyes redden as his pain matches mine. "Look, we need to get back out there. Nate and Ash, they're in the same boat. We need to find out what the police intend to do."

I swipe a tissue from the box resting on the back of the toilet and blot my face. "Yeah, okay." As Garrett opens the door, I grab his arm. "Wait."

He turns back to me. "What is it?"

"We say nothing about that night, okay? Nothing."

8

ASHLEY

Nate holds my hand as he balances on the arm of the chair where I'm sitting. The police asked us questions about where Nate and Garrett searched, and where I searched. All the while, they took notes in their little notebooks and eyed each other as if they shared some knowledge we weren't privy to.

"Excuse me, but I have to ask," I begin. "Has this happened in other places recently? It's just that you two look like this isn't the first time you've dealt with this type of scenario."

"No, ma'am," Blackwell replies. "We're not keeping any information from you. There's no rash of disappearances around Grant or Idaho, in general, if that's what you're asking."

Officer Riley regards him. "You already ran a report? I haven't seen it yet."

"I searched the database before we left the station," Blackwell replies. "I'll send you the details when we get back." He returns his attention to me. "My point is, there are other scenarios it doesn't appear you or the Metcalfs have considered."

At that moment, Garrett and Mara return, hand in hand. I

37

feel Garrett's eyes on me, but I avoid him, and Blackwell seems to pick up on the exchange.

"Mr. and Mrs. Metcalf, if you could please have a seat," Wiley says. "We'd like to stay focused on this situation."

"I apologize, Officer, but my wife is doing her best to stay strong. Under the circumstances, I'm sure you can understand." He helps Mara to the chair, then pulls up a footstool to sit beside her.

"Of course, Mr. Metcalf, I understand. But my partner and I were just about to discuss some other scenarios," Wiley replies.

"That's right," Blackwell adds. "Have any of you considered the possibility your girls might have run away?"

Am I hearing him correctly? Does this man really think Lexi ran away with Skye, of all people? "Officer Blackwell, my daughter is a straight-A student. Her studies are the most important thing in her life because she intends to get into a top-tier university. Running away?" I scoff. "That's not even a remote possibility. First of all, she wouldn't have dumped her phone. If she was running away, she would've turned off the phone's GPS locator so we couldn't track her."

I glance at Mara. "And no offense to the Metcalfs, but Lexi and Skye aren't close friends. They only walk home together because we all insisted on it for their safety. So your idea that this could be a runaway scenario..." I regard Nate for a moment, who nods for me to continue. "That would never happen. Not with Lexi."

"Yes, because your daughter is so perfect," Mara says, shooting me a look. "Maybe if you didn't pressure her so much into getting straight-A's, she might have some friends."

"Your daughters aren't friends?" Officer Wiley cuts in.

"Not really, no," Nate replies. "They used to be when they were younger, but not anymore."

"Did something happen?" Wiley presses, her gaze piercing Nate and me.

"No," I quickly jump in. "Nothing happened. They grew up and wanted different things. Our girls are gone. They didn't run away. So, what are you going to do about it?"

"Mom?"

Everyone's attention turns toward the hall, where Mara and Garrett's son, Milo, appears. Mara jumps up and heads toward him. "Hey, kiddo. We're still taking care of a few things in here. You must be starving. I know it's past dinnertime."

My heart sinks as I watch Mara with her son. He's only twelve. A sweet boy, too. Innocent. For the first time, I'm glad we don't have more children. Telling them something like this would be impossible.

"Why are the police here?" he asks, shaking away the brown hair that has fallen into his eyes. "Is someone in trouble?"

"No, no, of course not." Mara takes his hand. "Come on. I'll fix you a sandwich. Dad and Mr. and Mrs. Brewer can finish up here." She leads him toward the kitchen, glancing at the rest of us. "I'll be back in a minute."

Garrett drops his head into his hands. And for the first time in a long time, I feel bad for him.

"We have the girls' phones," Blackwell continues, as if there had been no interruption. "Which suggests foul play, so we'll open a missing persons case for each of them. This also means we'd like you to give us their laptops. We'll turn everything over to our Forensics team so they can start right away on accessing them, hoping to find answers. As soon as the sun is up, we'll have a team scour the woods. We'll talk to the girls' friends, reach out to the school, and talk to the teachers. Anything and everything we can do—we'll do."

"Thank you," Nate replies.

The officers stand, and Blackwell drops his notebook into his shirt pocket. "I won't tell you to get some rest tonight because I know that won't happen. But what I will say is I'd like you all..." His gaze shifts to Mara as she returns to the living room. "I'd like you all to find whatever you can. Either journals, their social media, if you have access, or anything you think might shed light on this situation. Maybe you can find out if either of them had planned to meet with anyone. Things of that nature."

"Our girls aren't the type—"

"Mrs. Metcalf," Blackwell cuts in. "In my experience, parents don't know nearly as much about their children as they think they do."

"And vice-versa," Wiley chimes in.

Garrett shows them to the door while Nate and I sit, motionless, frustrated by an impossible situation neither of us can comprehend. Though I didn't miss Officer Wiley's not-so-subtle jab. I doubt any of us did.

When the front door closes and Garrett returns to Mara's side, all we can do is sit in silence. The four of us—neighbors, former friends, each wondering if karma has finally come for us.

9
GARRETT

Ten Years Earlier

The moving truck is right behind us, so I pull onto the driveway and step out, while Mara gets the kids out of the backseat. I walk to the end and peer down the street. There it is—a semi-trailer full of our things. It was a long journey, but we're here now.

The truck is heading this way. Once it's close enough, I catch the driver's attention and point at the curb where I want it to stop. That's when I notice Mara ushering our daughter, Skye and our son, Milo, back toward the house.

As the truck pulls in, my gaze drifts to the neighbor's house. A man who looks to be about my age steps outside and walks to his mailbox. "Hey there," I say to him.

He smiles and walks toward me.

"Well, hello," he replies. "You must be the new neighbor. I'm Nathan Brewer, but everyone calls me Nate." He offers his hand.

"Garrett. Garrett Metcalf." I return the greeting. "Good to meet you, Nate. Yep, we just closed the day before yesterday and made the drive from Chicago."

"Chicago? Wow. This is a big change for you, then, isn't it?" Nate says.

"I guess so, but we're excited. My wife, Mara, and I wanted a more family-friendly, small town to raise our kids. And her parents live here."

"You have kids? Same here. A daughter. Five," he says.

"What a coincidence. Our daughter is five, too. And we have a son who's two."

"Sounds like you got your hands full, Garrett."

I nod and chuckle a little. "You got that right."

"Mr. Metcalf?" The driver approaches me, winded, hiking up his sagging gray work pants. A young man—he is not. "We'd like to get started unloading, if that's all right with you, sir."

I look back at Nate. "And now the fun begins. You'll excuse me, Nate?"

"Yeah, of course," he says. "I'll let you get to it." As he walks away, he stops and turns back. "Hey, once you get settled in, you and your family should come over. The wife would love to meet you and yours."

"Sounds great. Good to meet you, Nate," I reply.

"And you."

I size him up as he walks back into his house. He's plain. Average-looking. I wonder what his wife looks like.

"Garrett?" Mara calls out.

She's standing on the porch, Milo on her hip, as usual. "Yeah?"

"Are they going to unload the truck or what?"

That's when I notice the driver standing by, appearing to wait for instructions. "On it."

I t's almost dark by the time the truck leaves. All our things are inside. We've arranged the furniture, but boxes lie everywhere.

"Pizza should be here any minute," Mara says. "Skye, go wash your hands, sweetheart."

"Okay, Mommy."

Mara perches on the edge of our sofa, holding Milo's hands as he stands in front of her. I walk over and take a seat beside them. "So I talked to the neighbor earlier."

"I saw," she replies. "Did he seem nice?"

"Uh, yeah, I think so. He's married. They have a five-year-old daughter."

She looks at me with a smile. "Really? That's great. We should arrange a get-together after we're settled in."

"He mentioned doing something like that—Nate. He didn't offer his wife's name, but yeah, so we should set something up. Who knows? Maybe we can all be friends." I glance through the front window as the streetlamps flicker on. "Ah, hell."

"What's wrong?" Mara asks.

"I left a moving blanket on the driveway. I'll run out and get it." Stepping outside, I feel the warmth of the summer breeze breaking through the thick, muggy air. As I walk to the edge of the driveway, my gaze drifts next door. A woman stands in the yard, holding a garden hose and watering her flowers.

"Uh, hi, there," I say, walking toward her. "I met your husband earlier today. Garrett Metcalf." I extend my hand, and she looks at it a moment as though unsure she should shake it.

"Nate told me he'd met you. I'm Ashley. I'd shake your hand, but I've been pulling weeds. Mine are dirty."

"I don't mind dirty," I reply, a little flirtier than I intended.

"Oh, okay." She reluctantly accepts my greeting. "Nice to meet you, Garrett."

She's gorgeous. Long red hair, thick and wavy. A body that won't quit. Why the hell is she married to that nerd, Nate?

"I hear you're married," she says.

"I am. My wife, Mara, is inside with our little ones."

"Very nice. And I hear we have something in common," she adds. "Both our girls are five."

"That's right. My daughter's name is Skye. My son is Milo."

"Our daughter is Alexis, but everyone calls her Lexi," Ashley replies, glancing over my shoulder. "Looks like your dinner's here."

I turn around. "Oh, right. Pizza," I shrug. "No idea where the pots and pans are, so we figured this was a good choice."

"Don't blame you." She smiles. "Well, it was great meeting you, Garrett. I look forward to meeting the rest of your family soon."

"Same here. Have a good night, Ashley." I return to the driveway and reach for my wallet to pay the delivery guy. As he hands over the pizza, I glance back at Ashley next door. She quickly averts her gaze. But—she was looking.

10

LEXI

My head still hurts, my stomach is rumbling, and I have to pee. I don't even know what time it is, but it feels like we've been down here forever. It must be midnight or something. I think Skye is asleep. I don't want to wake her because being asleep is better than being awake in this place. Whatever this place is.

He hasn't come down again. Not since earlier when I thought he was going to hurt Skye. But he didn't. He just left. We screamed for what felt like hours, but no one came. I'm not sure anyone's coming. Not my parents, not Skye's.

We're alone down here, and I don't know who this psycho is or what he plans to do to us. I don't even know where *here* is. But I'm scared. Terrified, actually. I don't want to die. I just want to go home.

My bladder feels like it's going to explode. This asshole is going to make me pee in my pants, isn't he?

We shouldn't have taken the shortcut. All Skye had to do was leave on time. That's it. And we wouldn't be in this nightmare. But it's always about her. It's always been about her. She's the pretty one. The athletic one. The popular one. Me? I'm just the smart one. And look where that's gotten me.

My eyes sting as the tears well. *Where are you, Mom? Dad?* My lips quiver, and I know I can't stop it. The tears come, but I try to silence my sobs so I don't wake Skye. Then I feel it—the warmth in my pants spreading down my leg. I catch my breath, trying to calm myself down, but I can't. I have to get out of here. And now, I'm sitting in my own pee. I'm hurt and I'm scared. *Please, God. Please, God, get us out of here.*

"Lexi, you okay?"

"Skye, you're awake?"

"I think I was sort of asleep, but yeah, I'm awake now. Are you okay? I thought I heard you making a noise."

"No, I'm fine." My voice cracks. "But I peed my pants." The words barely come out before the tears spill. "I'm sorry... I'm sorry."

"Hey, it's okay, Lex." Her tone is reassuring, like I'm not some five-year-old who can't control her bladder. "Come on. It's not like this prick is letting us go to the bathroom. It's okay. Please don't cry."

But the fear is too much. I'm trying to be strong like Skye, but I want to go home. I want my mom and dad. "How are we going to get out of here?"

"I don't know," she whispers. "Do you feel any better yet, or does everything still hurt?"

"It's not as bad, but my head is still throbbing. My wrists hurt from these stupid cuffs. I mean, we're in chains, for God's sake."

"Yeah," she replies. "Everything still kinda hurts for me, too. I just wish I could see you. See anything. It's so dark in here. I have no idea what time it is, or how long we've been down here."

"I figure it's probably late. Like maybe midnight or something," I say. "Is he going to feed us or give us water?"

"I wish I knew, Lex. We won't last long without water."

"Three days," I shoot back. "Three days is all we can go without it, maybe up to five, but that's it. We'll start to get dizzy and super tired. Our heads will hurt worse, probably. Then, after a couple of days, our organs will start to shut down."

"Jesus Christ, Lexi, thanks for the pep talk."

"I'm sorry," I reply, my voice still shaking.

"No, it's fine. Look, I'm just as scared as you are, okay? I just wish I knew where we were. And who is this guy, huh? What a fucking creeper."

"Skye?" I ask.

"Yeah?"

"What if he—like—does stuff to us?" I can barely get out the words.

"Stop, okay?" she replies. "Nothing's going to happen to us. Nothing like that, all right? You can't think like that, Lexi. Come on. We need to start thinking about how we can get the hell out of here. You're the smart one. What can we do?"

I peer out into the darkness. "If I could see, I might find a way, but it's too dark in here." I stop for a moment. "Listen, if he does come in and starts...you know...maybe we can hurt him. Like fight him off and try to hurt him."

"Oh my God," Skye says, half in disbelief and half irritated by my suggestion.

"I know. I know, but that could be the only way."

"But how?" she asks. "I mean, you saw him. He's a big guy. No way we can fight him off."

"I don't know how else, then, Skye. We have to try to fight back, or we'll die down here."

The door opens, and a faint light shines inside, but not as bright as the first time. He walks in and flips the light switch. Now, my eyes sting as the room brightens in an instant. The pounding in my head worsens as I squint. But I see her. I see Skye.

She smiles a little, and seeing her makes me feel like I'm not alone. She looks bad, though. Her cheek is all swollen and bruised. The braid in her hair is loose and messy. Her legs are dirty, like he dragged her over the forest floor.

And then I think about my own injuries. My pants are ripped, dirty, and stained with my blood. I don't know what my face looks like. I see scratches and big bruises popping up on my arms. How did we even end up looking like this? I don't remember anything after he pulled the gun on us and told us to go with him.

"I thought you two might be hungry and thirsty." He walks down the few steps, still wearing that creepy mask.

"Let us go!" Skye demands. "Our families will come looking for us."

The man sets down the food. Sandwiches, I think, and a glass of water. Then he walks toward Skye.

"Get away from her!" I yell.

He stops mid-step and turns around. "So, you'd prefer I come to you, huh? I don't mind either way."

My chest pounds and my breaths are shallow, but I try to keep control, to not let him see how scared I am. He wants us to be afraid. He wants us to cry out for help.

"No, stop!" Skye screams.

"It's okay," I tell her. And with my gaze fixed on him, I continue, "I'm not afraid of you."

He tilts his head. That stupid mask on his face slips off his cheek a little, but not enough for me to get a good look at him. He reaches out for me, the tips of his fingers brushing my chin. "Oh, little girl, you should be afraid."

That's when he notices the wet beneath me. "Guess I should've let you go to the bathroom."

I want to cry, and it takes everything in my power not to. I say nothing.

"Stupid cunt." He stands again and takes hold of the tray,

leaving a plastic plate and a bottle of water next to me. Then he gives the same to Skye.

"We'll all get along a lot better once you girls realize there's no way out for you. And no one is coming." He walks back to the steps. "Night, night."

We're thrown into darkness once again.

11
SKYE

Am I still dreaming? I'm thirsty, my stomach growls... and is that...? My eyes flutter open. Darkness. Hazy. But something's wrong. Someone's here. Someone's touching me.

Wake up, Skye. Wake up.

"Mom?"

"Shhh. If you make a sound, she dies."

A sharp chill grazes my neck. Metal. A knife. I gasp. This isn't a dream. His hands roam. I freeze—every part of me locked in place. My voice catches in my throat. "Please..."

The knife presses harder, and I feel warmth slide down my skin.

"I will kill her. Is that what you want?"

He moves above me, breathing heavily. I can't see his face, just the glint of his eyes through the mask. His touch is rough, wrong, intrusive.

Please don't. Please stop. But if I say it out loud, he'll kill Lexi, and I believe him.

I squeeze my eyes shut. The tears come anyway. I feel myself breaking apart, disappearing into my own mind. *It'll be over soon,* I tell myself. *You just have to survive this.*

I'm not here anymore. Not really. Just a body.

The weight is gone from my chest. My eyes flicker open. The whoosh of the door opening and closing again sends waves of relief through me. He's gone. Lexi's safe.

But this silence now is louder than anything. How long do I just lie here? My body aches, but it's not the worst pain. The worst pain is inside—where something's cracked open.

Don't cry. Don't think. Don't remember.

I curl onto my side, away from the blood on my skin, away from the place it happened. I tell myself I'm still here. I'm alive. That has to be enough.

It wasn't your fault.

But the voice in my head argues back: You didn't stop him. You didn't fight.

I press my palms to my ears like I can shut out the noise. But it's all inside. Then I think of Lexi—safe, unharmed. And that's when the guilt really hits me. Because I'd do it all again if it means she gets to live.

I survived. I saved her. That has to count for something.

12

MARA

The smell of vomit clings to me. My throat is raw, and my mouth has a coppery taste. I lost count of how many times I threw up in the night. Each time I thought about what could be happening to my girl and where she could be, it sent waves of nausea through me.

Garrett tried to offer comfort, but nothing can console a mother's fear. You can't soothe it away with a whisper that everything will turn out fine.

Now, the sun is rising outside my bedroom window. What will happen today? Will we find Skye? Is she going to be alive? Will she be hurt? I'm worried for Lexi, too, of course I am. But she's not my daughter. The capacity of a mother's love is infinite —for her own children. Does that sound cruel? Maybe it is, but I can't exist without Skye. The mere thought of it makes my stomach clench, ready to push out whatever contents remain. I'm sorry to say that I *can* live without Lexi. That's the hard truth.

These are thoughts I'll keep to myself, though I have no doubt Ashley is of a similar mind. Instead, I'll force myself out of this bed, climb into the shower, and wash away the remnants of my body's gut reactions to inconceivable notions.

As I rise, Garrett stirs. "Go back to sleep. It's early," I say. I want to be angry at him for managing to find sleep, even if only a little. He tried last night, that much I know. So, despite everything that's happened between us, I do my best to remember he's still Skye's father.

My phone rests on the nightstand, and I snatch it before heading into the bathroom. The window lets in the morning light and distorts my features as I step into it, peering at my reflection in the mirror. My face is pale, and dark half-moons look airbrushed under my eyes. I look to have aged ten years. It feels like twenty.

A message arrives on my phone, pulling me away from a trance-like state. For a moment, hope swells in me. Is it the police? Do they have news? Of course not, you idiot. Why would they send a text?

It's from Ashley, and while I maintain a modicum of hope, wondering if maybe she's heard from Lexi, that hope vanishes in an instant.

Are you up? We're going over to the woods. Police will be there soon with the search party.

I let out a sigh, irritated that I let myself feel hopeful. And then I type my reply.

Meet you out there soon.

I press 'send' and step into the shower. While the hot water stings my skin, I hear the door open, so I peer through the obscured glass and see Garrett's naked figure. Jesus, when was the last time we showered together? I can't even remember.

He opens the shower door and regards me with an unbreakable stare. His eyes are full of regret and worry. He steps inside, pulls the door shut, and takes me into his arms. I'm too weak to be angry, too scared to think about our past mistakes. Instead, I melt into him and let my tears wash down the drain.

My mother is looking after Milo. Garrett and I still haven't found the strength to tell him what's happening. He idolizes his sister, and I can't break his heart. I know it can't stay this way forever because people in this town talk, passing judgment as if they, themselves, have lived perfect lives.

No doubt, the high school will be buzzing this morning. Officer Blackwell said they'd be talking to the students and teachers. There'll be no stopping the gossip then. Rumors will fly. Our parenting choices will come into question. Well, screw 'em. We're going to find our daughter, and that's all that matters.

I'm standing at the entrance to the woods, aiming my finger ahead. "I see him over there," I say to Garrett.

We start walking, preparing to join the team, which is bigger than I expected. And then I see Ashley and Nate. To be honest, Ashley looks about as bad as I do. I assume she didn't sleep much last night either.

"Officer Wiley," Garrett calls out. "Sorry we're late. We had to wait for Mara's mom to show up and look after our son."

"That's fine, Mr. Metcalf. We're just getting started anyway. Officer Blackwell will be here soon." She returns her attention to the five other officers. "You each have your assigned quadrants and volunteers. Let's get started."

I may have judged the town too harshly. There must be twenty people here, and at least half of the police force. Some people I know, some I don't. They've all come to help in the search.

"How'd you sleep?" Ashley asks as she approaches.

"Not great. You?"

She shakes her head. "A lot of people turned up to help. I didn't expect that."

"Me, either," I reply. "How's Nate holding up?"

"About as good as you'd expect. Garrett?"

"Same." I shrug. "Look, uh, I know we aren't as close as we used to be, but I want you to know that I'm still here for you. You're the only one who can understand what I'm going through right now. The guys—they won't get it—not fully."

"Thanks, and the same goes for me." Ashley glances at our husbands, who appear to be conversing several feet away. "And I just want you to know that I'm sorry for what happened back then. For—all of it."

I press my lips together in a tight grin. "No point in rehashing the past."

13
LEXI

The throbbing in my shoulder forces me awake. I didn't even realize I'd fallen asleep. I'm curled up, lying on my side, which explains the soreness. And as I try to sit up, pain shoots through my back from sleeping on this concrete floor.

The smell of my own urine makes me want to gag. My crotch is chaffing from the dampness, and it makes me feel even colder. I wonder if Skye had to pee, too. She must have.

I'd eaten the sandwich and downed the water last night. It's still dark in here, but I think it could be morning. A soft gray light is coming in from the bottom of the door. Faint, but noticeable.

I don't hear her. Maybe she fell asleep. As I sit up, I see the softest of silhouettes, though it could be the shadows messing with my eyes. Either that, or they're getting used to the darkness. "Skye?" My voice comes out hoarse. "Are you awake?"

I wonder if she's okay. I mean, we were both hurt pretty badly yesterday. She got it worse than me... I think.

I hear her moan a little, soft and quiet, like a baby, almost. The chains have enough give that I can sit up against the brick wall behind me. So, I reposition myself, every muscle in my body screaming at me.

"Skye, are you okay?" I see her features a little better, sort of. "Skye? Skye, answer me. Are you okay?" My words come out in a panic, wondering if I'm actually alone in here. But then I see movement. "Oh, thank God." Still, she says nothing. "Why aren't you answering me? Skye, you're scaring me now, come on."

She mumbles something. I can't understand her. "What? What are you saying? I can't hear you."

I hear her grunt, and then it sounds like she's trying to shift around. "You were asleep," she says.

I can barely hear her, so I strain to listen.

"He told me if I woke you up, made any noise at all, he'd kill you."

"What? No. No, no, no." My stomach clenches. I turn my head and throw up, the vomit splattering on my arm and leg. Tears spill down my face, my lips quiver, and a lump rises in my throat. I try to swallow it down, try to say something to comfort her, but there are no words.

"I'm—I'm so sorry." It's all I can manage to get out. She stifles her cries, and I swear I can see the pain in her face. Even in the dim light, I see her shame and embarrassment. "No. No way is this your fault, Skye. He's a sick fucking psycho, all right? And you and me? We're going to get out of here, okay? I swear to God, we will get out."

She doesn't reply, only sobs. I'm pissed now. Beyond pissed. So much so that anger twists in my already tender stomach. I might actually be sick again. I'm so mad, but I hold it down. I have to be strong for Skye. She needs me to be strong.

"I just need to figure out where we are." My gaze roams in search of anything recognizable. Any hint of a location, but all I see is the silhouette of an empty cellar. Brick walls, concrete floor, and wood beams on the ceiling where the light hangs down. It's like a dungeon down here. And I've read way too many fantasy novels not to know what happens in places like this.

"You saved my life earlier, Skye, getting him away from me like that. And now, I'm going to save us both."

"How?" she asks, her voice heavy.

"I don't know yet, but I—" The door creeks open, and I whip around to see. He's back. Skye gasps. I shake my head at her, and I know she can see me in the faint light he's let in. I need her to stay quiet. We can't let him see how afraid we are. That's what he wants.

He flips on the light again, and both of us squint from the pain in our eyes. He's wearing the mask. But then, I think he's wearing it so we don't see his face, right? Why else would he not want us to see his face unless he intends to let us go? A tiny spark of hope burns inside me. Yeah, that makes total sense, right? If we don't see his face, we can't identify him.

He lumbers down the steps. "It smells like puke down here. Puke and piss." He cocks his head as if considering just how bad it is and then keeps moving. The plastic doll's mask slips on his face, and he fidgets with it until it fits over him again. Slouching forward, he walks toward Skye.

"Get away from her," I say, though my voice comes out too small and afraid.

He turns to me, his eyes hard, but I swear I can see him smiling behind the mask. "You want to be next?"

"No," Skye shouts. "Stop. Let us go. You can't keep us down here forever." Her voice shakes at first, but her words get stronger. "The police are going to find us."

"Sure, they will," he mutters with a snort. "You hang onto that hope, sweetheart. And when I watch that hope drain from your eyes, I'll try not to tell you I told you so."

He looks us over like we're food and he's starving. His shoulders are relaxed, as if he's already decided our fate.

He approaches me and squats low, and I think he sees through the fake brave face I'm wearing. It's my mask—just like his.

"How about I take you next?" He caresses my legs, and I flinch, pain shooting up my spine. But he doesn't stop. His hand keeps moving up my thigh.

I fight back the tears, and I have to hope that the smell that surrounds me is enough to get him to stop. But if his goal is to scare me, he's already done that.

As he nears the top of my thigh, I hear Skye shout, yelling at him to stop touching me. To get away from me. But her voice seems distant, and I know I'm here alone. I alone have to act to stop this. At least try.

I keep my eyes fixed on him as he unzips my pants. My right hand slowly lowers until it touches the vomit. I can feel the chunks of lunch meat and soft bread crust, and the saliva comes—the way it does just as you're about to throw up again. But I don't. I keep it down. And I scoop up what I can of the mess.

As he's pulling down my pants, I raise my arm and toss it at him. The liquid splatters across the mask, landing in the little eye and mouth holes.

"The fuck?" He sits up and rears back his arm. "You stupid, sick bitch!"

I see his fist coming. I know it's going to hurt. But maybe he won't touch me again.

14
ASHLEY

They split us up for the search. Nate is in the first group. I'm in the second. Mara and Garrett are in groups three and four. The police reasoned that by placing one of us in each quadrant, we would be better equipped to identify any discoveries as belonging to one of the girls. I guess they have a point, and to be honest, I'm not sure I want Nate with me. I certainly don't want to pair up with either of the Metcalfs.

Last night didn't seem real. I couldn't sleep. I didn't eat. Still haven't eaten anything this morning. All I could do was sit on Lexi's bed and cry. Nate tried to comfort me, but there's still that thing between us. That thing that's never truly gone away, even after five years. I see it in his eyes whenever someone mentions Garrett, or when the Metcalfs leave their house as we're sitting on our front porch. That awkward wave he gives them.

It took two years after that night for us to find some sense of normalcy in our marriage. I imagine Nate wanted to leave me, but didn't in order to keep our family together. We considered moving, but he's built a successful business here. The pharmacy is one of only two in town. And I thought, in time, we would return to that place of love and trust. He says he's there, but I know he isn't.

Now our daughter is gone. Missing. Was she kidnapped? Is she dead? One thing I know for certain is that if we don't find her —it's hard for me even to think that—but if we don't, Nate and I won't survive. Most couples don't survive such losses, but with everything that's already happened between us, we won't stand a chance. So, not only do I have to find my daughter because without her, I'm lost, but I have to find her because I'll lose my husband, too.

I think back to that night, the night that changed everything, and I wonder...would we all be here if it had never happened?

Garrett's driving, which is good because I've had too much to drink. It's late, but I'm not ready to go home. He told Mara the client function was running long and that he'd be late. He's in Finance and is often required to attend these things, usually with his wife. Of course, he had no such function. It was an excuse for us to be together.

When Garrett and Mara moved in five years ago, I was glad their daughter and mine were the same age. Lexi was always quiet, and a little withdrawn, and Skye—well, she was the exact opposite. The two got along great, which meant Nate and I started hanging out with the Metcalfs, becoming close friends.

I didn't mean for it to happen. Garrett has a charming and dynamic personality. Not to mention rugged good looks. Thick brown hair with little waves on the top. A stubbled beard, not too thick. And a body that requires several hours a week in the gym to maintain.

I won't make excuses, like Nate doesn't pay me enough atten-tion, or he's always working. He is always working, but that's not the reason. I don't suppose I have a reason, actually. It just happened.

Skye's ninth birthday party. Something changed that day. The way we looked at each other. And that was it—we'd begun our affair.

That was a year ago. The guilt I initially felt over it has long faded. I guess the more you do it, the easier it gets. And so tonight is the first night we've had so much time to ourselves. Mara and their two kids are at her parents' house for the night. Nate is home, looking after Lexi. He thinks I'm at a girls' night. That's what I told him.

"Oh, I love this song." Garrett turns up the car radio.

He drapes his arm around my shoulder, and I shift closer to him. The center console is digging into my hip, but I don't mind. I'm just happy to be in his arms. The three glasses of wine don't hurt either.

We drive along a two-lane stretch of road, lined with trees on either side. Fall is in full swing, and the leaves are changing, but it's dark out. The trees appear like black shadows along the road. Street-lights are few and far between.

I know we'll be home soon, so we don't have much time left. I look at Garrett, and he smiles at me.

"What?" he asks.

"I was just thinking, maybe I could give you a little something? Something that will stay with you a while."

"What do you mean?" he asks, a hint of a smile tugging on his lips.

My fingers trace along the outline of his pants zipper, and I undo the button, then pull it down, revealing a glimpse of his boxers. Gently, I slide my hand inside.

"Jesus, Ash, are you serious? You're doing this right here while I'm driving?"

"Do you want me to stop?" I ask.

"No. Not a chance."

He groans as my lips wrap around him. My tongue darts out to tease his sensitive flesh. He gently places one hand on my head, keeping the other on the wheel... his hips buck forward, and I can feel him getting closer to release—

"Jesus!" Garrett slams on the brakes.

I'm jolted forward and thrust out my hand to brace against the steering wheel. My head almost slams into it. Then I bolt up and peer through the windshield. "Stop!" I scream, my fingers digging into his shoulder.

The tires screech, the smell of burned rubber fills the car. But he can't slow down quickly enough. Then...the thud.

"Mrs. Brewer?"

I'm yanked back to the present, standing in the middle of the woods, my gaze aimed at the forest floor. I look up. "Yes?" It takes me a minute to recognize the man in front of me. "Oh, Cash. Hi."

Cash Goodell is the owner of the local auto body shop and one of the volunteers. "Hi, Mrs. Brewer. The police want us to return to the staging area. I think they're ready to wrap things up."

"Oh, okay. Did they find something?"

"I don't know," he replies. "But we should head back. Are you okay?"

"Sorry, yes. As okay as I can be." I tug on my T-shirt and clear my throat.

"I'm so sorry about all this." He tucks his hands into his pockets. "It's just terrible. Really awful."

I manage a half-smile. "I appreciate that. Guess we should go back." And just as I start walking, he reaches for my arm, so I stop and turn back. "Yes?"

Cash licks his lips, lowering his gaze a little. "You know, it seems like you and the Metcalfs, you're pretty close, huh?"

"Yes." I say nothing more as I sense a change in his demeanor.

"And now with both your girls..." he trails off.

"We really should head back," I reply, starting again.

"Yes, of course." He nods. "You know, I probably should've said something a long time ago, but I recall now, when Mr. Metcalf brought me his car to be fixed after that unfortunate run-in with a deer..."

I stop in my tracks, my pulse quickening.

"I'd seen something in his car. It was under the floor mat on the passenger side. I had to rip all that up, of course, when I started working on it."

I spin around. "What is it you're getting at? Because I need to go back to base."

"Well, I won't keep you, Mrs. Brewer. You got plenty to worry about right now. I was just going to say I'd found a card from Mr. Metcalf—to you. Looked like it came from a bouquet of flowers or something."

My body trembles. I remember the card. Garrett had given me flowers that night, the card was tucked inside. I'd left them at the hotel we were in, but the card must've slipped out. "I'm sure you're mistaken. It must've been for his wife."

He nods. "Yeah, you know what? I'm sure you're right." He waves at me. "Let's go. I'll get you back to base."

We say nothing more as we rejoin the others in the staging area. I'm desperate to get away from him, so I search for anyone else to talk to. That's when I see Nate. He meets my gaze, and I approach him. "Hey."

"Hi," he says, peering beyond me. "Is that Cash Goodell?"

"Yeah."

"That's nice of him to come. We need all the help we can get."

I peer back at Cash. He nods and then walks away. "Yes, we do. So, do we know if anyone's found anything?"

"Don't know. I see Blackwell coming. Not sure when he arrived, but let's go see what he has to say."

Nate heads off, and I follow him. We pass by other neighbors and people from town. They pat our backs, offer sympathetic smiles, and tell us the girls will be found and that we shouldn't worry. They mean well. I understand that. But they can't possibly relate to us. Still, I'm grateful for their help.

"Officer Blackwell," Nate says, offering his hand.

"Mr. Brewer." He returns Nate's greeting, then regards me. "Mrs. Brewer. It's been a long day."

"Yes, it has," I say. "Did any of it help?" I notice Officer Riley coming up behind Blackwell. Her expression appears solemn, and I'm not sure what to make of it.

Blackwell turns to her. "Good, you're just in time."

"In time for what?" Riley asks.

Nate and I trade a glance, and then I regard Blackwell. "What are you talking about?"

He steps over to a nearby folding table and reaches for a plastic bag. Something's inside that bag, but I can't tell what it is. My pulse quickens. I feel Nate's hand on my shoulder.

"Just as we were wrapping up our search in the third quadrant," Blackwell begins. "I found this."

My eyes widen, my mouth falls open. "A knife?"

"A pocketknife, yes," Blackwell replies.

Nate squeezes my shoulder as if trying to steady himself. "Is there...blood..."

Officer Riley studies the knife while Blackwell dangles it inside the bag. "You say that was found in Quad three?"

"Just outside the perimeter, yes. In an area we almost overlooked," Blackwell replies. "We'll want to have it analyzed ASAP." He reaches into his pocket and pulls out a latex glove. Slipping it on, he then opens the bag and pulls out the knife. "This insignia."

He points to a small carving on the knife's handle. "It's the Utah state emblem—a beehive."

"Utah?" Nate asks. I feel his grip on me loosen. He lets out a grunt, and I look at him. It only takes a moment to see the dawning in his expression.

"Does this mean anything to you, Mr. Brewer?" Officer Riley asks.

"No," Nate says, shaking his head. "Nothing."

15
GARRETT

Five Years Earlier

Living in a small town has its downsides. Only two grocery stores. One hardware store. One body shop. So much for competition driving down prices. But one advantage remains—honesty. I trust Cash Goodell, the body shop owner, to give it to me straight. He doesn't sugarcoat things. And he doesn't get into other people's business.

I didn't tell him I was coming. Instead, it's early Monday morning, and I show up at the shop just as he's rolling open the overhead doors. I park and step out. He immediately sees me and walks over, eyeballing my car.

"Well, well. What happened here?" he asks. "Looks like your car got into a fight with a deer and the deer won."

I extend my hand, wearing a broad smile. "Morning, Cash. How are you?"

He accepts my greeting. "Doing all right, Mr. Metcalf. I'd ask you the same thing, but I think I get the gist of how things are going for you right now."

Cash studies the front-end damage on my Mercedes, his dark

eyes laser-focused. His rough hand runs along the grille, and then he groans, running his other hand through his naturally brown curls.

"So, what do you think?" I ask casually, hands in my pockets as if this is just some unfortunate side effect of living in the boonies.

"This happen over the weekend?" he asks, keeping his sights fixed on the damage.

"Yep. But the deer got the worst of it, I'm sorry to say." I join him at the front of the car, examining it alongside him. "Sorry to just turn up like this. I figured if I got it in early, you might be able to work on it straight away."

He brushes off his hands, then sighs loudly. And that's when I know it's going to be bad. But it's a problem I can't afford to ignore.

"Well, I'm going to have to order you a new grille. New bumper. New headlights." He shakes his head. "It'll take a solid week to get you those parts." He turns to me. "That's if you want OEM—original equipment, that is, or if you want aftermarket parts. Now, being that you got a Merc, well, I'd recommend OEM, but it'll cost you."

"I don't mind the cost." Of course I do, but I don't say as much. "Time is important, too. I can't be without my car for long because I hate paying through the nose for a rental." More importantly, I need the car to look exactly as it did before the accident.

"All right," he says. "I'll run you up a couple of estimates and see which way you want to go. Can you give me the day to knock it out?"

The sooner he gets started, the better. "You know what, Cash...why don't you just go ahead and order OEM and get started? I don't want to tinker around on price."

"I can do that." He starts toward the garage again. "If you want to give me your insurance details, I can get started on the paperwork for the claim. I'll bet they'll cover most of the expense in any case."

I follow him. "Uh, actually, I'm keeping this one off the radar." He looks back at me, his heavy brow furrowed. "I gotta be honest; my deductible is insanely high, and if I make a claim, my rates will go through the roof."

His brow relaxes as he waves off his concern. "Oh, yeah, sure. I get that. Goddam insurance companies. They aren't worth it half the time."

"No, sir."

He approaches the desk inside his shop. "So, I'll get those parts ordered for you after I've fully inspected the car. Never know what you're gonna find once you start taking things apart. Can you leave her here today?"

I didn't fully consider this scenario. "Sure. I'll call an Uber and take that to work."

Cash raises his index finger. "I'll do you one better. I got a loaner you can use today. It's not much, nothing like your Merc, but it'll get you from point A to point B. It'll give you time to sort out a rental because, given the state of your car, it's a risk driving it. In fact, you probably ought to have had it towed here, but I won't hold that against you."

"I'll take you up on that offer, Cash. Thank you."

He hands over the keys to the loaner, and we head back outside.

"Oh, hang on a second," Cash says, darting toward my car.

He opens the passenger door and leans in. I narrow my gaze, wondering what he's doing. And when he steps out again, he's wearing this look. The way he closes the door—slow and deliberate, casting down his gaze. My heart jumps.

He walks toward me, holding a piece of paper, still wearing that look.

"I figured you carried a copy of your insurance in your glove box. And that you might need it." Cash hands it to me. "You'll want to keep that in the loaner, just in case."

"Oh, yeah. Sure. Thank you. Almost forgot." Something's wrong. He found something. But why isn't he saying as much? Jesus. I rack my brain. What could it be?

"All right, man. I'll let you get to it," he says, turning away without another word.

I watch him until he disappears inside, then I walk toward the loaner, slipping behind the wheel. Stale smoke lingers in the older-model white Honda CRX. But right now, I don't care. Right now, I'm trying to figure out what Cash found. He didn't press me on filing an insurance claim or ask for details about the accident. I'd spent hours hosing down the front end, practically scrubbing it with a toothbrush. But something got his attention, and now, I don't know what to do.

I drive off, heading through town toward my office. I started a financial consulting firm when we moved here, and now I have a staff of ten. I lease a nice office building not far from Town Hall and have become a well-respected member of the business community here. I've created jobs, revenue for the city, and had a hand in putting this town on the map.

However, none of that will make a damn bit of difference if anyone ever finds the body.

16

SKYE

I can still feel him on me. The stench of his hot breath on my face, his sweat dripping on me. Every time I think about what happened, I want to throw up. I know Lexi feels bad about it. She even got sick, which did nothing to deter this creep. He doesn't care that we're sitting in our own filth.

Lexi is on the other side of the room, and I can hear her breathing heavily, like she's sleeping. I think it's daytime, with that tiny bit of light coming in from under the door. It's just enough to make out a few shapes. Lexi appears like a blob plopped down in the corner.

I don't know how long we've been down here. A day? Two? But with each passing moment, hope fades away, and I wonder if we'll ever get out of here.

Lexi thinks she can stop this psycho, attack him, or whatever. But we can't. He held a knife to my throat, and he would've killed me if I said anything. Then he would've killed her. We'd both be nothing more than rotting corpses down here. We can't stop this creep. There's no way out of here except up those stairs and through that door. What's on the other side? The psycho, for sure. But what else? Where are we?

I hear Lexi clearing her throat and shifting around a little. "Hey, are you awake?"

"Yeah. Are you doing okay?"

I shrug. "I guess. Listen, I'm not sure how much longer he'll keep us alive—"

"Don't talk like that," Lexi interrupts, totally alert now. "We're getting out of here, Skye."

"Listen to me." I raise my voice a little. "We have to be real about this, all right? This isn't some TV show or movie where the bad guy gets caught. We have to start thinking about what this asshole is going to do to us—like what he's already done."

"I don't understand," she says.

"Do you want to be tortured for God knows how long before this guy finally kills us? Trust me, you don't want to go through what I did last night, okay?" I sigh. "What I'm saying is that maybe we just fight back, you know?"

"That's what I've been telling you," Lexi insists. "If we fight back, we might be able to get out of here."

I raise my arms, jiggling the chains. "Look at us! We're chained to the walls, Lex. Come on. You're the smart one, here, all right? We aren't getting out."

"I don't get it. Then what are you saying?" she presses.

"I'm saying, unless you want to be tortured, just fight back so he doesn't have a choice but to stop us for real."

Lexi's quiet for a long time, and I know she gets my meaning.

"You want him to put us out of our misery," she replies.

"Not exactly," I say. "We go out on our own fucking terms— that's what I mean. The only thing we have control over down here is *when* we die. We make life hell for him, and he'll have no choice. That way, we win, Lex. You and me."

"There has to be a better—"

The door opens. Daylight spills in. He's coming.

"Good news, girls," he says, lumbering down the steps. "I hear they've formed a search party. Guess everyone's out looking for you two."

Hope fills my chest, immediately squashing the idea of letting this guy kill us. I think of my mom and dad, even my stupid little brother. They haven't forgotten about us.

"Too bad they won't find you," he says, standing in the middle of the room, still wearing that mask.

But I see something else. He's holding something in the crook of his elbow.

"Let us go!" Lexi shouts, tugging on her chains. "We didn't do anything to you. We can't even see your face. I swear, if you let us go, we won't say a word. Right, Skye?"

"Right," I say in a low tone. He's not going to let us go. Not ever. It doesn't matter that we don't know what he looks like. But as he approaches Lexi, my muscles tense. "Leave her alone."

"Relax," he shoots back, still moving toward her. He squats low, and all I can see is his back as he blocks her from view. "Lexi. Such a pretty name. A pretty name for a pretty girl."

I can't see what he's doing. Is he touching her? I wriggle around like I can break these chains or something. Instead, all I'm doing is hurting myself even more.

He reaches for Lexi's arm and yanks her to her feet. "Stand up, girl, and don't fight me. You won't win."

Shit. What's he going to do? What do I do? Telling myself to fight so that I can die on my own terms is one thing, but facing it —that's something else. I don't want to die, but I don't want him to hurt her.

He drops whatever he was holding and then reaches into his back pocket. "Now, I'm going to unlock these chains, all right? I want you to tell me you won't try anything. Can you do that, Lexi?"

She's quiet for a moment.

"Answer me, girl," he demands.

"I won't try anything," she whispers.

"Good."

It takes a second for me to recognize what he dropped. *Is that?...* I hear the chains move around and then see them fall onto the ground, a loud clatter echoing in their wake. Her arms are free.

Oh my God.

I want her to run. I want her to look at me so she can see in my eyes that it's okay for her to escape. That I'll be fine, but this is her shot, and she has to try. I know she can do it.

He lifts her shirt over her head, exposing her bra. I can't see his face, but I can tell he's breathing hard. Fucking prick. "Leave her alone!" I yell, kicking my legs and rattling my chains.

He ignores me.

"Don't touch me," Lexi says, her tone shaky with fear.

"I'll do whatever I want," he snaps back, reaching for what looks like a few pieces of clothing on the floor.

Tears sting my eyes, and I wonder if he's going to do to her what he did to me. *Please, God, don't let him hurt her. Please. I'm begging you.* Instead, he's putting another shirt on her.

"Here," he says. "I can't stand how bad you smell. Take off your pants and put these on, too."

I crane to see her face, but he's blocking her from me. Did he just give her clean clothes to wear? Lexi is quiet, and then I see her dirty and bloody pants drop to the floor. She steps out of them, pulling on the shorts.

He locks her up again and hands her paper towels and a trash bag. "Clean up your mess."

Then he turns to me, picking up what's left of the clothes. "You too, Skye." He stands me up, removing my chains.

My heart pounds. I cringe at the sound of my name coming

out of his mouth. Can I do it, though? Can I fight him? I'm scared. Lexi must've been scared, too. Jesus, how can I feel so confident one second, then when my chance comes, I wuss out?

I quickly change into fresh clothes, and he locks me up again. That's it. I've lost my chance. We both did.

He walks toward the steps again, but stops just before them and turns back. "I need you girls to be good now. Things will go much smoother if you are. If not—well, I sure would hate to be the one to tell your folks where to find your bodies."

When he leaves, we're cast in darkness again. I can't see Lexi anymore. I need a minute for my eyes to adjust. "What the hell was that?"

"I don't know," Lexi replies. "I'm sorry, Skye. I know I should've tried to do something, but I was too scared."

"Don't be sorry," I say. "So was I. But Lexi, he gave you a garbage bag."

"Yeah."

I close my eyes, not wanting to tell her the single thought that's running through my mind. But I have to. "It could be our way out."

"What do you mean?" she asks. "How can I use this against him?"

"Not for him, Lex. For us. We can make sure he doesn't hurt either of us again. It's *our* way out."

17
NATE

There must be something the police are overlooking. As I stand in Lexi's bedroom, my gaze roams. Her bed remains unmade, its blush-pink covers lying in a heap. Thick novels line the shelves I mounted on her wall last year. Science fair ribbons hang from her dresser mirror.

Looking around, I quickly realize Ashley and I aren't the parents I thought we were. We didn't have the passwords to get into her laptop or phone. We should've insisted on knowing them. For God's sake, she's only fifteen. What were we thinking?

"Hey."

I turn around and see Ashley leaning against the door frame. Her beautiful red hair hangs down her shoulders, unkempt. Defeat rests behind her eyes. "Hi."

She walks into the room. "It's only been a day, Nate. They'll find her."

"Why didn't we know her passcodes?" I ask. "Why didn't we insist on knowing?"

Ashley shakes her head. "Because we trusted her. I don't think we were wrong in doing that. Lexi is a smart girl. She's not prone to getting caught up in social media."

"We buried our heads in the sand. We should've been more engaged." I turn to her, eyes stinging with tears. "Where is she, Ash? Where the hell is she?"

"I don't know, honey." She walks over to Lexi's dresser, opening the drawers. "Maybe we just need to look harder. Maybe there is something in here we missed."

"Like what? Without access to her computer, we're not going to find anything useful." I join her in her search for—something —anything that might point to where Lexi is right now. "Do we know if Garrett and Mara have gone through Skye's bedroom? Have they searched for answers?"

"I don't know."

"You mean you and Garrett haven't talked about this?" I ask, knowing full well I'm pushing buttons that shouldn't be pushed right now. But I'm pissed. I want my daughter back. Someone must pay for what's happening, and Ashley is the easiest target.

"What?" she asks, her brow knitted. "I've talked to Garrett as much as Mara. What are you trying to say? Because this isn't the time, Nate. You understand? Lexi is gone. I know you're angry, same as me, but that doesn't give you the right to throw the past back into my face."

Anger balls in my gut. This isn't fair. Haven't I suffered enough? Now, my daughter is gone, and I'm just supposed to accept it? *Screw that.* With a guttural roar, I pick up Lexi's mattress and flip it over her bed.

Ashley rocks back on her heels, thrusting her hand over her mouth. I turn to her, my face heating with the kind of rage I haven't felt in five years. "I can't go through something like this. You don't understand."

"*I* don't understand? She's my daughter, too, Nate."

I turn back to look at the bed, out of breath, my pulse racing.

That's when I notice something on the floor, next to the bedframe—something that wasn't there only moments ago. I bend over to pick it up. A wave of nausea courses through me when it begins to register. "Oh my God."

Ashley walks toward me again with cautious steps. "What is it?"

I return to full height, the plastic card between my thumb and index finger. "Where the hell did she find this?"

She looks at it, tilting her head a little. "What is Lexi doing with some random guy's driver's license? Nate, who the hell is that?"

18

LEXI

Three Weeks Earlier

I step out of the high school auditorium, my debate team's final prep session running longer than expected. As much as I like the debate club, I hate it when we have to come in on Saturdays. And now, as I walk out, a storm is coming. Ahead, the clouds are dark and look like they'll soak me through before I get home. I could call Mom and ask her to pick me up, but I don't.

My backpack slouches on one shoulder. I feel my flashcards poking out of the side pocket and quickly push them back in and zip it up. I need those and have spent hours putting them together. No way am I going to let the coming rain ruin them.

Albertson's is just down the block, between the hardware store and the laundromat. Might as well grab a Coke and a candy bar for the walk home.

When I reach the entrance, the glass doors slide open, and I walk inside. The fluorescent lights flicker overhead, and the air conditioner blows above me, messing up my hair. I make a beeline for the fridges in the back, grab a cold soda, and snag a Reese's cup from the display when I reach the checkout.

"Hey, Lexi."

One of the teacher's aides, a senior, works here on the weekends. "Hey, Adam."

"Were you at school?" he asks, glancing at my backpack.

I nod. "Debate club."

"Oh, cool."

"It's really not," I say, poking fun at myself because I know what they all think of me.

"Better than working here, though," he says, smiling.

His comment makes me happy, like maybe not everyone in this school is an asshole. "Yeah, I guess, but at least you get paid." I hand over my money. "Thanks."

"Sure. See ya later, Lexi," he replies.

I step out under the store's awning, pulling back the tab on my can of Coke. The breeze picks up thanks to the approaching storm, pushing a rogue shopping cart across the pavement. I watch it careen toward someone's nice SUV. "Dang it." I set down my things and run into the parking lot to grab the cart seconds before it hits the car. I manage to snatch it just in time, and that's when I spot something on the ground. A small rectangular piece of plastic, just lying there as if someone had dropped it. A driver's license.

"Oh, no." I glance around and notice a guy, sort of young I guess, maybe in his twenties, stepping into a dark blue sedan. He's kind of cute, but obviously way too old for me. It could be his, so I shove the cart into the corral and head toward him. "Hey! Excuse me, sir?"

I hear the roar of his engine. His window is rolled up, and he must not hear me. "Hey? Sir, I think this is yours," I call out, louder this time. I expect him to roll down the window, maybe thank me for saving him the trip to the DMV. Instead, he pulls out, barely glancing my way.

"Okay then," I mutter, the license still pinched between my fingers.

Curiosity eats at me as I walk home. Staring at the license, this guy's face is frozen in the tiny, laminated square. Brown eyes, dark hair. Not smiling. He's twenty-two. The name reads Eric R. Downey, and he's not from around here. This license is from Utah. What the heck is this guy doing here?

When I arrive home, I walk upstairs and head down the hall toward my bedroom, spotting Mom on her exercise bike in the spare room. Dad's at the pharmacy because Saturdays are always super busy.

The spare room has all their workout stuff inside, but I think only my mom uses it. It was supposed to be for another kid they'd wanted, but that never happened. I'm not supposed to know that, but I'm not stupid. I pick up on a lot of things they don't realize. Despite what we show other people, my family is just as messed up as everyone else's.

Once I'm in my room, I drop my backpack on the floor and peel off the paper on the Reese's cup. Snatching my phone from my back pocket, I slip off my shoes and plop onto the bed. "Time to do a little recon on Eric R. Downey."

Rain begins to tap on my window, and I'm happy to have beaten the storm. My bedroom is quickly cast in shadow. The light pink paint on my walls turns dark, and my Lana Del Rey posters somehow appear more ominous. I glance over at my decorative pillow, all fluffy and white, and grab it for comfort.

"Okay. Here we go." I open Instagram and type in his name. The results are instant. I scan through the several profile pics that pop up until I see the one. It's him. At least he isn't wearing the same "I don't give a shit" look that's on his ID.

I debate whether this is a good idea, but then chuckle at the fact that I just left a debate club meeting and can't seem to shut off the practice. Regardless, my parents are always telling me I shouldn't talk to strange people on social media. That it's usually some weirdo who's pretending to be someone he or she isn't.

Still, I know they won't bother checking my posts because they never do. They trust me. Or maybe they only say they trust me when, in reality, it's an excuse not to be the parent. I'm not entirely sure they give a shit what I do. Still, I'm hesitant because I am smart. Then again, he's cute, so I should do the right thing and get his license back to him.

I slide into his DMs.

Me: Hey, weird thing happened. I think I found your driver's license.

Seconds go by, then a minute. Just as I'm about to toss my phone aside, it vibrates.

Eric: No way. Where?

Me: Albertson's parking lot. I tried calling out to you, but you drove off.

Eric: Seriously? Wow. You're a lifesaver.

Me: Glad I could help.

Eric: I owe you one. Maybe I can grab it from you soon? Treat you to coffee or something?

I hesitate, biting my lip. No one's ever asked me to join them for coffee. I've never even been on a date. So cringe. I mean, he seems cool. And it's not like I'd be going to his house or anything. I'm not stupid. It's just coffee—in public.

Me: Maybe. I don't know. I could always mail it to you.

Eric: Sure, yeah. I guess that'd be cool, too. So are you, like, in college or something? You look college-age in your profile pic.

Do I tell him I'm a fifteen-year-old who's still in high school? Should I blow this shot I have at meeting a cool college guy?

Me: Yeah, just community college this year. I'll transfer out of state next year. Can't wait to get out of this town. Where do you go to school?

Am I being sus? How do I even talk to a college guy?

Eric: I graduated earlier this year, actually. I'm in Grant now, living with my parents. They moved from Utah while I was in college. But I've been looking for a job. I totally want to get out of here, so I get it.

We talk more about what kind of job he wants. He asks me what I'm studying. I know I'm a complete fraud, but I like talking to him. Is that so bad? I catch myself smiling at his clever comebacks.

Eric: Listen, I gotta go, but if you want to mail my license back, don't send it to the address listed. I don't live there anymore.

Me: Oh, okay. Hey, if you are hanging around for a while, maybe we could meet up? I mean, if you have the time. And I could bring your license back to you.

Eric: I'd love that, Lexi. Thanks. How about next week? Say, Wednesday? Unless you're busy with school.

Me: No, I can do that. So, I guess just send me a message where you'd like to meet, and I can do it any time after 4 pm.

Eric: Cool. I'll find some place near the grocery store. I figure you must live around there somewhere.

Me: Yeah, I do. Just down the street on Lexington Drive.

Eric: Perfect. And hey, it was great talking to you. Gotta run.

I close my laptop, feeling amazing. Yeah, he's older than me, but not by that much. I mean, it totally won't even matter in a few years what our age difference is.

19
LEXI

At first, I waited for him to do something—something to hurt me. But he didn't. All he did was get me to put on clean clothes. Should I ask? "Hey, Skye?"

"Yeah?"

"Where do you think he got these clothes?"

"I'm not sure I want to know," she replies. "It feels weird wearing them. Like maybe they came from other girls who were down here before us."

"That's what I was afraid of." I turn my gaze toward the steps and the door that's surrounded by faint light. "Will he go after them? Our parents?"

"No," Skye shoots back. "No, he won't do that. He doesn't know where we live. He doesn't know anything about our families. Don't say stuff like that—"

"Okay. Okay, I'm sorry. I didn't mean to." But he has to know more than she thinks. After all, he found us in the woods. I doubt he just hung out there waiting for unsuspecting kids to walk by. Then I feel the tears sting my eyes. "I'm losing my shit in here."

"Well, don't," she demands. "We can't lose it now. We have to think of how we can get out of here. There has to be a way."

"I'm glad to hear you say that because, after what you said before, I thought you were ready to give up."

She scoffs. "I don't know, Lex. I want to fight, but I'm afraid, you know? Shit, this is so messed up."

And then, it occurs to me...Something I hadn't considered until right now. I'm not sure why it's just now coming to me. Maybe because he stood inches from my face. Did I see something in him? Something recognizable? I mean, is it possible all of this is my fault? "Hey Skye, there's something I need to tell you."

"Yeah? What is it?"

"Um, a few weeks ago, I sort of met this guy." I glance at her, but it's too dark to see her face. "And we sort of started talking online. I—I think he's older than me. I found his driver's license in the parking lot at Albertson's. Then I found him online."

"Oh my God, Lexi. You were talking to some rando online? Are you crazy? Holy shit. It's him, isn't it? You met some stalker or killer or something, and he came for you. Only, stupid me, I was with you. Oh my God."

I hear her click her tongue, and if I could see her face, she'd be rolling her eyes and shaking her head at me. She's mad. "Wait. I don't know if it's him. We never met in person. We were supposed to, but it didn't happen. Something always seemed to come up. He doesn't know where I live, Skye, I promise. Besides, it doesn't look like him."

"How can you tell?" she shoots back. "You said you never met him."

"Yeah, but this guy, I don't know, he's older."

"This psycho is wearing a mask, Lexi. You have no idea if it's him. Oh my God. I can't believe this. It's your fault. I'm going to die, and it's your fault."

"Please don't say that." My voice cracks. "It's not him. It can't be. It's not possible. I literally never told him anything about me." But hang on...that's not true.

"Then why did you say anything at all?" she asks. "You must've thought it could be him, or you wouldn't have bothered to open your mouth."

That lump in my throat is back, and I try to choke it down. Maybe this is all my fault. Maybe it's the same guy. How could I be so stupid? Of course no college guy is going to be interested in me. No guy is interested in me at all. Only Skye. They all love her.

"Look," she says, her tone calmer. "I don't mean to blame you, Lexi. I mean, if it is this guy, it's not your fault he's doing this. You didn't bring this on, okay? And I'm sorry for saying you did." She takes a breath and goes quiet for another moment. "Did you tell your parents?"

"No. They would've freaked out," I reply, suddenly understanding why I wasn't allowed to talk to strangers online. "But if it's him, I know his name."

"What is it?" Skye presses.

"Eric Downey." I hear her sigh, like she's thinking hard about the name and wondering what to do about it. "Like I said, I don't know if it's him. But it's definitely someone who lives here. No one except for locals knows about the cut-through, right?"

"I guess," she replies. "But it's not that hard to figure out, Lex."

"No, probably not."

"Even if it is him," Skye continues. "It's not like we can do shit about it."

"Hang on. What if there is?"

"What do you mean?" she asks.

"This is going to sound totally gross, but what if, like, one of us tells him we need the bathroom really bad?" I hear a small chuckle coming from her. "No, I'm serious. What if I tell him I have a stomachache, and I'm going to crap all over the place. That would gross him out, right? He couldn't even handle it when I threw my puke in his face."

"That was pretty good, though," she says, a hint of pride in her tone. "So, you think he'll let you go upstairs to use the bathroom? You could always say you're on your period, too. He already knows I'm not."

I don't want to think of how he already knows that about her. "That would for sure freak him out. If you'd rather do it, I'm okay with that," I insist. "I'm just saying one of us could try, don't you think? The whole stomachache thing? I mean, what choice do we have?"

"Even if you can get upstairs, he's not going to take his eyes off you. Not a chance," Skye replies. "And he'll know you're lying...unless you have to—"

"No, I don't. But you're right. One of us gets up there and then what?" We're both quiet again for several moments. "What if maybe I could find a weapon to use? Something in the bathroom. I don't think he'd come in there with me. That could work, right?"

"Depends on what you find. He isn't going to leave behind something you could use against him, Lex. He's not stupid."

"Well, then, if I can't find something, I'll deal with it. I'll tell him it was a false alarm."

"So he can beat the shit out of you, or worse, for lying?" she asks. "No. That's not happening."

I close my eyes for a moment, regretting every nasty thing I've ever said about Skye Metcalf. This is the girl I once called my best friend. No matter what happened between our parents, whatever it was, none of that matters now. "Skye, if this is my fault, I won't let you suffer for it. I'm gonna do this and it's gonna work."

20

GARRETT

We were out of milk. The perfectly normal function of going to the grocery store to buy more suddenly seems surreal and out of place. My daughter is missing. How can I be standing at the checkout counter, swiping my card to buy a gallon of milk? Because I still have a son. A twelve-year-old who knows nothing of what's happened, only that his sister is off somewhere, probably having to do with cheerleading.

"Here's your receipt, sir," the cashier says. "And I'm so sorry about..."

I take it from her. "Thanks." I leave the store and notice the late afternoon sun sinking behind the trees. Skye's been gone for a full twenty-four hours. They say that's the critical time—those first twenty-four hours—and if no leads develop, chances grow slimmer with each passing day of finding my daughter alive.

As I retrieve my keys, heading into the parking lot, I spot someone standing near my car. Almost immediately, I recognize the man. "Cash? Hi. Everything all right?"

"Mr. Metcalf, hello." He pushes his hands into his pockets. "How are you holding up?"

I shrug. "About as you'd expect. But I have to thank you for coming out this morning to help with the search. It meant a lot to my wife and me."

"Yeah, of course," he replies. "I'm just sorry not much came of it."

"It all helps." I'm ready to open the driver's side door, but I wait a moment. "Saw you checking out my car. She's holding up like a champ."

"I see that." He walks around it as if assessing its worth. "Surprised you held onto it, to be honest."

"Oh yeah? Why is that?" I press, wondering where this is going.

"Well, it's getting up there in age. Had some pretty serious front-end damage a while back." He turns down his lips. "Figured you might want an upgrade."

I narrow my gaze. "Are you trying to sell me a new car?"

He laughs. "Not exactly. I'm simply pointing out that people such as yourself, with successful businesses and nice homes, usually upgrade, particularly if something is damaged, unless there's a reason to hold on to it." His face turns serious. "So, do you? Got reason, Mr. Metcalf?"

"No, sir. But you forget, I'm in finance. I make financial decisions for my clients every day. The same goes for my own finances. And buying a new car just for the sake of it isn't a smart decision." I open my door. "So, no, I'll be keeping this car for a while. She's been good to me."

Cash nods. "Yes, she has, Mr. Metcalf. She knows you pretty damn well." He turns and walks away. "You and your family take care now. I'll be praying for you."

"Thank you." I slip behind the wheel, peering through the rearview mirror as Cash heads toward his car. "The fuck was that?"

. . .

"She's all fixed up, Mr. Metcalf. Good as new." Cash wipes a cloth over the door handle, polishing it up for me.

I walk around my car, inspecting it. No one would ever know how badly it had been damaged in the accident. "It looks as good as the first day I bought it."

"Well, that's the goal." He walks toward me, crossing his arms over his chest. "I will say, though, there was a heck of a lot more damage behind the bumper than I expected. That deer must've been built like a damn brick house."

"I suppose it was," I reply, hesitant to elaborate. Cash didn't ask for details when I brought him my car, and I sure as hell didn't offer any. But the look in his eyes now suggests he's got his suspicions. Just how deep those suspicions go, I can't be sure. And I wonder if he's looking for some sort of payoff to keep those notions to himself.

"Should we settle up?" I press, wanting to get out of here quickly.

"Yes, sir." Cash heads inside the shop and takes a seat behind his desk. "Sorry it took as long as it did. Parts had been on back order. You know how it goes."

I sit down across from him, the scent of motor oil and metal hanging in the air. "I get it. I'm just grateful for the work you've done. It looks fantastic."

"Hmm," he says, eyeing a piece of paper in his hand. "This is the revised estimate I gave you over the phone. You know, I found all that internal work needing to be done as well, so here's the updated invoice, per our discussion."

He hands it to me, and I take a look. It's more than I expected. I look at him and he smiles, saying nothing. But something about his expression—yeah, he knows. He knows I didn't hit a deer. The question is, how much does he know? Is this extra fee meant as payment to keep him quiet? Of course, I'd pay a hell of a lot more and quickly realize he's not as smart a businessman as I would've thought.

Still, there's no way he could prove anything. I washed away the *hair and blood. Bleached everything I could. No, Cash Goodell has nothing on me except a hunch—a gut feeling.*

I sign the invoice. "Looks good to me."

That was five years ago. He's never said a word since, so why now? Why make a point to discuss my car after so much time has passed? Did he talk to the cops this morning before the search? Even so, what would they have said to make him reconsider our unspoken arrangement?

I drive home, almost forgetting about the milk that needs to be put into the fridge. As I arrive and step out of my car, I see Nate next door, getting something out of his. He notices me and I wave. He tosses a nod at me before walking back into his house, acting like nothing's happening. Like our girls aren't missing. How we're all supposed to get through this, I have no idea.

With a deep sigh, I glance through our front window and notice Mara standing in the living room. Just standing there. I head inside. "I got the milk."

Mara turns away from the window, eyeing the bag in my hand. "I just talked to Ashley."

For a moment, I feel a surge of hope. "Does she have news?"

Mara shakes her head. "No. Not from the police." She wraps her arms around herself as if it's cold in here. "Apparently, though, she and Nate were searching Lexi's bedroom, feeling desperate, I guess. Anyway, they found a driver's license belonging to a man from Utah."

"What?" The word catches in my throat. "Why the hell does Lexi have something like that?"

"That's why Ashley called." Mara approaches me, alarm masking her face. "Utah, Garrett. After what Officer Blackwell found today? What do you think that means?"

21

ASHLEY

Five Years Earlier

Stunned, I peer through the cracked windshield for what feels like forever. The headlights illuminate the empty road, capturing the billowing smoke from beneath the hood of Garrett's Mercedes. I touch my fingertips to my throbbing temple, realizing the airbag must've hit me; the deployment forceful enough to cause the injury. And when I look at my hands, blood covers my fingers. My ears are ringing, drowning out my rapid breaths.

No cars are coming from either direction. It's just us out here and whatever lies on the road behind us.

"Are you okay?" Garrett asks.

"Huh?" I turn to him and realize he appears uninjured.

His brow knits as he reaches out for my face. "You're not okay."

I pull back. "I'm fine. Are you?"

He nods, wearing a shocked expression I'm sure mirrors my own.

Every move I make sends a wave of pain through me, but I

need to get out of this car. I have to see if whatever we hit...whatever I think it was...is okay. I shift back onto the passenger seat and reach for the door handle.

"Wait." Garrett grabs my arm. "Where are you going?"

"What are you talking about?" I tighten my brow. "We have to get help. We need to go see what's out..."

"It was a deer," he cuts in. "Nothing we can do about it. We need to go."

My eyes widen, and my mouth drops. "Are you insane? I'm not going anywhere." I open the door. "Except out there to see what we've done."

I stumble out of the wrecked car, bracing myself against it as I walk toward the back. My heart pounds, and my throat turns dry as the reality of what has happened sets in. We're out here alone, the car hissing. And now, I prepare for the worst.

When I reach the back, I see a foot, then a leg, wound gaping, bloody, and unnaturally bent back. Then the rest comes into view. "Oh my God." I brace against the car as my legs wobble.

Lying in a pool of blood, the man is still. The impact crushed his right leg. His left arm lies over his head, and blood trickles down his face. But what is most alarming is his eyes—still wide with shock. Oh, God, is he dead? I already know the answer, but don't dare say it.

Footsteps on the asphalt draw my attention, and I look over to see Garrett walking toward the man. Tears fill my eyes. "What have we done?"

Garrett doesn't respond. Instead, he squats next to the man, checking for a pulse at his neck. He's large, at least 200 pounds. Older, I think. Possibly in his fifties.

"Is he...alive?" I ask.

Garrett stands again, rubbing his hand over his face. "No. He's gone."

Knots tighten my gut, and I feel sick. "What are we going to do? I don't understand where he came from. No other cars are out here. Was he walking?"

"Maybe his car broke down. It could be up the road some-where." Garrett walks toward me, pulling me close. "It's okay, Ash. We'll figure this out."

I push him back, anger rising in my chest. "How? We killed a man, Garrett. You and me. We aren't even supposed to be here. What the hell are we going to tell Nate and Mara? What are we going to do?" Tears stream down my face. Not only is this man's life over, but so is ours. Life as we know it is over. "He must have a family." I clear the emotion from my throat, forging fresh resolve. "No. No, we have to do something. We have to call the police so they can figure out who he is and where he came from."

Garrett grips my arms tightly, his fingers digging into the tender flesh on the underside. "Listen to me, Ashley. We've both been drinking. We weren't exactly paying attention to the road. This man didn't walk out in front of us. I swerved and hit him." He aims his index finger. "You see my tire tracks and the ruts in the shoulder? If the cops come, they'll arrest me. I'll go to jail. No...I'll go to prison...for manslaughter."

I look at the dead man again. "We can't pretend this didn't happen, Garrett. We can't do that."

He lets me go and stands back, folding his arms over his chest. "Then call the police. Call them and tell them what I've done. What *you* were doing when it happened."

His words cut through me, and I see a reality I don't want to accept. "Our kids. Our families," I say, fixing my gaze on him. "We'll lose everything."

"Yes, we will."

I close my eyes, summoning the strength not to throw myself off into that nearby gully. It would be so much easier if I did, rather than face the truth of what I know must be done. "We can't do this alone. If this is going to work, the story, the body…it can't just be us. We need them."

"Nate and Mara," he says, already appearing to know what I'm about to say next. "Alibis."

"Not just that." I point at the body. "We need their help to take care of him. We have to find his car and get rid of that, too."

"Who says they'll even agree to help?" he asks. "Would you if you learned Nate was having an affair with Mara? Would you want to help him get rid of a body because he struck someone with his car while getting a blow job?"

His face heats with anger. Anger at himself and me for what we've done, for how we've deceived the ones we claim to love. He's not wrong. And neither one of us will ever forgive ourselves. But in this moment, self-preservation takes over. I can't lose my husband and daughter. I won't.

The life we've built, I only now fully appreciate. I know how that makes me sound, and it's not something I ever believed I could be capable of doing. But here I am. Here we are. In a situation so utterly inconceivable, it's farcical. Yet, the body on the ground suggests otherwise.

We must make a decision because we won't be alone on this road for long. I pull in a cleansing breath. "We come clean to both of them and beg for forgiveness. Then we beg for their help."

"You don't know if they'll agree," he says.

"Maybe not. Maybe this is the end of everything for us, and rightly so. But I think a part of Nate, probably Mara, too, already knows what we've been doing, and has chosen to live with it. Maybe I'm wrong. But they're smarter than we've given them credit for. All we can do is ask, praying they love us enough to risk everything. Because that's exactly what we're about to demand of them."

22

NATE

Ashley and I don't question the need to bring the driver's license we found in Lexi's room to the police's attention. It's clearly the best lead we have in our daughter's disappearance, along with the knife discovered in the woods. But how easy will it be for Blackwell to connect the license to that night's events, given it's from Utah?

I wait for Ash to join me at the kitchen table as I sip on a cup of coffee, knowing it's much too late for caffeine. She'd spoken to Mara a few minutes ago, telling her what we'd found. Now, with Garrett having just returned, Mara called again. We don't need their approval to do anything, but this still involves all of us, so I don't know which way it will break.

Ashley enters the kitchen, clutching her phone. Her face is unreadable. "What did she say?" I ask. "I assume she told Garrett what we found."

"Yes. She also told me Garrett ran into Cash Goodell at the store. In the parking lot."

I tilt my head. "What's he got to do with anything?"

"Garrett told her that Cash was acting strangely, implying he knew something."

"Knew something. Such as?" I press.

"What do you think?" She pulls out a chair and sits across from me at the table. "He was asking Garrett about his car and when he planned to sell it. Cash suggested, in a roundabout way, that he knew the cause of the accident wasn't a deer."

"For God's sake." I slouch down in the chair. "You don't think...no." I shake my head.

Ashley narrows her gaze. "What?"

"The timing seems convenient. First, the pocketknife, then this driver's license. Cash showing up, acting cagey. You think he knows this guy?" I tap my index finger on the ID as it rests on the table.

She stares at the picture. "I'm not sure how that's possible. Even if Cash does know the man, it doesn't explain why Lexi would have had that ID in her bedroom."

I sip on my coffee again and peer through the window at the setting sun. "Maybe Cash knows more than we think. Maybe he knows where the girls are, too."

"Are you serious?" She points at the license. "That's not him, Nate. That's not the guy."

"Well, you'd know better than me." I wince, immediately regretting the comment. "I'm sorry. I'm sorry, Ash. I didn't mean it." Her eyes redden as she looks away. "Our focus should be on getting the girls back. I know that. But we have to consider the possibility that Cash knows the truth. Maybe he'd found something when he fixed Garrett's car, I don't know."

Ashley's expression shifts, her gaze darting away from me. "Okay. Say you're right. Why wait five years to act on it? It doesn't make sense. What makes sense is the man in this picture, staring back at us like he knows something. Like he has our daughter. I'm not ignoring the obvious—it's a Utah license, then we have the pocketknife. A connection exists regardless of whether we want to admit it."

"What are you saying?"

She closes her eyes. "If we give this to the cops, they'll figure it out."

"No one knows what happened back then," I reply. "No names, no missing persons. Nothing. So, I'm not keeping this from them. The guy in that picture—he could have Lexi right now, doing God knows what to her and Skye. No, screw that. I'll call Blackwell myself and tell him."

"You're right. Of course you're right," she replies, rising from the chair. "It's the only logical solution."

"What are you going to do?"

"Find out what it is Cash Goodell thinks he knows. I'll leave the cops to you. If Cash is involved, we should figure that out right now."

"Jesus, Ash." I get to my feet. "You're not going to see him tonight. What, you want him to call the cops on you? Don't you think they'll wonder why you're harassing him?"

She pushes her hand through her thick red hair. "I can't sit here and wait for something to happen, Nate. I can't wait for that call from Blackwell, telling me our daughter is dead."

I approach her, grabbing her arms, wanting to shake some sense into her, but I lock onto her gaze. "Then let's take the license to Blackwell tonight. He can find out who this man is, test that knife for prints, and see if it matches this guy. Look, just because it's a Utah license doesn't mean he's connected, all right? Even I can admit that's a leap."

"You can't be that naïve, Nate," she replies.

I loosen my grip on her, letting my arms fall to my sides. "I don't want to sit around any more than you do. But I'm not convinced what's going on now has anything to do with the past. It's been five years. Come with me. Please. Let Blackwell look into it. There's no possible way he can connect any of this to what happened."

She nods, and I realize I've convinced her to see reason. "Yeah. Okay. What about the Metcalfs? Should they go too?"

The last thing I want is to be around Garrett Metcalf. "Let's wait to see what Blackwell finds. It could be nothing."

"But they already know about it, Nate," Ashley replies. "If we talk to Blackwell, they're going to want to be there. As much as you don't want them involved in this, they are. Their daughter is missing, just like ours. And if we don't put all this shit behind us, we're never going to find them."

23
GARRETT

Mara and I are sitting in our living room. Both of us, on the sofa, watching the muted television. The side table lamps burn a soft white, and the wall clock ticks away, reminding me I have yet to save my daughter. Meanwhile, I'm thinking that something is wrong here, besides the obvious.

"Should we tell them to take it to the cops?" Mara asks.

I lean over and rest my elbows on my thighs, rubbing my hands together. "I can't believe this is a coincidence."

"No, me either," she replies. "And it could be our best shot at finding the girls. You get that, right?"

"Yeah, I do." I regard her. "And I want Skye back more than anything."

"So do I, Garrett. So, we agree? We all go to the station and talk to Blackwell?"

"What about Cash?" I ask, sitting upright again. "What if that son of a bitch knows the truth?" I don't tell her I suspect he's known all along. "Maybe the guy on the license, whoever he is, talked to Cash. What if they're working together?"

"Working together?" Mara shrugs. "Then it makes all the more sense to get the cops looking out for him. Garrett, I need my girl back home. This might be our only shot. None of what happened before matters right now. You know that."

"Of course I do." I rise to my feet. "Look, you three should go to the station. I'm going to make sure Cash doesn't have a hand in any of this."

"How?" Mara rises to join me. "How are you going to do that without giving yourself away?"

"I don't know, but I'll figure it out. We'll go next door and tell the Brewers the plan."

"And if they don't agree?" she asks.

"They will. All any of us want is to get our girls back. No matter the cost." I head toward the door, grab my car keys, and wait for Mara to catch up. "You ready?"

"Just give me a minute. I need to check in on Milo." She grabs her phone and makes the call.

I hate that we're doing this to our son. Milo's still with Mara's parents. Neither of us has the nerve to tell him what's really going on. And I admit, a part of me is glad he's not here. If all of this is happening because of...then Milo is safer somewhere else.

"Hi, sweetheart," Mara says into the phone. "I just wanted to see if you're enjoying your visit with Grandma and Grandpa."

Tears prick my eyes as I watch her speak. Mara's a wonderful mother. I wish I was a better father.

"That's great," she says. "Don't you worry about your school-work. I'll make sure you don't get behind on anything." She nods. "Not much longer now, baby. I promise. Okay. You have fun. Dad and I love you, and we'll speak tomorrow. Bye, sweetheart." Mara pockets her phone and slings her bag over her shoulder. "I'm ready."

We walk to the Brewers' house under a dark sky. I don't know if I can survive another night without my daughter. I'm certain

Mara can't. Yet the four of us are about to rip open a wound that nearly destroyed us all. None of that matters in the face of losing our children. I know who we are and what we've done. But we'd still do anything for our kids. No matter what.

Mara knocks on the door. Nate opens it, and only a moment later, Ashley approaches. "We're here about the license," Mara says.

Nate casts down his gaze for a moment. "We take it to Blackwell?"

Mara and I nod, and I glance at Ashley. "You three should go. I need to take care of something else."

"I'm sorry, you have something more important than this?" Ashley asks, barely hiding her irritation.

"Cash Goodell," Nate replies, seemingly already knowing my intention.

I nod. "That's right. He could be involved in our girls' disappearances. After my encounter with him earlier tonight, there's not a chance in hell I'm brushing it off as meaningless."

"We get what you're saying, in fact, Ash and I just discussed this," Nate continues. "But he was there this morning, helping us search for them. If he is involved, why would he risk showing up like he did?"

"To make it look like he's on our side, helping us," Garrett replies. "He could also have been out there this morning to see where the investigation is heading."

"I suppose that makes sense," Nate adds, trading a knowing look with Ashley. "All right. The three of us will go, and when Blackwell asks where you are, Garrett, what do we say?"

I look at Mara, and we appear to reach the same conclusion. "I had to go to the office. Hand over some files to my staff while I'm dealing with all this. It sounds reasonable enough, and I don't think he'll question it." I regard the others and then eye Mara again. "Okay. You guys should get this over with and pray to God

Blackwell finds something useful." I give Mara a peck on the cheek and return to my car, leaving her with the Brewers.

After climbing behind the wheel, I press the ignition and head out. I'm not exactly sure where. Cash's body shop? It's probably closed for the night. Maybe that's a good thing. After all, if he knows more than he's saying, the answers could lie in there. Did I just convince myself to break into the body shop?

If I'm going down, I'm going down knowing my daughter is safe. Besides, what's another felony charge?

24
MARA

We say nothing as I sit in the backseat of the Brewers' car, driving toward the police station. Instead, I peer through the window at the blur of silhouetted trees against a dark sky, wondering where my daughter is and who the hell has her.

I try my best not to place blame. This could be some twisted psycho who Lexi had met thanks to that license, which I suspect was left for her to discover just for that reason. But I can't ignore the obvious—if it was left intentionally, then Lexi was targeted. Then the question becomes—why? Targeted out of some obsession, or targeted because of the actions of her parents? And then, where does Skye fit into this? Well, it stands to reason she's a target for precisely the same reason as Lexi—us.

I worry about what Garrett will do, but I worry more about what's happening to Skye. No doubt, Nate feels the same about Lexi. Both of us were thrust into an impossible situation, and we gave in. So who's really to blame?

"We're here," Nate says, pulling into the parking lot.

"Do we know if Blackwell is on duty?" Ashley asks.

"No, but if he's not, Wiley probably is." Nate cuts the engine. "Either way, we'll get someone to help us. I'm not leaving here until we do." He steps out of the car.

I climb out of the backseat, joining them as we walk onward to the precinct's entrance. Somehow, I should've known that our past would catch up to us.

We don't talk about what happened—the affair, or the accident. We've excelled at keeping it under the rug. I wonder, though, if Skye knows more than she's let on. After all, it became pretty obvious that our families stopped hanging out. Then the girls drifted apart. I know my daughter, and she's smarter than she realizes. I hope to God that's what saves her if we can't.

I don't know what will happen now, except that I'll do anything to get her back, even if it means we all go to prison for our crimes.

Nate opens the glass door for us, and I walk inside behind Ashley. The lobby is quiet. Chairs, empty. The bitter odor of stale coffee drifts in the air. Our footsteps echo against the tile floor as we continue inside. Soon, we're recognized by the officer at the counter.

"Evening," he says, his eyes holding compassion. It's a stark contrast against his crisp black uniform and crew cut hair. "What can I help you folks with tonight?"

Ashley steps forward, taking the lead as she always does. "We'd like to talk to Officers Blackwell or Wiley, if either is available."

He types something on his keyboard and stares at the monitor in front of him. "Officer Blackwell is here. I'll let him know you'd like to see him." He picks up his phone. "Why don't you all take a seat over there?"

We walk toward the narrow waiting area. Two rows of black metal chairs with vinyl seats facing each other. Grant, Idaho, is a small town with a police force of less than twenty. Many of the officers came out this morning and helped with the search. I've lived here for ten years now, and this is the first time I've stepped foot inside the police station. I don't like it. I feel exposed, like everyone knows what we've done.

"Officer Blackwell."

I return to the moment and notice Nate with his hand extended, approaching the officer. This is it. What happens in these next several minutes will decide the rest of our lives.

"Mr. and Mrs. Brewer." He looks at me. "Mrs. Metcalf. What can I do for you?"

Nate holds out the license. "We found this in Lexi's bedroom a little while ago."

Blackwell raises a single brow and takes the license. He examines it, turning it over, studying the back of it. "Any of you folks know this gentleman?"

"No, sir," Nate says. "None of us, which is why we're here."

Blackwell regards us for a moment. "Come on back. We'll talk in my office." He leads us into the hallway and glances back at me. "Where's Mr. Metcalf?"

"Oh, he had to run into his office. He's handing off several clients to his staff so he can keep focused on finding our daughter."

"I see." Blackwell reaches his office and gestures inside. "Why don't you all take a seat?" He follows us into the somewhat cramped space.

There are just enough chairs to go around, so I take my seat while the Brewers sit next to me. Tension fills the air, like we're all afraid of what will happen next. Can Blackwell sense it? Any cop worth his salt probably could. The four of us stand to lose a great deal, but it's nothing compared to losing our daughters.

Blackwell rounds his desk, taking a seat behind it. "All right.

So, you found this driver's license. I suppose that means Lexi never mentioned it to you before."

"That's right," Ashley begins. "Never said a word. In fact, Nate found it under her mattress, so she was clearly hiding it. We just don't know why."

"Our forensics team is still working on gaining access to the girls' phones and laptops," Blackwell adds. "That might shed light on this situation, but in the interim, leave this with me. Between this ID and the knife, we could have a substantial lead. I'll dig up anything and everything I can on this gentleman and see if he's someone we should be talking to. And when I get the prints back, I'll run them through the database and pray for a match." He hesitates a moment, glancing between the three of us. "I will say that this is the best lead we have at the moment, and I'm pleased to see you're doing what you can to help us find your girls. That said, I'll keep you posted. It won't take me long."

"You'll look into this tonight, right?" I ask. "Another night for these girls could be their last, Officer."

"Yes, ma'am. I understand where you're coming from. I won't waste any time, that's a promise. But I would like you all to go on back home. Let us do what we can, and like I said, I'll let you know if this means something."

He stands up as if he, alone, has determined this meeting is over. I glance at Nate and Ashley, who appear to mirror my expression. We all thought we'd get answers, and we're about to leave without a single one. "That's it? You want us to sit and wait for you to find out who this guy is?"

"Yes, Mrs. Metcalf," Blackwell says. "That's exactly what I want you to do. Look, this license is out of state. It's not like I can drive to this man's house and ask him if he took your daughter. And I need time for the prints to be processed. Now, I understand what you're going through."

"Oh, I don't think you do, Officer," I reply, sensing I've crossed a line. I can see it in Ashley's face.

"Come on, Mara." Ashley reaches out to me. "He's going to get answers for us. We need to let him do his job."

I scoff, nodding along, just like they all want me to. "Yeah, okay. Fine."

25

GARRETT

If there's another way in, I can't find it.

I've circled the building twice now, my flashlight cutting through the darkness in search of anything. The beam lands on locked doors, shuttered windows, and those damned bay doors —closed tight and secured with heavy bolts. I mutter under my breath, frustration bubbling under my skin. Every corner I check feels like another dead end, keeping me on the outside.

The grounds are quiet, save for the crunch of gravel under my shoes. I'd scanned the perimeter earlier for security cameras, sweeping my light along every eave and corner of the building. Nothing. Not a single suspicious glint of glass or the faint red blink of a recording device. That doesn't mean there aren't cameras inside, though, watching from shadows where I can't see them. But at this rate, I'm not getting in there to find out. Not unless I'm willing to make some noise—smash a window or two —and that's asking for trouble.

I press my palm against the cool metal of one of the bay doors, leaning into it as if sheer willpower might force it open. "What the hell did I expect?" I whisper to myself. "Of course it's locked up tight." My voice reverberates in the surrounding stillness. A sigh escapes me as I pull back, running my hand through my hair. "Now what?"

My gaze flicks toward the chain-link fence at the back of the property. The faint metallic glimmer draws my attention, and I squint at it. That must be where he keeps the cars he's working on. A storage yard for vehicles waiting to be fixed.

I make my way around the side of the building, keeping close to its walls as I approach the fence. My flashlight casts a halo over the cracked asphalt and pea gravel I trample on my way over. When I reach the fence, I aim my light inside.

Three rows of cars sit in various states of disrepair, their distorted bodies shining faintly under my light. Some are missing bumpers; others have doors with mismatched paint. Still others have crumpled front ends and look like they aren't worth the trouble of fixing. It reminds me of an emergency room waiting area. Except here, there's no urgency. But even as I take it all in, something else gnaws at me.

Why now? Why would Cash come at me now, after all this time? Five years have passed since he fixed my car. He didn't ask questions then, didn't pry into why I needed his help so desperately or why I seemed so hush-hush about it all. And his employees? They never said a word to me beyond polite pleasantries.

So what changed?

The question spins in my mind as I step closer to the gate and inspect its lock. A thick chain weaves through the aluminum posts, secured by a padlock that looks sturdy. I give it a tug anyway —half out of habit and half out of hope that maybe someone was careless enough to leave it undone.

No such luck. "Great. Just great."

I glance over my shoulder, half-expecting someone to pop out of nowhere. But then an idea strikes—a risky one, sure, but better than standing here doing nothing while questions worm through my brain. I keep wire cutters in my trunk. It's part of a kit I use when I go mountain-biking. They're small, but sharp enough to cut through this chain-link fencing. Will Cash notice? Probably. But when he sees nothing's been stolen, he'll chalk it up to kids messing around.

That's what I'll be banking on.

Returning to my car, I rummage through the kit in my trunk, every sound around me setting my nerves on edge. And when I find the cutters, I walk back to the fence. The metal handles feel solid in my grip as I position the cutters against one section of chain link and squeeze hard.

The first snap echoes in the night air, followed by another and another until there's just enough space for me to slip through. Sweat beads on my brow even though it's gotten cooler since I arrived. My nerves stand on end. I swear I'm not a criminal, yet evidence would suggest otherwise.

Crouching low, I shimmy through the opening carefully—or at least I try to. The jagged edges catch on my shirt as I move forward, and pain slices across my shoulder.

"Son of a bitch!" I reach back instinctively, my fingers brushing against wet warmth. Blood—not much—but enough to remind me how easily things can go wrong when you're trespassing.

I glance back at the fence and spot the torn strip of fabric hanging from one of the cut lines. Blood, too—glaring pieces of evidence. "Perfect," I grumble as I yank it free, then use it to wipe off the blood. Am I even up to date on my tetanus shot? Fuck it. I need answers. I stuff the fabric into my pants pocket before moving forward again.

Once inside the yard, I sweep my flashlight across it. Shadows bounce off the rows of vehicles, and that Stephen King book pops into my head—that one with the old car with a mind of its own.

"What am I even looking for?" The question tumbles out as if hearing my own words might bring me answers. But no answer comes—not yet anyway—and so I walk down each row despite doubt and fear of being caught gnawing at me. And then... I stop cold. My flashlight lands on a single vehicle tucked near the far end of the lot—a dark sedan with Utah plates glinting under its beam. Blue? Black? I can't be sure.

"What the hell?" Realization clicks into place like puzzle pieces.

Every other car here bears Idaho plates—all except this one. I guarantee that's not a coincidence.

26

ASHLEY

We're no closer to finding our daughters than we were an hour ago. Officer Blackwell insisted we go home and wait while he looked into the driver's license. Easy for him to say. He doesn't have to go another night not knowing where his child is or if she's even alive.

Nate pulls onto our driveway, and the three of us step out. I notice Mara glancing at her home. Still no sign of Garrett's car. I regard Nate for a moment, wanting to question why he didn't push back on Garrett's decision to dig into Cash Goodell when I'd suggested the very same thing. But it occurs to me now, Nate might've been laying some groundwork. Leaving Garrett to confront Cash, rather than either of us doing it. I don't hate the idea, if that's the case. Especially since I'm positive Cash knew about the affair, recalling his words to me during the search. I said nothing to Nate about it. What would have been the point? I didn't believe it had anything to do with the girls—at the time. Now? I'm not so sure. Still, sometimes, Nate surprises me.

Mara is still staring off toward her house. I reach for her shoulder. "What do you want to do? Wait at our house for him to get back?"

She turns back to me, seeming to ponder whether it's worse to wait with me, who she hates, or wait alone in her house for her husband, who I doubt she's fond of anymore.

"If he found anything," Mara begins. "You should probably hear it too. I'll hang out with you two until he returns."

I nod, a tender smile on my face. "Good. You shouldn't be alone right now. I'll pour us a glass of wine."

She follows us inside, and we head into the kitchen. Nate said nothing on the drive home. Then again, what is there to say? "I'm opening a bottle of wine," I call out to him. "Care for a glass?"

He drops onto the dining chair. "Sure. Why not?"

In the quiet of our house, I pour three glasses and offer one to Mara, then one to Nate. We say nothing for several minutes when headlights shine just beyond our front window. "That could be Garrett," I say.

Mara jumps from her chair and rushes toward the door, pulling it open. Nate and I trade a glance, and I imagine he's thinking the same thing I am—what did Garrett find?

We rise and join Mara outside. She's already next door, waiting for Garrett to step out of his car. He peers at us, and then the two of them head back our way. I widen my stance, preparing to hear, well, probably nothing.

"Cash either took our girls," Garrett begins, "or he knows who did."

"What makes you think that? What'd you find?" Nate asks.

Garrett holds up his phone, the screen open to an image. I step closer for a better look. "A Utah license plate."

He nods. "Yep."

"That's all you found?" Mara asks. "After what he said to you earlier, this is all you managed to find?"

"It's not like I could break in, Mara," he snaps back. "I got into his yard and had a look around, then spotted this dark sedan. No damage that I could see, which is strange for a guy who runs a body shop. Why would he keep a car there that didn't need work? And how many Utah plates do you see around here?"

"Still." Nate shakes his head. "It's a stretch to think there's a connection. We could go talk to him. You and me. Tonight."

"What are you going to do, Nate?" I press. "Accuse him of kidnapping our girls?" Suddenly, I'm thinking I was wrong in my earlier assessment. I look at Garrett's phone again. "No, he'll see what Garrett did tomorrow, then press charges against him for harassment."

"It's not too late to talk to him tonight," Garrett adds, setting his sights on Nate.

"So, you'll just knock on his door and show him that picture?" Mara asks. "The one you took while trespassing on his property? Breaking into his yard? Think about it, Garrett."

"And what do you think we should do, Mara?" he asks, irritation growing in his voice.

"Okay, okay." I raise my hands and look around. "The neighbors are going to hear us out here. Let's just all take a breath and go inside to talk about this."

As I place my hand on Nate's shoulder, he pulls away. "What's wrong?"

He regards me, pursing his lips and shaking his head. "Garrett's right. After what Cash said to him, now this car in his yard? Look, I was leery before, but now? We aren't taking any chances with our daughter's life by cutting Cash Goodell slack." He looks at Garrett. "Let's go. You and me. We'll talk to him and find out what the hell's going on."

"Do you both want to get arrested?" Mara asks.

But before she gets an answer, they're already heading toward Garrett's car.

"Let 'em go, Mara," I say. "There's nothing we can do. Maybe this isn't a bad thing."

"Are you serious?" Her eyes roam over me like I'm crazy.

"Blackwell is going to do what he has to do...by the book, right?" I ask. "How the hell long do you think that's going to take? Another day, maybe two? Our girls could be dead by then."

"Not you, too." She turns away for a moment, then whips back around. "I should've known you'd be on their side."

"I'm on the side of our kids," I reply, although I didn't know where Nate was going with this. And while I'm not sold on the idea, it may be the only way to get Cash to talk while Blackwell takes his sweet time looking into the ID we found.

"Then what are we supposed to do in the meantime? Sit on our asses, drinking wine, pretending as if we like each other?" Mara asks.

I peer out over our quiet street. "No. But there is something else we can do." I set my gaze on her. "We go make sure no one's uncovered our mistake."

27
SKYE

He hasn't given us any food or water for hours. My stomach is eating itself, and my mouth feels like I've been chewing on sand. Now, all I can think of is what Lexi said about dying from dehydration—that terrifying fact she casually tossed my way.

On the upside... I haven't peed my pants yet since I got this fresh change of clothes. The thought makes me want to laugh, but my body is too sore and too exhausted to do even that much.

Lexi's grand plan for taking down this psycho asshole is insane. Completely insane. And yet... part of me admires her for dreaming it up. But admiration won't save her if she tries something crazy like that. If she goes through with it, he'll kill her without a second thought. And then I'll be next, after he's finished with me. If it comes to that, I'd rather die outright than go through whatever he has planned. I'll use that bag he left down here to do it.

But how do I stop her? How do I convince her to give up this idea when she's so damn stubborn?

Somewhere in the darkness, I hear her humming a song that

barely reaches my ears. I know the tune but can't place it. My mind is too busy telling my body to conserve resources. "Lexi?" My voice is gruff, barely a whisper.

The humming stops. "Yeah?"

"If he comes back down, please don't go through with it, okay? Promise me you won't. He'll kill you."

Her silence stretches so long that I wonder whether she's ignoring me or just doesn't have an answer.

"What choice do I have, Skye?" She breaks through the quiet. "No one's going to find us down here. You know that as well as I do...Hey, you remember that time...one of our last sleepovers when you stayed at my house?"

"That was, what, the fifth grade?"

"Summer of the fifth, I think," she replies. "Anyway, we snuck outside and walked down to the store for candy?"

I laugh a little. "Yeah, I remember. Our parents didn't even come check on us."

"I know. They were all acting weird back then. But you remember how, when we came back, we couldn't climb up to my bedroom window?"

"Oh my God." I rear back my head. "That's right. I totally forgot about that. I was freaking out, and you were super calm about it."

"Because I knew we could find a way back inside without ringing the doorbell—without letting my mom and dad know we'd left the house."

"And you did—you figured out a way." We're both quiet for a moment. I take a deep breath before continuing. "But this is different, Lex. If you can't stop him. If you get up there and can't pull it off, or can't find anything to use against him. Things will only get worse for both of us, worse than we can imagine. Is that what you want?"

"No."

"Then don't do it. Please. I couldn't stand knowing something happened to you. It's not even so much that I'd be next..."

She sighs. "Look, just like when we were ten, it's up to us to do something. To find a way through this. Skye, it has to be us."

Lexi's right—we're alone in this basement with no one coming to save us. "You know, it's been hours since he came down here last. What if his plan is just to leave us here until we rot?"

"If that's what he's planning, then there's nothing we can do about it. But I don't think he'd put us in clean clothes if that was the case," she replies. "All I'm saying is that if he gives us an out, even a slim chance, I'm taking it. I let the last chance slip away. That won't happen again."

"Fuck it. Maybe you're right," I say. "One of us has to get out of here, or neither of us will. You're probably the best one for the job anyway."

A creak from the top of the stairs stops us both cold. The basement door swings open. Light spills into the room, blinding after hours spent in near-total darkness. Heavy boots stomp down the wooden steps.

He's back.

Shit. Did he hear us? Does he know that we're planning something? But then I see them—two plastic water bottles swinging from his hands—and relief swells in my chest. Thank God.

As he approaches, his towering frame looming toward us, I force myself not to flinch or cower. I glance at Lexi, and her gaze appears locked onto him. What is she going to do?

He stops in front of me first, blinking hard behind that stupid mask. Then he holds one bottle toward me without a word.

My instincts kick in. I yank it from him like some crazed animal, twisting off the top and gulping it down so fast I start to feel sick.

He's watching me, sizing me up to see just how desperate I've become. My body tenses, but I don't stop drinking the water. I can't.

When I empty the bottle, he doesn't say a word. Instead, he turns toward Lexi, then walks to her. She stiffens as he approaches, her wide eyes darting at me for reassurance.

"Just drink," I mouth. "Don't fight."

She nods—just a little, but I see it. Her lips tremble when he hands her the bottle. She drinks slowly at first, and I don't know how she's able to control herself. I could drink another bottle just as fast as the first.

While she drinks, her eyes stay deadlocked on his mask, appearing suspicious of what he'll do next. When she's finished, he steps back, shifting his gaze between us.

"Good girls," he says, his voice low and muffled behind the mask.

He turns back to me then, and for just a second, our eyes meet. I know what's about to happen. This time, it's not only about me. He wants Lexi to see it. To understand how powerless we are against him. Maybe he heard us after all, and this is our punishment.

My eyes redden, filling with tears, but I blink them away. I'm not giving this asshole the satisfaction of seeing me cry again.

He grabs my ankles without warning, his grip bruising as he yanks hard enough to send me sliding off the wall I've been leaning against. My back slams onto the concrete floor with a dull thump that knocks the air from my lungs. Pain shoots up my spine like I've been stabbed, but I grit my teeth and stay silent.

Lexi gasps. "No! Leave her alone!" With desperation in her voice, she yanks on the chains.

"Take note, girl," the man says without even looking at her. "You're next."

He hovers over me now, blocking out everything else. His hands move to loosen his belt buckle, and when he unbuttons his pants and pulls down the zipper, my stomach turns. I'm going to puke up all that water I drank.

But then... I hear it. A strangled, gurgling sound, wet and choking. The man freezes mid-motion, his head whipping back toward Lexi.

"The fuck?" He straightens up and marches toward her. "What the hell are you doing?"

I crane my neck to see around his wide frame. Lexi is twitching in her restraints—her head jerking back so hard it looks like it might snap off. Foam bubbles at her lips as her body twists against the chains.

It hits me like a bolt of lightning. This is a seizure. Or at least, it's meant to look like one. I've known Lexi for most of my life, and she doesn't get seizures. Instead, this is what she's chosen to do to protect me. Lexi found a way, just like she said she would.

"She's having a seizure!" I shout, faking panic. "She's going to die if you don't help her!"

The man takes a step back and stands there like he doesn't know what to do.

For a split second, I catch Lexi's eyes through all the chaos. And I see it. This isn't real. This is her plan. I do my best to hide my smile. I knew she could do it. I never should've doubted her. And he believes it too. He's falling for it.

"She needs help!" I cry out again, trying to sell the act with everything I have left in me. "Do something or she'll die!"

28

LEXI

He's standing over me, and it feels like the air's being sucked out of the room. I can't breathe. I literally can't breathe. He's just there, and I don't know what he's going to do. So I keep going. I keep flopping around, making sure his attention stays on me. Skye is doing her part by screaming at him to help me. She knows this isn't real, and yet she's playing along so that if I do this, if I convince him to get me out of here, I might stand a real shot at getting us help.

I'm scared to death, but I shove it down, locking it away. I can't let it show. This was the only thing I could think to do. The only move left to make. If he realizes I'm faking, if he catches even a hint of hesitation or doubt in my act, I'm probably dead. No, not probably. Definitely dead. And so is Skye.

My limbs jerk and twist on the concrete floor, and I'm sure I look crazy or possessed. I feel like I'm insulting actual epileptics, but my knowledge of seizures comes from TV shows and movies, and I bet they're overly dramatic for that reason. Never mind that now. I'm not trying to win an Oscar. I need to survive—to make sure we both survive.

Just as I'm about to shift again, his boot digs into my back, shoving my entire body toward the wall.

"Hey." He sounds pissed. "The fuck is wrong with you, huh?" The toe of his boot twists harder into my spine, grinding deeper and sending pain up my back.

"I told you!"

It's Skye. She sounds desperate. Oh God, he doesn't believe me, and she's trying to convince him.

"She's having a seizure! You have to help her!" Skye says.

"Shut up," he yells, his voice bouncing off the walls.

I have to level up, or I've lost, so I bite down on my tongue. Pain shoots through my mouth like an electric shock, and then the coppery taste of blood fills it. It pools there for a minute before I let it spill out, dripping down my chin. He has to see it now—see that this is real. The pain is real, that's for sure.

Before I know it, his hands clamp hard under my arms. He hauls me up like I weigh nothing, and my legs dangle in his grip. My instinct is to fight back and try to escape—but I can't. Instead, I go limp, letting my head slump forward, like I've passed out.

He's gotta undo my chains now, right? Maybe take me upstairs and lay me on a couch or something? This is way better than the bathroom idea—this is working.

I don't know what to think as he holds me there, like he's debating what to do with me. Which way is this going to go? Is he going to throw me against the wall and kill me, or is he going to take me out of here?

"Goddam it," he grumbles.

My bare heels scrape against the rough concrete as he drags me across the room. For just a second, I shift my gaze toward Skye. It's risky, but I need to see her. Her wide eyes lock onto mine instantly. I feel her fear and panic like it's part of me. Her lips open a little like she's about to say something—to scream or beg or plead—but nothing comes out.

One thing is clear. Neither of us knows what's going to happen next, or if this is the last time we'll ever see each other.

He pulls me to the steps, dragging me up as I twitch, still playing the part. I don't know what else to do. If I stop now, he'll leave me down here, chaining me back up, and all of this will have been for nothing. I at least have to get upstairs. Maybe I can figure out where we are.

When the door opens, I feel the fresh air on my face. Oh my God. It's cool and doesn't smell of vomit and pee. He steps inside, pulling me backward, and I look at Skye again. She nods just a little—just enough for me to know I have to keep going no matter what.

He drags me into a hallway, and now I see I'm in a house. But where? It has wood floors that are scratched up and old-looking. White walls, but they're dirty and have scuff marks everywhere. I don't see pictures or anything on them.

It occurs to me now that seizures don't usually last that long, I don't think. So, I moan a little, trying to make it seem like I'm coming around. I move my feet, and he stops pulling me.

We're in the living room. And that's when I realize the place smells like dirty laundry and rotten food. Better than in the basement, but not by much. I take in everything I can. The crappy furniture, the layout of the rooms, how far I am from the front door, and anything around me I can use against him.

He tosses me onto the sofa, and its springs dig into my back. Then again, I've been lying on a concrete floor for I don't know how long, so this is a huge improvement. But then he just stares at me, his eyes narrowing behind the mask. My heart feels like it's going to beat right out of my chest.

"You done?" he asks, hands on his hips like I've been throwing a tantrum.

But I don't have to pretend to be scared. I'm pretty sure he sees it. "Water."

He snorts, tilting his head. "You had me there for a second. But don't for one minute think this changes a goddam thing."

He lays his hands on me.

My stomach knots, tight and sick, but I stay still. I got him away from Skye. That has to count for something. Even if it means I pay the price.

He fumbles at my shorts. Tears well, but I shut my eyes—tight. I'm not here. I'm not *me*. I'm somewhere else.

I'm back in our yard. Dad's laughing, yelling "Nice shot!" as the volleyball sails over the net. The sun's warm on my shoulders. Mom's clapping from the old wood deck.

Then he's on top of me. Heavy. Suffocating. His breathing is loud and harsh. I feel the pain begin, deep and burning, and a cry rips from my chest.

Make it stop. Please, just make it stop.

I scream—but his hand crushes over my mouth. I freeze, locked in panic—but then I see his eyes. Just for a second. Not a monster. A man. A coward. And something shifts.

No. Not like this. Not without a fight.

I twist my body, panic giving way to fury. My leg breaks free, and I slam my heel into the back of his calf—hard.

"Goddamn it!" he yells.

He falters. Good. I don't stop. I drive my foot into him again, writhing underneath him, refusing to be still, to be silent.

His balance slips. His grip loosens. I scream again—louder, stronger.

And then—he falls. A heavy crash against the floor.

I scramble upright, yanking my shorts up with shaking hands. He's moaning, clutching his leg, writhing in pain. I can't tell what happened—maybe he hit something. I don't care.

This is my chance. Move, Lexi. Move now.

I crawl to the other side of the couch, ready to hoist myself over the arm, when I feel his hand clutch my ankle. He yanks me hard, and I fall off, thumping onto the floor next to him.

He leans into my ear. "Did you think I was finished with you?"

29
SKYE

I hear movement up there, and I think I heard her scream. Is she hurt? Is she still alive? I strain to listen for any sign that Lexi is okay. But I'm left with silence. My eyes flick to the door. He didn't lock it this time. It's shut, but not locked. That should feel like hope, but it doesn't, not when I'm still chained up like an animal.

I tug at the chains again, like maybe this time they'll magically break, but all I get is the same clinking sound and a sting around my wrist. Stupid.

Okay. *Think, Skye. Think.*

The light shines overhead. He left it on when he went upstairs, and for the first time, I really *see* the room. I wish I didn't.

The walls are rough brick, stained dark in some places, with what—I don't want to know. At first, I think the marks near the floor are just cracks or dirt—but when I lean closer, I see them for what they are. Scratches.

I turn slowly, the metal cuffs pinching at my skin. Every part of me wants to look away—but I can't. There are scratches everywhere. Fingernails? Oh God. I can't think like that. I blink fast, trying not to cry. Lexi. I have to keep thinking about Lexi.

But it's like the room is swallowing up my hope. The door is unlocked, but I can't reach it. The light is on, but I don't want to see anymore. Even if I could get out, what then? Does he have a gun? Will he shoot Lexi first, then me?

He's smarter than us. He's done this before. But then, where? Not in our town. We would've heard about other people—girls—going missing. So, where are we? God, there has to be something I can do to help Lexi—to help me.

And as if by some miracle, I see it. Tucked in a crack in the floor—a bobby pin. I haven't seen one of those since I was a little girl. Mom used to put them in my hair when she braided it because it was so baby-fine with little flyaways everywhere.

I think I can get to it. I tug on the chains—yeah, if I stretch as far as I can, I can touch it with my fingers. Then—maybe then—I can use it to get out of these cuffs. But I have to do it fast. I could already be too late.

I press my shoulder against the cold floor and stretch out my arm, my fingertips brushing the edge of the bobby pin. Just a little closer. Come on, come on. My fingers scrape against the concrete, bending back my nails. Almost there.

Just need that extra inch, so I press my face into the floor. That's it. The tip of the bobby pin shifts. It moves toward me. I almost have it.

I inch it closer, dragging it with the edge of my middle finger, slow and careful like it's made of glass, like my life depends on this tiny hairpin—because it does. My other wrist screams from the pull of the chain, but I don't stop.

Then—footsteps. Heavy. Measured. Coming from upstairs. "Oh no." I freeze, my breath caught in my throat. No voices yet, just footsteps. And as I listen, I hear only one set.

No Lexi.

My stomach drops.

I fumble with the bobby pin, almost losing it, but clamp my fingers down just in time. The footsteps get louder. Closer. I clutch the bobby pin in my palm and curl into myself, shoving it up the sleeve of the shirt he put me in, fast, before he gets here.

The doorknob turns.

I squeeze my eyes shut. Please let her be with him. Please let her be alive.

30
MARA

Five years have passed since I've been back here. I never thought I'd step foot in these woods again, yet here we are, searching for the body we buried so long ago. The night all our lives changed.

I remember the devastation I'd felt. The call from Garrett telling me that not only was Ashley with him in his car, but that he'd hit a man, killing him instantly. The memories flood back in a torrent as I walk through these woods with the woman responsible.

Yes, it takes two to tango, but Ashley was my friend. Our families haven't been the same since. Nate and I took on their terrible secret. He didn't have to. He and Ashley could've walked away, leaving Garrett to face the consequences.

To this day, I can't be sure why Ashley didn't, but it has occurred to me she could still be in love with my husband and didn't want to see him thrown behind bars. Saying nothing of the fact that their affair would've come front and center at a trial, dragging the Brewer name through the mud in our small town.

Lexi would've figured out just exactly the kind of woman her mother was, and I think that was the real reason behind Ashley's cooperation.

"It's too dark out here," I say to her. "Are you sure we're heading in the right direction?"

"Yes. It's another fifty yards ahead," Ashley replies, aiming her phone's light at the ground.

I want to ask how she remembers so precisely, but I already know she forgets nothing. Meanwhile, I've done my damnedest to put this whole thing in the rearview. A fat lot of good that did me.

"What are we looking for, exactly?" I press. "If they found the body, we would have heard about it on the news."

"That's what I want to make sure of—that it's still here," she replies. "This isn't a coincidence—Lexi having that driver's license."

"Even so, why now?" I ask. "Why wait this long to come for us?"

Ashley stops and squares up to me, pulling rogue strands of her red hair off her face. "I wish I knew. Maybe it's for revenge. Maybe someone who couldn't accept what happened to their loved one kept digging and finally found the truth. Either way, let's make sure we know what we're dealing with first. Then we can think about how we hit back." She makes her way deeper down the slope, off the road, and into the gully where we left him.

Hit back. I trail her a few steps, wondering what she means by that. Rage and anger consume me just as much as it does her, but hitting back? Jesus. I just want my daughter. That's how I hit back.

The deeper we head into the gully, the darker it gets until it's almost black. No more light from the adjacent highway. Nothing. For a moment, I think about the possibility. The real possibility of putting an end to all of this, of putting an end to her.

I could do it, you know—kill her. Right here. Right now. Tell everyone it was an accident. She fell, tumbled into the ravine, and smashed her head on a rock. Then, of course, the police would come here and probably find the other body. But would that be so bad? No one needs to know Nate and I were there that night, helping them like the idiots we were.

I could do it. I even have a gun now. Garrett doesn't know. I took it from my father's gun cabinet when I dropped off Milo. Dad doesn't know, either. Or at least, he hasn't checked his cabinet in the past couple of days. See, I refuse to be defenseless anymore, in light of Skye's disappearance. I refuse to put myself in a position of being taken advantage of again. By this woman here, or anyone else.

That moment five years ago changed my life. My family's lives were changed because of what *she* did. And we're in this situation because of *her*.

Nate and I pull off the side of the road, the soft earth rutting under the tires as the car comes to a stop. My stomach twists as my eyes land on Garrett's car. Shining in the headlights, I see the front end crumpled inward like a crushed soda can, smoke trails winding upward into the black sky. Glass shards on the asphalt. It looks like a scene from a movie. This can't be real. This can't be happening.

And then there they are—Garrett and Ashley. They stand side by side a few feet away from the car, their bodies stiff. No doubt, filled with guilt and regret. But is it because they killed a man, or because they got caught cheating?

Garrett's hands are tucked deep into the pockets of his black suit pants, his shoulders hunched forward in his white button-down shirt. At least he dressed well for his date.

Ashley's arms are crossed, her head lowered just enough that her disheveled hair obscures most of her face.

A man's body lies sprawled on the road behind the car, lifeless, with dark blood pooled around him. He's someone's husband, someone's father, someone's son. And they killed him.

I glance at Nate beside me. His knuckles are white where they grip the steering wheel, his jaw clenched so tightly his facial muscles twitch. Neither of us has said much since leaving the house—barely two words exchanged during the entire drive. But we didn't need to speak to know what was on each other's minds. We'd read it in each other's faces when we got that call. We knew exactly why our spouses were out here alone together tonight. And now this... this mess is just another layer to it all.

Nate cuts the engine, and for a moment, neither of us moves. The silence unfolds between us until finally, he exhales through his nose and opens his door. I follow, stepping out into the cool night air that raises goosebumps on my skin. The closer we get to them, the heavier my chest feels—like it's being squeezed in a vice. Each breath becomes more labored. I don't want to be here. I don't want to know about any of this.

Garrett shifts awkwardly when he sees us coming, his gaze darting between Nate and me like a child caught lying to his parents. Ashley doesn't even lift her head. She just stares down at her feet. The sight of them—guilty and silent—sends a surge of anger through me so hot and sharp it nearly takes my breath away.

For a moment, I want them to suffer—to feel every ounce of betrayal and shame they've inflicted on us tenfold. Let them deal with the wreckage they've created—the affair, the accident, this poor dead man—all of it. Let them bear it alone while Nate and I walk away, leaving them to rot in their guilt. But then... then I think about the kids.

I see my daughter's face in my mind—her bright smile when she runs into Garrett's arms after school or begs me to let her stay up late because Dad said it was okay. Our son, who's much too young to understand any of this. I think of their daughter, too. A sweet little girl who doesn't deserve to carry the weight of this scandal for the rest of her life in a town that thrives on gossip. No matter how much I want to hate Garrett and Ashley right now, I can't do that to our kids.

Garrett steps forward, his hands now held out in front of him like this is a stick-up. I kind of wish it was. "Mara," he starts, his voice cracking. "Mara, I'm so sorry."

I take a step back—an instinct to protect myself from this man I no longer recognize. "Get away from me. I'm not here for you or her." My eyes flick toward Ashley before settling back on Garrett. "I'm here for our kids."

Out of the corner of my eye, I see Nate circling to the back of Garrett's car. He pauses there, staring down at what I assume is the body on the ground, before covering his mouth with one hand as if he might be sick. When he looks back up at Garrett and Ashley, his expression is a mix of disbelief and fury.

"Did either of you bother checking to see if this man was still alive after you hit him?" Nate demands, his voice cutting through the crisp air that surrounds us. "Or were you too busy trying to figure out how to cover up your goddam affair?"

Ashley recoils at his words, but still doesn't look up. "He died instantly." Her voice is barely audible over the sound of the woods that border the road. "It was an accident, Nate."

Nate lets out a laugh as he turns his attention to Garrett instead. "An accident? Did you run off the road? How do you even manage to hit someone out here?"

Garrett hesitates for a fraction too long before glancing sideways at Ashley—a fleeting look that says more than any words ever could.

"For God's sake." I move toward Nate, unable to stomach their silence any longer. My eyes fall to the body on the ground—a man

who probably had car troubles and was looking for help. And this is what he got.

"We have to do something," I say, forcing myself to look away from the bloodied body. "Before someone sees us."

Ashley takes a tentative step forward, her movements jerky and uncertain as if she doesn't quite know how to hold herself. "The gully," she suggests, pointing toward a shadowy dip in the landscape nearby. "We'll take him down there... make sure to take his wallet too."

Her words hit me like a slap across the face because who the hell even thinks this way? This woman, who used to be one of my closest friends. The same woman who helped me plan birthday parties for our daughters and spent countless Saturday afternoons gossiping over coffee is now standing here calmly suggesting how best to dispose of a dead body.

"You were my friend," I whisper.

Ashley finally looks up at me, her eyes red-rimmed and swollen from crying, but still holding onto some faint glimmer of defiance, or maybe desperation. "I know. And I'm sorry."

Something inside me snaps. Before I can stop myself or even think twice about it, my fist connects with her jaw in one swift motion.

Pain shoots through my hand immediately, but I don't give a shit because the sense of satisfaction outweighs it. Ashley stumbles backward, startled by my actions.

"Jesus Christ." Nate rushes forward to steady her before shooting me an angry look.

I meet his gaze head-on without flinching. "Now," I say flatly as I shake off the pain. "Now, we can deal with the body."

. . .

"Here." Ashley aims her index finger toward the edge of the halo of light on the ground. "We hid it here."

"How can you be sure?" I ask.

She turns to me. "Because I put two large stones near the top of the hole we dug."

I look down and see the stones, now covered in moss and dirt. "So, it appears he's still here. Now what?"

31
NATE

We've been sitting in Garrett's car watching Cash Goodell's home for almost ten minutes. The porch light burns, casting an amber glow over the front door. Lights shine through the front windows. People are inside, and they're still awake.

"What do you want to do?" I ask him. "If he sees us, he'll come out and ask what the hell we're doing here."

"You're right." Garrett opens the driver's side door. "So, we'll go to him."

I step out, knowing full well it would be so easy for me to let Garrett stew in his own shit. Let him suffer the consequences of what Cash might do. Does he have our girls? I don't think so. But he might know something about the man in the ID. So, I'll play along for now. But if Cash does have something to do with the girls' disappearances, I don't know what'll happen. If he doesn't? Well, we will have opened Pandora's Box, and God knows what will happen to any of us.

We head toward the front porch, climbing a couple of red

brick steps before standing under the overhang. I glance at Garrett. "Are you going to knock, or should I?"

He doesn't respond, only raps his knuckles on the door, not too hard, but not soft, either. It takes a few moments before I hear footfalls. Someone's coming. I brace for impact.

The locks disengage and the door opens. Cash stands before us, dressed in gym shorts and a T-shirt. His eyes narrow as he darts his gaze between us, clearly unsure of why we're there, yet seeming to have at least an inkling.

"Mr. Metcalf. Mr. Brewer. What can I do for the both of you?"

I swipe open my phone and retrieve the image of the driver's license found in Lexi's bedroom. "We're here to ask you if you know this man." I hold it out for him.

Cash takes my phone and squints at the picture. "This guy? You're asking if I know this guy?" He raises his gaze to us. "No. Should I?"

I glance at Garrett, who doesn't appear to believe him. I'm not sure I do either, all things considered. "Ashley and I found that ID in Lexi's bedroom. We've already informed the police and they're looking into it—"

He hands back my phone. "Then why the hell do you think I'd know him?"

"You didn't work on his car?" Garrett asks. "Take another look. It's a Utah license. Doesn't ring a bell at all for you?"

Cash presses his lips into a thin white line and takes my phone again. Staring at the screen, he shakes his head. "Sorry, guys. I got nothing for you." He returns it to me. "But I'll ask you again, why do you think I know him?"

Before I can answer, Garrett lunges at him, gripping him by the collar of his T-shirt. "Don't play with me, Cash. After what you said earlier tonight, did you really think I'd let that shit go? My goddam daughter is missing. So is Nate's. You know that. So don't fucking lie to us, you hear me? If you know this guy, you'd better say so."

"All right. All right." I pull Garrett off him. "Knock it off." I turn back to Cash. "Look, man. You were out there this morning for the search. You said you wanted to help. Well, this is how you do it. If you know this guy, and you're lying, I swear to God, I'll let Garrett do whatever the hell he wants to you, understand?"

"Listen, I get what you're both going through, but you're acting crazy right now." Cash tugs on his shirt and smooths it down. "I don't know that guy, got it? And you're right, Nate. I was out there trying to help you all find your girls, and this is the thanks I get?"

"Then why the hell do you have a car in your yard with Utah plates, huh?" Garrett blurts out. "Just like this driver's license."

I close my eyes. *Goddam it, Garrett.*

Cash steps outside, closing the door behind him. "How the hell do you know that? Did you break into my yard? What the hell is wrong with you, man? I should call the cops right now."

I raise my hands. "Cash, don't. Please. We're desperate for answers, all right? Surely, you can understand that. The cops have zero leads on our girls, so, yeah, we started taking matters into our own hands to find them. And after what you said to Garrett earlier..."

"Hold on." Cash eyes Garrett. "What do you mean by that? What do you think I said, Garrett?"

"No, you don't get to play dumb right now," Garrett replies. "You came up to me and started talking about my car and the damage from my accident years ago..."

Cash folds his arms, tilting his head. "You mean the damage that wasn't done by any deer I've ever come across? Come on, man. It doesn't take a genius to figure that out."

Garrett's face twists, heating a dark shade of red. "Tell me what you know, or I swear to God, I'll kill you where you stand."

Cash scoffs and returns a crooked smile. "You're threatening me now? How about I make that call to the cops and tell them you broke into my property? Would you like me to do that, Garrett?"

This time, I step in. My breaths come in quick gasps, and anger rises under my collar. "You say one goddam word to the cops about this, and you'll be looking over your shoulder from here on out, you got that? We want our girls back. And if we figure out that you're involved in any way, I'll kill you myself." Without waiting for a response, I turn and walk away, leaving Garrett behind. Then I hear the door slam and footsteps come up on me.

"He knows something, doesn't he?" Garrett asks.

"Oh yeah. Or he would've called the cops right then and there." I stop as we reach the car. "The question is, what are we going to do about it?"

32
SKYE

My head snaps toward the steps just as I hear the handle jiggle. Hope flutters in my chest as the door opens. And then I see her. Oh God. She's okay. She's okay.

"Lexi." I call her name like I thought I might never say it out loud again.

He's dragging her down the stairs by her arms like a rag doll, her feet stumbling over each step. My stomach drops at the sight of her face. Dried blood streaks down her chin, but it's the look that I recognize. Weak and broken. Shame and embarrassment. And then I know exactly what he's done.

"Oh my God," I breathe out. My chains clatter as I lurch forward, tugging against them with all my strength. "No! No! What did you do to her?"

He doesn't answer me, not with words, but I can see it in his posture, in the way he tilts his head a little as if our pain is funny to him. He's smiling under that mask; I know he is.

"Lexi?" My voice wavers as tears cloud my vision. "Are you

okay?" It's a stupid question, of course she's not. But I can't stop myself from asking it because seeing her like this...

He shoves her against the wall hard enough that she crumples onto her backside, but still, she doesn't cry out or make a sound beyond her heavy breathing, like she's out of breath altogether.

"Lexi," I choke out again, fresh tears spilling over as guilt crashes down on me. "I'm so sorry...this is all my fault."

She doesn't look at me—not at first—and for a moment, I think maybe she's broken for good. Broke beyond repair...until he grabs her wrist to secure her chain again.

And then she moves.

It happens so fast that it takes me a minute to process. One second, she's leaning toward him like she's too weak to resist, and then the next, his shriek pierces through the air like a bullet whizzing by.

"What the—" My words catch in my throat as he stumbles back, clutching his arm—and that's when I see it—blood dripping from Lexi's mouth—and something dangling between her teeth.

Oh God. She bit him. She actually fucking bit him. And from the look of it, she took out a chunk of his flesh.

For a brief moment, a split second, I see pride flash across her face as she spits out the chunk of skin onto the floor.

But then his hand comes down hard and fast. A brutal backhanded slap sends her head snapping back against the wall with a crack that echoes in my ears.

"Stop!" My voice rips from my throat, raw and ragged, as I yank against my chains. "Stop it! Leave her alone!"

He turns toward me in a slow and calculating move—and even though his expression is hidden behind that damn mask...I can feel rage radiating off him. He doesn't like it that he got beat by her, by either of us.

"Do it!" I spit at him as he looms closer. "I dare you! You fucking coward—"

His hand is all I see before everything goes black.

33
ASHLEY

I don't recognize this. A few feet away is another set of stones, placed in exactly the same manner as the marker I left for the body. "What the hell is this?"

Mara steps closer, and I aim my index finger at the ground. "These weren't here before." With the tip of my shoe, I push away the debris—leaves, sticks, and small stones. "This ground was recently disturbed." Finally, I drop to my knees and use my hands to claw at the ground.

"What are you doing?" Mara asks.

"Someone else put these rocks here. They put them here to mark something, just like I did. I have to know what's down here."

She looms over me. "You're not going to uncover anything this way. We need the shovel."

Mara hands it to me, and I start digging into the soft earth. "You don't have to stay here for this."

"Where am I going to go?" She shrugs. "Besides, I'm here to make sure you don't screw us."

"What's that supposed to mean?" I stop for a moment and glance at her.

Mara raises her chin. "Who's to say you won't use this opportunity to get Garrett? Maybe plant something here that points back to Garrett and me."

"Are you serious right now? Is that why you're here?" I press.

"What, you think I'm here out of the kindness of my heart?" she replies. "You think I trust you enough to do this alone? Not a chance in hell, Ashley. We may have glossed over this shit from before but that doesn't mean I've forgotten any of it. I haven't forgotten who you really are."

"Me?" I laugh, returning to digging the hole. "It wasn't just me that night, Mara."

"You're right. It wasn't. But I swear to God, if all that's happening right now...if our kids were taken because someone found out what happened...Cash Goodell, or whoever else...you'd better believe that body isn't the only thing that'll be in the ground."

"Whatever you say, Mara," I reply, thrusting the shovel deeper into the overturned earth. But then I stop, feeling like I've hit something. "Shit." I squat low again, pulling away the dirt. "Aim your light down here." Mara shines it on the spot as I brush away dirt and leaves, digging in with my fingers to peel back what remains. "I'm sure I hit something. Hang on. I think I see it." I keep brushing away the dirt until...

Mara leans closer. "What the hell is that?"

I shake my head. "I can't tell yet. It's still partially buried. But..." I keep digging, holding my breath until I get a clear view because I think I know what this is. "What the...?" I pull back, resting on my heels, and I look up at Mara. She sees it too. "How the hell did that end up in here?"

"You tell me." Mara drops to her knees and reaches into the hole to retrieve it.

I stare at it like my eyes must be betraying me. "That's the plate from his car. I don't understand. How the hell did that get in here? We got rid of the car."

"But we didn't remove the plates," Mara adds. "So how are they in here, right next to the body we buried?"

I fix my gaze on her. "Someone who knows the body's here did this. It's a message. A warning."

"A warning? So, what, maybe this guy isn't really dead. Maybe there isn't a body buried over there."

My face twists in confusion. "He died, Mara. We all saw that. We buried him for Christ's sake."

She shrugs. "Well, I can't explain this."

I laugh at the absurdity. "How did they find his car? We towed it for miles and pushed it into the ravine. No one knew where that car was."

"Someone did," Mara replies. "And someone figured out where we put the body."

34
MARA

The only thing we succeeded in uncovering tonight is the painful truth. We have no idea who took our girls. No clue who ripped Skye and Lexi from our lives or how to get them back. And in the process of fumbling for answers, we uncovered the real possibility that someone knows our secret. I don't know if the two events are connected, but I'm betting they are, which makes our guilt all the greater.

I can feel it in the restraint that follows our words. Unspoken accusations hang in the air, yet, as much as we're tearing apart at the seams, I know one thing for certain—if we don't find a way to work together, to push past our strife long enough to comb through every detail of the past five years, then we'll lose them. We'll lose Skye and Lexi to whatever shadow from our past has come back to haunt us.

That is…if we aren't arrested first.

Garrett breaks through the quiet, his voice rough and raw as he tips back a glass of whisky neat. The amber liquid catches the tremor in his hand that he probably thinks no one notices.

"Someone's screwing with us." He slams the empty glass onto our dining table.

Ashley and Nate don't flinch—they're too used to Garrett's theatrics.

"You think?" Ashley says—to no one's surprise. She's the type who has to get in the last word. "We found the car's license plate. That's enough to make it clear—someone else knows."

"It has to be Cash," Nate interjects. He leans forward, his elbows resting on his knees as he glares at Garrett. "The way he came at you tonight? He's in on this."

I shake my head, unwilling to let him spiral into another baseless theory without challenging it. "Why?" I ask. "Why would Cash be involved? He fixed the car when it happened. If he suspected something back then, if he thought there was foul play, why wouldn't he have said something, or gone to the police?"

Garrett rakes a hand through his hair, leaving it sticking up in wild brown tufts. "Because someone got to him. Someone came to him and started asking questions, maybe even threatened him if he didn't come clean. It was probably whoever owns that car in his yard. The one with the Utah plates. Makes sense."

His eyes are bloodshot and glassy, but there's an edge of reason beneath them that makes me take note.

"Someone was able to track down Cash after realizing he worked on my car and then sold him some kind of story," Garrett adds.

"It wouldn't take much convincing," Ashley replies. "But we have no idea who *someone* could even be."

"Did you think you could kill a man, and no one would care?" I ask. "No one would come looking—ever?"

Nate bolts up from his chair, scraping it loudly against the wood floor. He walks toward the kitchen window; his hands balled into fists as he stares out into the darkness beyond the glass. "This is crazy. All that happened—it happened to us. To the four of us. It had nothing to do with the girls." He turns around. "No...this can't be related. It's not possible."

"You just said—" Garrett cuts in.

Nate raises his hand. "I know what I said! Maybe Cash does know something. Maybe he even knows the truth about what happened back then and thought stirring the pot would mess with us because of what's happening now—I don't know. But digging into the past isn't helping our kids." His gaze sweeps across all of us before landing on me. "Not one damn bit. Can any of you honestly tell me you'll be able to sleep tonight? Not knowing where they are? Not knowing if they're...if they're still alive?"

Ashley moves toward him and places a hand on his shoulder—a gesture meant to comfort, but one that seems to only fuel his frustration.

"Honey. This is hard for all of us."

"Is it?" He jerks away from her touch, his voice rising again as anger overtakes whatever restraint he had left. "You know what, Ash? You have no damn clue how hard these past few years have been for me—or Mara either, I imagine."

I say nothing in response but feel a momentary connection to Nate I haven't felt in a long time.

"The only reason I'm even still here—the only reason I'm still with you—is Lexi," Nate spits out before stopping abruptly, seeming to realize he's gone too far.

The silence that settles over us is deafening.

He doesn't finish what he was going to say—but he doesn't need to because we all know exactly what those unsaid words are: If she's gone...we're done. I don't disagree, except I still have my son to consider.

"There's nothing more we can do right now," I say. "In fact, I think we've already done enough damage for one night."

35
NATE

It's been hours, but it looks like Ashley finally fell asleep. Her breathing has evened out, and the furrow that's been etched into her brow all night has finally smoothed. I regret what I said earlier—about leaving her if Lexi is gone for good.

It's just that the weight of today, of every hour since Lexi disappeared, presses down on my chest like an anvil. My daughter is gone, and my marriage is crumbling under the strain after living under a black cloud for years.

I slip out of bed, quietly moving inch by inch until my feet touch the wood floor. The faint creak of the bedframe makes me freeze mid-step, my eyes darting to Ashley. She doesn't stir.

I hover over the dresser, pulling open a drawer with painstaking care to avoid waking her. The contents are a mess—hastily folded shirts tangled with shorts and socks—but I grab whatever's closest. A plain grey T-shirt and a pair of drawstring shorts.

As I step into the bathroom and close the door, I catch a glimpse of myself in the mirror. The man staring back at me looks... hollow. My eyes are bloodshot, rimmed with dark circles that reveal the sleepless nights and too many unanswered questions. I splash cold water on my face before changing, trying to shake off my exhaustion and worry.

When I reemerge, I pause in the doorway. Our bedroom is awash in moonlight. It catches on Ashley's face, softening her features in a way that almost makes her look like the woman I married—the woman who used to laugh until she cried, and hummed along to her favorite 80s songs on the classic radio station. But all I see now is Lexi in her face: the same delicate nose, the same curve of her jawline. And I see her betrayal as though it happened only yesterday. If Lexi doesn't come back... if we don't find her...

What I said before—the words echo in my mind, harsh and unrelenting. What kind of man am I? What kind of father? Then again, I stayed after what Ashley had done. So, the real question is —what kind of man am I at all?

I tiptoe across the room, careful to avoid the spots in the floor that creak under pressure. When I reach the bedroom door, my hand hesitates on the doorknob. I glance back at Ashley one more time, her figure small and vulnerable beneath the covers. How did we get here?

Affairs don't happen in a vacuum—that much I know for certain. Marriages crack and splinter under the weight of life until they finally shatter. And maybe I didn't see those cracks forming soon enough. Maybe I didn't try hard enough to fix them when I did. But this—Ashley and Garrett—this betrayal is something else entirely. If they brought this nightmare into our lives, if their lies cost me Lexi, then to hell with forgiveness.

The quiet of the house feels heavy as I make my way downstairs, every creak of wood beneath my feet amplified in the stillness. Memories hang in every corner—Lexi's laughter echoing down these halls when she was young. Ashley's voice calling us to dinner. Family game nights where we'd bicker over Monopoly rules until someone inevitably quit mid-game. Usually me. Now those memories feel like they don't belong to me anymore. Like they were never really mine, but something I'd seen on TV.

However, now isn't the time for regret or nostalgia. Tonight was supposed to bring clarity, but all it's done is push the wedge deeper between us.

Stepping out of my front door into a pre-dawn, I draw in a deep breath of damp air. The world is still asleep. Our quiet street, undisturbed by headlights or voices or any signs of life.

I unlock my car and slide onto the driver's seat. Lexi is out there somewhere—scared, alone—and while this town sleeps, I'm certain she suffers in ways I can't even begin to imagine. I don't want to imagine. Rest isn't an option for me—not until she's home.

The drive to the pharmacy is short but feels endless as my thoughts spiral. Where could she be? Who could have taken her? Why haven't we found her yet? Do I even want to think about what Ashley and Mara found in the woods? The damn car plates? *For God's sake.*

When I pull into the empty parking lot, I feel like it's a reflection of my life. This place was our dream. Well, my dream. Ashley just went along for the ride. For a while.

I walk inside. The red glow of the emergency lights cast down over rows of locked shelves and clean counters. A sign near the entrance reads: 24/7 Surveillance. It's a necessity these days. Pharmacies have become prime targets for desperate people chasing pills.

I meander through the darkened aisles until I reach my office at the back. Unlocking the door, I step inside, and memories take over. Lexi's face when she hugged me goodbye that morning. Ashley's tears when we realized Lexi was missing.

Inside the office, everything looks as it should. Neat rows of supplies, waiting for another day of transactions and prescriptions filled. But nothing about this moment feels routine.

Hidden beneath paperwork and clutter, sits what I came for —a flash drive taped securely to the bottom of a drawer in my credenza. As I hold it in my hand, its weight feels insignificant compared to everything riding on what it contains.

When I insert it into my computer and press play, the old footage fills the screen. Garrett's wrecked Mercedes, illuminated by my car's headlights. Mara's determined gaze as she steps out to investigate. Ashley, standing beside Garrett, eyes downcast, her body radiating guilt.

And then my own voice cuts through. "There they are."

"There they are," I say, stopping behind Garrett's wrecked Mercedes. Then I look at Mara, who sits in the passenger seat. "I'm sorry."

"Why are you sorry?" she asks. "You're not a cheater. They are." She aims her finger ahead. "And now, they've killed someone."

"And we're here to help them cover it up," I add. "Are you sure this is what you want to do?"

She regards me, firm and unwavering. "I am, for my family. Are you?"

I'm quiet for a moment, staring at Garrett and my wife, standing side-by-side on the road. "And what about the real victim in all this?"

Mara peers ahead again. "Just another casualty of their lies." She steps out of the car and walks toward them.

I glance at the dashcam, making sure it's aimed at the right spot. "Just in case."

36
GARRETT

The sun is peeking out over the horizon. I've been here for two hours, waiting. Mara was asleep when I left. Nevertheless, it's only a matter of time before my phone rings, and it's her, asking where I am, telling me not to do anything stupid. I think I'm well past that now.

Cash Goodell knows where the girls are, and without Nate Brewer here to stop me, I'll be able to get answers. So, I'm waiting for him at his shop. The fact that he didn't call the cops on me last night proves he's hiding something.

It's not a coincidence—that car with the Utah plates sitting in his yard. Not now, when Mara and Ashley found the original plates next to the goddam body. I can't piece it together yet, but I will, and soon. And then Mara will forgive me. She'll forgive me for the affair and, more importantly, forgive me for doing this to Skye. I'll bring her home. Hopefully, Lexi, too, but I will find my daughter.

A dog barks in the distance, sharp and insistent. The sound bounces off the sheet metal walls of the body shop and then fades away. I glance at the front door again. Still locked. Still quiet.

My palms are sweating. I wipe them on my jeans and remind myself why I'm here. Not for revenge. Not for redemption. Just answers. Just Skye.

The rumble of an engine sounds behind me. I peer into the rearview. "There you are."

Cash's truck slows, making the turn into the parking lot. The old Ford F-150 he so lovingly restored. Shiny red, gleaming beneath the sun's morning rays.

He pulls into the lot like a man with nothing to fear. I wait until he cuts the engine, then step out.

"Morning, Cash."

He flinches. Just a twitch. But I see it.

"Well, shit," he says, pulling the car door shut behind him. "Guess you didn't fully appreciate the fact I didn't call the police on you last night 'cause here you are."

"I thought you might've used the time to drum up something close to the truth," I reply.

He sorts through his keys, finding the one for the front door. "You think I'm scared of you, Garrett? It's you who should be scared of me—of what I know."

We're face to face now, only the length of the truck's hood between us. Cash's eyes dart to the shop door, then back to me. There's a flicker of something—calculation, maybe. I press on. "And what is it you think you know?"

He ignores me and walks toward the entrance. I trail him. "That Utah plate. Don't see too many cars with them around here, even fewer that need body work done. Who is he? How long has he been here?"

"Hell if I know," Cash replies. "For the love of God, Garrett, I don't know where your girl is, all right? Despite what you might think of me, I wouldn't let those kids suffer, not for anything."

"Maybe you don't know where they are, but you sure as hell know something."

He hesitates.

I step closer. "If you're lying to me, Cash, I swear—"

"You'll what?" he snaps. "Beat it out of me? You've already blown up your life. Don't drag me down with you."

I grab him by the collar and slam him against the door. The frame rattles, the glass seemingly ready to shatter.

"I don't care what happens to me," I say. "But I'm not leaving here without some answers. You *know* something. Who is this guy, huh? Where is he?"

"Get the hell off me."

Cash shoves me back, but I still have a fistful of his shirt. "Where's Skye? Where's my daughter?"

"Garrett!"

Her voice pierces my ears, reminding me of my mother when she'd yell at me. I let go. Cash stumbles, rubbing his neck. I don't even look at him. My eyes are on Mara, standing at the edge of the lot, wearing denim shorts and a T-shirt. A short ponytail tightens her hairline, making her features appear older, and the scowl she's wearing ages her even more.

"Goddam it," she says, walking toward us. "This is what you've been doing? Running off before dawn to start fights in parking lots?"

"I'm trying to find our daughter," I shoot back.

"You think this helps her? Attacking Cash? Threatening him again?" She sets her sights on Cash. "I'm out here defending you, but if you know anything about our girl, you have to tell us."

He shakes his head, shoulders hunched like a scolded child. "I already told him. I don't know where she is. I swear to God, I'm telling you the truth."

Mara stares at him, then at me. "Why did you come here, Garrett?"

"I just want to know about whoever owns that car," I say.

She turns back to Cash, softer now. "Please, Cash. Who is he?

You know we found a driver's license from Utah, too, right? If you know anything—*anything*—please."

Cash doesn't speak. His jaw clenches. His eyes flick toward the shop. And that's all I need. I shoulder past them both and head straight for the entrance.

"Garrett!" Mara calls after me, but I don't stop. The lock's old and the door gives way with a hard shove.

The inside still reeks of motor oil and metal. I see invoices tacked to a corkboard behind the cluttered desk, which is piled high with paperwork and fast-food wrappers. I tear into it.

Cash is behind me now, footsteps pounding across the floor. "Hey! You don't get to just storm in here like—"

I slam a drawer shut and rip open the next. "Watch me."

"Garrett, please," Mara says from the doorway. Her voice is quieter now. "We need the truth, but not like this."

"This is the only way I know, Mara."

Receipts, parts orders, DMV records. I'm knee-deep in desperation when I see it; the corner of a manila folder peeks out from under several repair estimates with a phone number written on it—one that isn't local. I yank it free and flip it open. There it is. An invoice.

2015 Ford Taurus- dark blue

I read on, finding the license plate number, which I recognize as the same I'd seen in the yard. "You tell me you don't know anything," I shout, "and yet here it is—your name, your shop, your signature. But no customer name. So whose car is it, Cash?"

He freezes, his face turning pale. Mara looks between us, lips parted.

"Who is he?" I ask. "*Where* is he?"

Cash swallows hard, then looks at Mara, then back at me. Defeated. "I don't know where he is. Look, he came here a few weeks ago, dropped off his car. I'm still waiting on the parts. Until last night, I knew nothing about what the Brewers found in their daughter's bedroom—that driver's license." He shakes his head. "I suspect you got a lot of secrets you're keeping, and I'm not asking, all right? And with those girls missing—if I thought this guy had anything to do with that, I would've gone to the cops."

"You seemed interested in me selling my car down at the Albertson's last night. Why?"

He shoots a look at Mara. "I'm not an idiot, okay? But how about we let all that go? I'll give you this guy's name. Maybe he's involved, maybe not. It's not for me to say. In fact, it's not for you to say either. This should go to the police. But you want to run with this? It's on you."

"A few weeks ago?" I say, looking at Mara. "He must've been watching them. Learned their routines."

"Then he found a way to get to Lexi," she adds, looking over at Cash. "Give us his name—right fucking now."

37
LEXI

The taste of his blood in my mouth won't go away, like I ate a rusty nail or an old coin. It's almost gross enough for me to forget the throbbing pain on the side of my face. I can hardly open my mouth at all. Still, I got him pretty good. He wasn't expecting it. Not that it helped.

We're still here in this basement, chained to its walls, still prisoners. And I'm losing hope that we'll ever leave this place.

I've lost all sense of time down here in the dark. Moonlight came in through the windows when I was upstairs, so I'm guessing it was nighttime. I don't really know. I don't think I slept, not much anyway.

All I went through was for nothing. I'm in exactly the same place I was before. Only now, I feel different. Pain—yeah, for sure. But there's something deep inside me now that feels hollow. I need Skye to wake up—to talk to me and remind me that I'm still alive.

"He should've come back down by now."

My eyes widen in the dark, desperate to absorb enough light to see her. "Skye, you're awake?"

"Are you okay?" she asks.

I don't want to answer. I'm too afraid.

"I keep replaying it. Over and over," she whispers. "Like if I remember every second, maybe I'll finally understand it."

"I don't think it'll ever make sense," I reply.

I hear her fight back her emotions, sniffling, her voice cracking. "I didn't fight. Not like you did. I just froze."

"You didn't freeze," I say, wishing to God I could see her face. "You protected me. You saved me."

"I was so scared."

"Me too," I say. "Still am."

A pause stretches between us. The kind that aches in your chest.

"I feel like I'm not me anymore. Like... he took something I can't ever get back."

My throat tightens. "He hurt us. But he doesn't get to keep us. We won't let him."

"How do you know?" she asks, her voice so tiny now I can barely hear it.

"I don't," I admit. "I just keep breathing. And when I can't, I think of you. I think, Skye's here with me, so we're going to be okay."

I hear her sigh, as if a weight lifted from her. And I feel like we are going to get through this, but it's going to take all our strength. "What did you mean before when you said he should've come down by now?"

"I mean, I've been timing him because what else is there to do? I've figured out that he comes down here at specific intervals. Like, what I think is morning, like now, he comes down and checks on us. Then, he comes down like four hours later. And then again, after about six hours."

I smile, though she can't see it. "How did you figure all this out? You don't have a watch or phone or anything."

"How come you didn't, smarty pants?" She chuckles and then coughs a little. "I counted the first hour, then sort of winged it from there. So, where is he, and why hasn't he come down yet?"

"I don't know. Maybe he's still pissed that I bit off a chunk of his shoulder," I say, as if that's some everyday occurrence.

"That was seriously cool, Lex." She laughs a little again. "But it was dumb, too. He could've killed you."

"He could kill us any time he wants, Skye. He just hasn't, and I'm not sure why."

"Maybe that doesn't matter right now," she adds. "Maybe what matters right now is that something's kept him from checking on us on his schedule."

"What do you think it could be, then?" I ask.

"What did you see up there?"

"I was in a living room. This brown wood paneling covered the walls. Stained brown carpet. The furniture was all shitty and old. Kinda velvet-like. It smelled up there, too, like an old person's house or something."

"Did you see outside?" I hear the hope in her tone. "Could you tell where this place is?"

"Not really," I reply. "I kind of saw out there, like the street or whatever, but I didn't recognize it."

"So we're in a neighborhood?"

"I don't know. I didn't see any houses. Just a street."

She's quiet for a moment. "Okay, so maybe the houses are far apart, or he's at the end of a street or something."

"Yeah, maybe." The door opens, drawing my attention. My heart pounds as he flips on the light, and I see his masked face. He's wearing a T-shirt, so I can't tell if he's bandaged the bite.

"Good morning, girls," he says, walking down the steps. "I hope you both had a good night's rest." He stands in the middle of the room, planting his hands on his hips.

He looks different to me somehow. Shoulders slumped. Hang

on, did he favor his right leg just now? I glance at Skye, wondering if she notices, but I can't read her face.

My stomach growls super loudly, and he turns to me. "Hungry?" He walks over, and that's when I really notice it—a limp. Did it happen when I was upstairs yesterday? I remember him falling off me. He did sort of clutch his leg.

"Yeah, I'm hungry," I say, my tone hardened. "We both are. You haven't fed us in forever or given us any water. If all you wanted was for us to die down here, why not just kill us?"

When he moves closer, I feel a lump rise in my throat. My pulse jumps even faster, and while I do my best to keep my expression firm, inside, I'm shaking so hard I could break into pieces.

He stops about a foot in front of me, looming like he's about to pick me up and throw me across the room. Never thought I'd be happy to be chained to the wall. I look at Skye again. She's shaking her head, silently warning me to stop. I don't know what's gotten into me, other than I don't think there's anything he could do now that would hurt me any worse than what's already happened. So, what do I have to lose?

"You want food? Water?" he asks, staring down at me. "All you have to do is cooperate, and I'll give you what you want. Both of you."

"Cooperate how?" Skye asks.

He turns to her. "Just do as I say, and you'll both be fine." He heads toward the steps again, climbing them until reaching the door. "Keep your mouths shut, or I'll cut out your tongues." The room goes dark again as he leaves.

"Did you see that?" I ask her.

"Yeah. He's hurt," Skye replies. "But I don't get why he's telling us to be quiet, like we don't already know that."

I glance at the door as though he's going to walk through it again and clear up the entire matter. "Is someone else coming? Could it be the cops?"

"Hard to say," Skye replies. "But I think...I don't think we're the only people who've been down here."

I look down at my clean clothes. "Yeah, I kind of figured that."

"I saw stuff, Lexi. When you were up there with him, and I didn't know if you were dead or alive. He left the light on, and so I got a good look around."

"Oh my God." Suddenly, I'm feeling better about our situation. "Did you see something that could help us?"

"Maybe. I mean, I saw a lot of shit that made me think people have—not survived this—before. Scratches on the walls and floor. Bloodstains, or what I think were bloodstains." She draws in a deep breath. "But then I saw something else...a bobby pin."

My face drops. "That's it? A bobby pin? How is that going to help us?"

"If we can use it to pick our locks, I don't know, maybe we can break free."

Seems like a stretch, but I don't want to crap all over her idea. I mean, I faked a seizure, thinking it would help, so what do I know? "He's injured," I remind her. "How can we use that to help us?"

"I'm not sure yet. So, let's figure it out. Between the bobby pin, that garbage bag, and now the fact that he's injured...maybe all that together, and his timing...I don't know, Lex. Maybe we can figure this out. Unless you have something else on your calendar?"

38
NATE

The dashcam had been on the entire time. At first, I thought all it captured was the four of us standing around, panicking in the dead of night, our voices raised as we argued over what to do next. The memory makes my throat tighten, the way we struggled to form a coherent plan. Except Ash. She had a plan.

My dashcam hung from the rearview mirror, and everyone was so wrapped up in the situation, no one noticed it was running. We stopped on the side of the road, behind the vehicle. Garrett had taken the dead man's car keys.

Now, as I sit here replaying the footage, I see it clearly—clearer than I wish I did. The license plate. My breath catches in my throat as I pause the video and lean closer to the screen. The numbers and letters glare back at me like an indictment. I'm almost certain it matches what Ashley found when they went back to the spot where we buried the man.

If I'm right—and God help me if I am—then someone has come looking for him. Someone, somehow, knows what we did. Why they waited, I can only speculate. Maybe it just took that long to figure out what happened. It wasn't like there were any police reports. The man's phone was smashed, and we got rid of that too. We did everything we thought possible to make sure no one ever discovered him. And yet, here we are.

What I need to figure out now is whether any of this connects to Lexi's disappearance. The timing feels too perfect to be a coincidence. But why? Why now?

I remove the flash drive and pocket it before locking up the store again and heading home. The sun is peeking through the trees, and I dread going another day without my girl. A small spark of hope ignites as I remember that Blackwell might get answers today about the mysterious Eric Downey. And if the man in that license matches the owner of the car in Cash's yard, then all doubt will vanish about his intention. Eric Downey, and whatever connection he has to the dead man, has come back to make us pay by taking the only things that matter to any of us—our kids.

When I pull onto the driveway at home, I notice the curtains are still drawn across every window, leaving the house in shadow despite the growing daylight.

I unlock the front door and step inside, greeted only by silence. It smells a little stale in here as the air outside grows more humid.

I set my keys inside the bowl on the foyer table, and glance toward the hallway. The distant sound of running water reaches me. Ashley must be in the shower.

I make my way into our bedroom, hearing the shower, and then I notice our bed is still unmade. I don't dare walk into Lexi's bedroom again, the mattress still flipped over, the drawers on the floor, emptied. The painful reminder that she's gone and our helplessness to do anything about it.

The water shuts off. I stop at the door, listening for Ashley's movement, wondering if she's stepped out. I wait for some sign—a shuffle of feet or anything.

After what happened, the intimacy between us had become complicated, a strange mix of desperation and denial that neither of us wanted to acknowledge. In the immediate aftermath of her affair, our sex life flourished as if we were trying to drown our pain beneath layers of forced passion. We tried things we'd never done before, played games like we were teenagers. In time, we realized it did nothing. It provided nothing but a brief reprieve from reality.

Now? Now, we're back in the same old rut as before, and I wouldn't think to interrupt her shower with the prospect of sex even while my heart is breaking and I'm desperate for her touch. As much as I don't want to admit it, I need my wife. I need her to love me.

I knock on the door. "Ash? Can I come in?"

"Yes," she replies.

I open it to find her wrapped in a towel, wet hair resting against her shoulders. Drops of water still cling to her face, making her appear young and innocent. Not like a wife and mother whose child is missing, who hasn't slept and barely eaten in days.

"Where did you go this morning?" she asks, peering at me through the mirror.

"The pharmacy. I was just making sure everything was set for Josh." Meanwhile, my fingers fidget with the flash drive still in my pants pocket. "I wanted to know where you put that car plate—the one from—"

"It's in my nightstand. I didn't know where else to put it. Why?"

I wrap my fingers around the flash drive, pulling it from my pocket. "I need to show you something."

She eyes the device. "Let me get dressed. I'll be out in a minute."

I nod and step out of the bathroom, closing the door behind me. The moment she lays eyes on what I'm about to show her, she'll know my intention. I've kept this information secret from her since it happened, prepared to use it in the event things went sideways. Threats, attempts at retribution. Divorce papers. I was prepared because this evidence damns us all. One of us steps out of line? We all suffer.

I take a seat on a chair in front of our bay window. The sunlight shines behind me, warming my skin. It takes another few minutes before Ashley steps out of the bathroom, still with wet hair that's now combed back. She's dressed in a T-shirt and shorts. It's the first time in a long time that I see her—really *see* her. "Come sit down."

She sits in the chair next to mine, and I place my laptop on the small round table between us. Then, I press play. Holding my breath, I gauge her reaction. The slight creasing of her brow, her lips parting just a little. Then I see her chest rise and fall with greater intensity. She looks at me. Not like any regular look. No. It's the look of betrayal. I recognize it because I looked at her the same way five years ago.

"What did you do, Nate?" she asks. "Why do you have this?"

I take a breath. "At first, it was for insurance. *My* insurance. Now? It's something we can use to protect ourselves."

Ashley shakes her head and closes her eyes for a moment. "How? I'm on here, or did you forget my part in this?"

"I didn't forget." I close the lid of my laptop. "The license plate you and Mara found is definitely from the victim's car. The video proves that."

"Okay. So, who found it? Who put it next to the body and didn't go to the police?" she presses.

"I also have this." I open another file. A picture. "That's the victim's ID."

"Jesus, Nate." Ashley jumps up from the chair.

I raise my hands in surrender. "I'm not showing you this to scare you, Ash. I swear it. Like I said, this was for my protection. And I'm showing you because the last name on that ID is Downey."

She slowly lowers herself back down onto the chair. "Eric Downey."

I nod. "Could be the guy's son."

39
MARA

I thought he was going to kill him. The way Garrett came after Cash like that. Maybe I should've let him. Then again, I'm not sure if Cash knows anything—not really. Why would he have kept it to himself rather than go to the police?

Still, as I drive home, trailing Garrett in his car, I wonder if Cash has an angle. Blackmail? Did he overhear something? If so, it didn't come from any of the four of us. We've kept this secret for a long time, and we aren't about to let something slip now.

But I must keep focus on the fact that what Ashley and I found in the woods leads me to believe our girls are being used as leverage, but by whom? The idea turns my stomach. The certainty of knowing that they're gone because of us, because of what we did.

Garrett got the name of the man who owns the car with the Utah plates, but no address. Eric Downey. Yep, the same name as what's on the driver's license found in Lexi's bedroom. Cash conveniently didn't have the address, but he did have a phone number. Will Officer Blackwell track him down for us? We have yet to hear from him about any leads based on the license.

But Downey has left us with no doubt that he came after Lexi to get back at us. Maybe she'd been the easier target. He could've gone after Skye, just the same. Nevertheless, if we call and alert him that we know who he is, it could backfire on us—on the girls, assuming I'm right. Still, the time's come to tell the Brewers what we know.

The impossible situation consumes my thoughts as we return home. I glance next door, noticing Nate's car in their driveway. As much as I want nothing more to do with them, I know we have to work through this together if we want to find the girls.

Garrett steps out ahead of me, and just as I get out, I see Nate and Ashley heading over. "Speak of the devils."

Garrett reaches into his shirt pocket and pulls out the invoice. "That car in Cash's yard? We know who it belongs to."

"What?" Nate comes to an abrupt halt. Ashley, still a few steps behind.

"I went to see Cash this morning—"

"Really?" Nate interrupts. "After last night? Jesus, Garrett, what the hell were you thinking?"

"I was thinking one of us needed to figure out what happened to our kids, so I thought it better be me."

I sense the rising anger in his tone, and given the growing tension, I suspect Nate's reacting in kind.

Nate lunges toward him, twisting his fist in the fabric of Garrett's shirt. "You son of a bitch. This whole goddam thing is your fault. Don't you dare suggest I'm sitting back and doing nothing."

"That's enough." Ashley steps between them.

Figures she would.

"We don't need this right now, from either of you," I say, turning to Garrett. "Tell them what Cash said. What you found out."

He fumbles for his phone.

"Now, Garrett!" I shout.

"All right, for crying out loud. Give me a second." He grabs his phone and swipes open the screen, pulling up the images he'd taken. "This is the car and plate in Cash's yard. I also found an invoice of who it belongs to." He swipes the screen to the next photo. "This is the invoice with his name. Eric Downey."

"The same guy from the license in Lexi's room," Nate says. "So he is here."

Garrett and I trade glances when I continue. "We should be out there looking for him. We can't let the cops find him first." That's when I see Nate's expression shift. He swallows hard, like he knows something he doesn't want to say. "What's going on?"

Ashley takes a step forward. "It came to me last night."

"What did?" Garrett asks.

"I remembered his name. I remember looking at his driver's license that night. We were all in such a hurry to hide and destroy all the evidence. We were all so panicked."

"What are you saying, Ashley? You actually remember his name?" I turn to Garrett. "I didn't even look. I didn't want to. Did you?"

Garrett shakes his head.

"We all wanted to pretend he wasn't a real person," Ashley continues. "But he was. And his name was Theodore Downey."

"Downey?" I ask, and then it dawns on me. "Eric is his son, isn't he?"

She nods. "We think so. And he's got to be the one who's taken our girls."

40

SKYE

We've run out of things to say. It's a waiting game now. Wondering whether he'll come back down at his usual time, or if someone is coming here to this house. Will we hear their voices upstairs? Do we scream at the top of our lungs so whoever it is will help us? Or do we do as he told us and keep our mouths shut, believing him when he says he'll cut out our tongues? I sort of feel like he's a man of his word. Still, in the back of my mind, I consider what we might do if he is injured. How can we use that against him?

Maybe I'm putting too much thought into this. First things first. We wait and see if we hear anyone else upstairs. I just don't know how long that will be—if it happens at all.

I look at Lexi and see her faint silhouette in the darkness, regretting how I'd treated her for, well, a long time. I guess it started when our parents stopped being friends. They never told us why, but it changed the way I felt about Lexi. It's not fair, I know, but that's what happened.

I miss her—her friendship. If we ever get out of here, I'll change that. I swear to God, I will. "Hey, Lex?"

"Yeah?" Her voice is soft but steady.

"Did your parents ever tell you why they stopped hanging out with mine?" I ask.

"No, not really. I mean, I guess I never really asked. It seemed to just sort of happen." She's quiet for a moment. "What made you think of that?"

I shake my head. "I honestly don't know. I guess I was thinking about how things used to be between us—how our families used to do everything together."

"Yeah," she says. "I remember. It was fun for a long time, and then—it wasn't."

"I'm sorry for that," I say. "Just so you know. It was my fault, Lex."

"No, it wasn't," she replies without hesitation. "I think it was just that I'm not as pretty as you are. You're popular, and all the boys like you."

"Stop it." Now, I'm feeling guilty and wishing she could see herself through my eyes. "You are pretty. Don't say that."

"Well, I guess none of that matters right now, huh? We're stuck down here."

"If we don't..." Tears sting my eyes again, blurring the edges of everything around me. "I just want you to know that I love you like a sister. I always have and I'm sorry I was such a dick to you all this time."

She laughs—a sound so unexpected in this place that it feels surreal. "You were kind of a dick."

We both start laughing as I wipe away my tears, a welcome break from the fear and worry. But when I hear a sound upstairs, I raise my index finger to my lips. "Shhh." My gaze rises to the ceiling as if I have X-ray vision and can see exactly what's happening up there. But I can't. It's the first time we've heard anything, which makes me wonder why now? What's directly above us? The creak of floorboards, the faint sound of movement.

This is why he warned us to be quiet. And now I feel like all I want to do is scream, praying that if there is someone else up there with him, they'll hear us. The urge to shout bubbles up inside me.

I look at Lexi, but I can't see her face, and she can't see mine. She must be thinking the same thing. Do we act, risking our lives even more, or do we accept that our lives are already at risk, no matter what?

"Lexi," I whisper. "If we do this, we do it together."

"What? Scream?"

"Only if you want. I won't risk your life for my own selfish reasons."

"I'm scared," she whispers back.

"Me, too." I raise my fingers like she can see me. "On the count of three. One. Two. Thr...

"Wait," she whispers. "Listen."

I strain with my ear aimed toward the ceiling. The sounds—possibly footsteps—I'm not sure, but they're fading. Like someone's walking away. I lower my gaze and close my eyes. "We just lost our window, didn't we?" My lips tremble, and I feel the tears coming again.

"It's okay, Skye. If we'd acted, it would've been for nothing, and he would've made us pay."

We turn quiet again, both of us seeming to realize how afraid we are of this monster. For all our brave talk of escape, of plans to take him down, this is how it ends—two scared teenage girls, knees to our chests, crying for our parents.

The locks on the door disengage. It swings open, and he turns on the light. It stings my eyes every time.

"You were both such good girls today that I thought I'd repay you with food and water."

Gee, thanks, asshole. Words I won't bother saying out loud—if I want to live.

He walks down the steps, and I notice he's still favoring his right leg. I glance at Lexi, and I know she sees it too. He sets down a paper plate with a sandwich on it. Nothing else. I think it's peanut butter and jelly. And then he places a plastic cup full of water beside it. I'm desperate for a drink, but I won't give him the satisfaction of seeing my desperation. I'll wait until he leaves.

Then he approaches Lexi, setting down her food and water, too. "Not much longer now, girls." He turns around and heads back up the steps. I see what appears to be a stain on his pants, on his calf. It looks like blood.

With his back still turned, I wave my hand at Lexi to get her attention. It takes a second, but she looks, creasing her brow. I aim my finger at him, at the stain, and mouth *'blood.'* She squints, trying to get a better look, but I can tell she doesn't see what I'm seeing. But now, he's at the top and turns around a final time.

"Not much longer now, and this will be over for you two." He flips off the light switch and secures the door as he leaves.

"You didn't see it?" I ask her before even taking a sip of the water I'm so desperate to have.

"I saw something, but I couldn't tell from here," she replies. "Maybe blood, but from what?"

"He definitely hurt himself, which is why he's limping. It must've happened when you were upstairs with him. You don't remember if he hurt himself?"

She's quiet for a moment, but I can't see her reaction. "I mean, no, not...well, maybe."

"Maybe what, Lex? What happened to him?" I press, but I know she would rather do anything than to have to relive the event. Still, I need answers.

"I sort of made him go off-balance. He fell to the floor. I noticed then that he clutched his leg, but I didn't know what happened."

"It had to be more than just a fall from the couch to the

floor." I shake my head, knowing that's nowhere near enough to cause him to limp. "There has to be more to it."

"I—I don't remember, Skye, okay? I don't want to remember."

I hold out my hands. "Okay. Okay, you don't have to think about it anymore. Whatever it is, whatever happened to him, it's clearly hurting him still, and maybe, just maybe, he'll be forced to leave to see someone about it. Maybe he'll be gone long enough, or whatever, I don't know."

"Long enough for what?" she asks.

"To try to get out, Lex. Because I think I know what happens to girls down here."

41

ASHLEY

I kept it from them—Nate's secret. If they'd known he had that video, I don't know what Garrett would've done. Killed him? Maybe. And despite my shock and disbelief, we now know who he is—the son of the man Garrett and I killed. His car is sitting in Cash Goodell's yard right now.

I hear Nate's footsteps in the kitchen, and I turn away from the window above the sink.

"Blackwell called," he says. "He wants all of us down at the precinct ASAP."

A bolt of electricity shoots through me. "He found the girls?"

"No." His face masks in defeat. "He wants to talk to us about Eric Downey. Which makes me think he found out who he is."

My mind spins with the implications. "Okay. So maybe he knows where we can find him. Has a current address or something, right?"

"Yeah." Nate nods. "This could be what we need to get Lexi back."

He's hesitating. I can see it. "What?"

"Look, I know we're desperate to get Lexi. And it seems

highly likely this man has her. But you have to know what's going to happen when Blackwell finds him."

"Yeah, I do," I reply. "We'll get her back."

"And it'll all come out," he adds.

"What are you saying, Nate? We blow off the police? Because I don't think that'd be a good look for any of us. And if there's even the remotest of chances it could lead to us finding Lexi, you'd better believe I'll be the first one down there."

"I know, and you're right. But I think we should all come to an agreement that we say nothing about what we know. About Downey being the son of..." He swallows hard. "We just listen to what he has to say. Because if Blackwell gets any whiff of what we know—Eric Downey's car in Cash's yard—whatever—he'll be all over us. Tailing us. Watching us. Waiting for us to do something wrong. We'll have to keep lying until we get what we can from him. But if he picks up on it, we're toast. So, the four of us need to go in clear of all this other shit that's happened."

"So we get Blackwell to tell us if he knows where Downey is—and then we get to the man first," I add.

"That's our only way out of this." Nate swipes his car keys from the kitchen island. "Garrett and Mara are waiting."

I follow him outside and see the Metcalfs. I let my gaze roam over them, each of us understanding what we're about to do. "Like Nate says," I begin. "Let Blackwell do the talking. We don't tell him we already know Downey's car is at Cash's shop. He might already have that information."

Mara looks at me, her lips pursed into a thin line. "I think we all know what's at stake. Regardless of what Blackwell says, we will find this man."

I say nothing more, and the four of us split up. Nate and I are in our car, and Garrett and Mara are in theirs. We head out to the police station. Peering through my side-view mirror, I see Garrett's Mercedes trailing behind us. He should've gotten rid of it long ago. But, at the time, he said it would only draw more attention. Maybe. However, now it's become a serious problem.

Right now, though, I just want my daughter, yet it's becoming impossible to separate the two situations. Cause and effect. These next few hours will determine how the four of us proceed.

Nate turns into the precinct and parks near the front. I glance over my shoulder and see Garrett pulling up close behind. And when I turn back to Nate, he's quiet, just staring at his hands that still clutch the steering wheel. "Hey, we'll get through this." I reach for his shoulder. "He'll tell us where Downey is."

He turns to me. "And then he and a bunch of other cops will storm the place—wherever it is—before we get a chance to."

"Maybe. Either way, we're getting her back." I shrug. "I've been living on borrowed time, regardless. If it comes down to me or Lexi, I'll always choose her." I open the door and step outside. For the first time in days, I notice how warm the air has gotten. Spring is here, and we should be picnicking at the park and taking evening walks. Instead, I don't know if I'll ever see my daughter again, or if I might still end up in prison for who knows how long?

The Metcalfs approach Nate and me, and the four of us head into the station. I don't take the lead, as I usually do. Instead, I hang in the background, letting Garrett and Nate handle things. It's not my M.O., but I'm losing hope, and with that, my desire to do anything other than hide out in my daughter's room and wait for her to come home.

I hear them talking to the officer behind the counter. Mara is standing next to me, but we say nothing to each other. The moments go by in a blur. Officers traverse the lobby. A few people come and go, lawyers probably. I stand frozen while the world spins around me.

"He's on his way."

Nate's voice travels toward me. "Ashley, did you hear me?" he asks.

I shake out of it, and the sounds around me grow clear again. "Sorry?"

"I said Blackwell is on his way up."

"Oh, okay." I wrap my arms around myself, feeling a chill in the air that wasn't there a moment ago. I see Mara and Garrett huddled together in conversation. Are they plotting ways to pin this on us? I wouldn't put it past either of them. I could've left Garrett that night —left him to deal with the fallout. But I stayed like a fool, dragging my innocent husband into the mess. And now they're going to find a way to stick it to us. I'll be damned if I let that happen.

"There he is." Nate approaches Blackwell with his hand outstretched. "Officer Blackwell."

"Mr. Brewer. Thank you for coming down." He eyes me. "Mrs. Brewer." And then he regards Garrett and Mara. "Mr. and Mrs. Metcalf. If you all follow me, we can talk privately in the back."

Again, I lag, feeling the weight of what might happen, wondering if the Metcalfs are looking to screw us over.

"Are you okay?" Nate whispers as he walks beside me.

"Not really. I feel like we're walking into a trap." He looks at me with doubt but says nothing more because we're here. We walk into Blackwell's cramped office, sitting in the chairs he's placed around his desk.

Nate sits down next to me, Mara on the other side, and then finally, Garrett sits on the end.

Blackwell rounds his desk and drops onto his chair. "All right. First of all, thank you for coming down this morning. I do want to update you on what I found regarding the driver's license discovered in Lexi's bedroom." He opens a manila file folder that rests on his desk. "The license, unfortunately, is no longer valid."

I run through the image in my mind, certain I'd seen an expiration date on the license that hadn't yet come to pass. "I'm sorry. It's no longer valid? As in—expired?"

"As in—revoked," Blackwell replies. "Turns out, Mr. Eric Downey lives in Salt Lake City and had his license revoked last year for felony DUI. I have no idea how or why this young man is in Grant, or if he's even still here." He regards us, almost sizing up our expressions, wondering if we're hiding anything. At least, that's how it feels to me.

"So you don't know for sure if he's here in Grant right now?" I ask.

"No, ma'am. According to the background check I ran on him, his last known address matches what's on his driver's license. I'd have to contact Salt Lake PD to see if he's on their radar at all. He's currently unemployed, with no immediate family. None that I could find, anyway."

"You're telling us that this man means nothing?" Nate asks. "That Lexi's possession of his license means nothing either? Because to me, it proves he's here and that he'd been in contact with our daughter."

"I don't dispute that," Blackwell adds. "And we will be on the lookout for this young man, I promise you. I was, however, hoping we'd have something more definitive to go on. I am still, however, waiting on those prints. Don't lose hope yet. I feel we'll get results from that."

I glance at Garrett, thinking about the car he found in Cash Goodell's yard. Will he mention it?

Garrett picks up on my stare, returning his gaze. If he says something to Blackwell, it'll open up that can of worms we've been trying so hard to keep shut. And when Garrett looks away again, I have my answer. He intends for us to find Downey ourselves. Fine by me.

"You want to add something, Mrs. Brewer?" Blackwell asks, narrowing his gaze like he's just noticed our unspoken exchange.

I feel the eyes of the others on me, almost willing me to keep my mouth shut. We all know what Eric Downey looks like. We just need to find him. And when we do, we'll get our girls back—and then kill him.

"No, sir. Nothing to add."

42

GARRETT

An old address. That's all Blackwell had. A part of me wonders how the hell this guy is even a cop. But then, this is probably the best possible outcome. It frees us up to find Downey on our own, doing what's required to keep our secret safe and get our daughters back. And there's Nate. I could see the son of a bitch eyeballing me back there as if this was all my fault.

As we were walking out of the precinct, he'd mentioned having to stop by his pharmacy to check in on things. Sure. Except that I don't believe him. I'm not sure I can believe him about anything now. He'll be looking out for his family's best interests. But so will I.

I pull onto our driveway. "Why don't you go inside and call your parents? See how Milo's holding up."

Mara shoots me a look, already seeing straight through me. "What are you going to do?"

"I need to run out."

She purses her lips. "Where are you going, Garrett?"

"I'm just going to drive by Cash's shop and see if that car is still there," I reply, lying through my teeth.

"If you cause him any more trouble, he'll have you arrested. You get that, right?"

"Blackwell didn't do shit for us back there, and you know what? Fine by me. We have a name and a number. I'm not going to sit on my thumbs while Eric Downey has our daughter."

She turns away and then opens her car door. "Find him, then."

I say nothing and watch her walk inside. That's when I see Nate pulling onto his driveway. Perfect. I can't follow too closely, or he'll pick up on it. But I know where the pharmacy is, and I'll drive around a few minutes first, then see if that's where he's actually going.

Nate doesn't waste time dropping off Ashley. I watch her head into her house, regretting how things ended between us. There'd been a time when I thought the two of us would wind up together. We'd talk about traveling and the future. Never mind how it would've screwed with our kids' heads. We didn't think about the consequences. Then everything changed. She wants nothing to do with me. Can't hardly bear to even look at me. And now this. I can't change what happened back then. I can only work toward finding Skye and Lexi. This is how I do it.

As Nate pulls out again, my hands tighten around the steering wheel. I think about Blackwell's words while they're still fresh, churning over them.

"We'll keep an eye out for this young man."

If those aren't the words of a cop who's given up, then I don't know what are.

And Nate—Nate sat there stiff as a board. Didn't say a word. Just stared at the wall behind Blackwell. But there was a moment —one single moment. I caught it—the look Nate gave me. He thought I was going to screw everything up again by mentioning Cash Goodell. Like I'm that stupid.

Once Nate's gained some distance, I take off, following him, making sure I know what he's up to. And to my surprise, I see him turn into the pharmacy. "Well, shit. You did come here." The best thing for me to do is park down the street and wait. I suspect he's here because if any of his staff gets asked if he'd stopped by, they could answer truthfully. But I'm still not convinced he's staying put. No. He came out for a reason, and I'll find out what that is.

For all I know, he was the one who put the license plate where Ashley and Mara could find it. Planned it out to throw me off. So what's his game plan? Good goddam question.

It's been fifteen minutes, and in the distance, I see Nate step out of the store. He's heading toward his car. "Now we're talk-ing." The thing is, he knows that Eric Downey could be our guy, too, and yet he's not out there looking. Why is that? What's so important that he doesn't want to follow up on finding Downey?

Nate steps into his car and drives off. I follow, keeping two cars between us. "Where are you going, buddy? Don't suppose you know where Downey is? I swear to God, if I find out you're keeping something from me, I'll kill you."

He pulls off into a strip mall. Most of the storefronts are vacant. Just a dollar store, a nail salon, and a mobile phone store. The parking lot is mostly empty. Now, I have to decide whether to follow him. He'll see me. But I have to know why he's here.

I have about two seconds to decide, or I'm going to pass the entrance, and he might see me anyway. "Screw it." I make the turn and drive straight toward him. He sees me and steps out of his car.

Too late to change my mind now, so I park and step out to join him. "What the hell are you doing here, Nate?"

He walks toward me—no, saunters—like he's got something

on me and is about to use it. "I should be asking you the same thing. Why are you following me?"

"Because I saw that look you gave me back at the station," I reply. "Right in front of Blackwell, too."

He chuckles, fiddling with his car keys. "And what look was that?"

"You're going to tell him, aren't you?" I press.

"Tell who what? What are you talking about?"

I plant my hands on my hips, shaking my head. "Blackwell. You're going to tell him what happened and that all you guys are certain that our daughters were taken because of it." I square up to him. "That's the look I'm talking about, Nate. Like you were about to tell Blackwell everything. Am I wrong?"

"You're crazy, is what you are," Nate replies. "You go after Cash twice, now you're following me? Don't you think your time would be better spent looking for your kid? I know mine is."

I step closer, and now we're only inches apart. My gaze shifts around. No one's outside watching us. And if anyone's inside these stores, I don't see them coming out to investigate. So maybe now's my chance. I'd give anything to punch Nate square in the mouth right now, but all that'll do is ensure I end up in a holding cell. "And what are you doing to find your daughter, huh? Tell me, Nate. What the hell are you doing?"

He lowers his gaze, shaking his head and smiling. "I was checking into Lexi's phone records. Blackwell's people are still working to get into the damn thing, so I figured this was something I could easily do to help. I contacted him and gave him the number of the last call she'd made. He ran it through whatever program they have, and he told me it pinged to this location, but that it must've been a burner because no name popped up."

I stand still a moment. "Why the hell didn't you tell any of us this? Does Ashley know?"

"Blackwell insisted his people were still looking into the girls' records. But I didn't want to wait, so I came here." He looks around, glossing over my initial question. "Whoever Lexi called was in this vicinity."

I raise my chin. "You think it was Eric Downey?"

He shrugs. "I don't know. You're the one who has the phone number Cash gave you. You tell me."

"Oh shit. You're right." I reach into my back pocket and pull out the invoice I got from Cash. Unfolding it, I hand it to Nate. "Here. Take a look. See if it's a match."

Nate opens his phone and scrolls through the bill from his carrier. He looks at the number and then at the records. "Son of a bitch." He eyes me. "It's a match. It's the same guy for sure. Eric Downey."

"So, what the hell does this mean? He's here somewhere?" I look around like he's going to walk out and announce his arrival.

"I don't know." Nate scans the area. "But what this tells me is that Downey must've used Lexi to get both our girls. He has them, Garrett. I've never been so sure of anything in my life."

"We need that goddam address from Cash." I inhale a deep breath. "I think we both know he has it. Which means he's in on it."

43
MARA

Ashley's house stares back at me like it's waiting for me to do something. Daring me. I stand in the kitchen, peering at it through my window. The cup of tea in my hands has gone cold, though I don't remember making it. I'm just glad it's not a photo of Skye, one of her stuffed animals, or her favorite T-shirt. All those things I've been clinging onto until now, afraid that if I let them go, then I'll let her go.

My thoughts shift to Garrett. God only knows what he's really up to. I'm not stupid. I know how to tell when he's lying to me—now. Too bad I ignored the signs in those early days.

I don't know what he thinks he'll accomplish. We can't go back to Blackwell and point it out to him. 'Hey, by the way, Officer, go check out that car in Cash Goodell's body shop. We're pretty sure the owner is the same guy on the driver's license.'

My eyes flick back to the Brewers' house. I wonder what Ashley's doing. Probably crying into her hands, or praying, or rehearsing the next lie she's going to tell.

I hate her. There it is. No sugar-coating it. No polite nods and strained smiles like we've been doing for the past five years.

Before she slept with my husband, before she stepped into my life like it was hers to take, we were close—close enough that I considered her more like a sister. But what kind of sister would do what she did?

I hate her. And maybe I didn't want to admit it before, but now? Now my skin crawls every time I see her, every time I hear her name, especially when it comes from Garrett's lips.

I think about that night—the phone call. Garrett's voice trembling, telling me I needed to drive out toward the highway and help him. But not just him—help her, too. That was how I found out.

She caused the accident. Or he did, but she was there, distracting him, doing God knows what. And someone died because of it. We had to bury the problem, just like we had to bury the affair. Dug a deep hole and shoved it down into the dirt, just like the body.

And now—now my daughter's gone. And Ashley still gets to breathe? Her daughter is gone, too, yet she doesn't see that it's all her fault.

I slam the mug into the sink. It shatters, and ceramic shards fly, one catching my palm as if punishing me for my thoughts. Blood spills instantly, trailing into the stainless steel sink, the crimson veins sliding into the drain.

Let it hurt. Let me feel something other than grief over my missing daughter, over the hatred I have for Ashley Brewer, and how I wish we had never moved here.

I rip a paper towel from the roll on the counter, pressing it against the cut, and step toward the front window. I see her silhouette—Ashley, standing in her kitchen. She can't get rid of me. She took something from me long before our girls vanished— my husband. My trust. My peace. And now? I glance at my purse lying on the kitchen island, the gun still inside. I've got nothing left to lose, so I don't think. I move.

Out the front door, across the lawn. No shoes, just the paper towel still pressed to my bleeding hand. It's soaked through now. The warm air heats my already heated brow, but I ignore it. Then, I pound on her door.

She opens it too fast—like she saw me coming. Her mouth opens, probably to say my name, but I'm already inside, pushing past her into the foyer.

"Mara—wait—what are you—"

I turn around to face her. "How dare you."

She recoils like she thought we'd just keep playing the grieving mother card and never talk about why this is really happening. "You want to pretend none of it's your fault? That our girls aren't missing because of what you and my husband did."

She stares at me, wide-eyed. "I can't change the past, Mara."

I scoff, eyeing her like the piece of trash she is. "No, maybe not. But you two dragged us into this nightmare, kicking and screaming. You couldn't keep your hands off Garrett, and now our daughters are gone, and you think you get to stand there and cry and act like you're the victim."

She shakes her head, tears spilling down her cheeks. "Mara, we don't even know if the accident has anything to do with—"

"Really? You're the reason it happened," I snap back. "He never said it directly, but I know. And I know—God help me— that if he hadn't been so distracted by you, maybe none of this would've happened. And our girls would be here now."

Ashley stumbles back like I just hit her. The thought had crossed my mind. She doesn't even realize the best thing that has happened to her today is me leaving the gun in my purse.

"You think I haven't punished myself every day since?" Her voice comes out small. "You think I don't wake up every morning wishing I could change it?"

I laugh. "No. I think you wake up wishing you hadn't been caught."

She covers her face with her hands, sobbing now. "I didn't mean for any of this—"

"Oh, spare me. You meant every bit of it. You wanted him. You got him. And now everything's broken. My daughter is gone. And I look at you and all I see is a woman who ruins lives and walks away clean."

"You think this is clean?" She presses her hand against her forehead. "Lexi's gone, too, or don't you remember? You've been so concerned about Skye, never bothering to think twice about my daughter. Oh, no. It's always been about Skye."

I move past her, pacing now, breathing hard. "I should go to the cops. Tell them everything. Then you'll pay the price you should've paid long ago."

She lifts her chin in defiance. "And what about Garrett?"

We stare at each other, and the silence swirls around us. She knows I won't do it. Not yet. Not while there's still hope our girls are alive. But that hope is fading fast. I step close again. "If my daughter doesn't return, I'll make damn sure you and Garrett both pay."

44
LEXI

Skye is right. He's not keeping to his schedule. He's late again, after coming in earlier this morning. Or was it late last night? Time means nothing down here. But now—yeah—something's changed. Now, every minute that passes, we're holding our breath, wondering what he's planning. His last words to us echo in my ears. *"It'll be over soon."*

Even though I can't see Skye, I feel better knowing she's here with me. Sounds crappy, I know. I should be wishing she was free, not being held captive in a basement. She's smarter than she thinks, and finding the bobby pin—hiding it—it could be our way out. And not the way out we first thought of. This could actually help us.

"He's late again," she whispers.

"Yeah. I get what you mean now." His routine made us think he wasn't going to kill us or let us die. Sounds crazy, but somehow, we sort of felt okay getting regular food and water. "Skye?" We hear it then. The footsteps above us. "Someone else is with him."

"What do you think?" she asks. "Do we yell? Scream?"

"Maybe. Yeah." I hesitate, and my throat tightens. But before we decide, the lock clicks. The door opens.

And he's there, hiding behind the doll mask. Same as always—Shadowed eyes, lips that peek through the mouth hole. Creepy shit. But now we know we were right. He's not alone. Another man steps out from behind him. Taller, broader. Jesus, he's wearing a mask too. Different, but no less creepy. It looks like it's from some old costume of a Raggedy Ann doll. I remember my mom reading me those books because her mom read them to her. The pictures—yeah, that mask looks the same. Red hair, and everything. But this man—his hands are gloved, and he doesn't say a word.

I chance a look at Skye. I think we're both wearing the same expression. Who is this freak, and what does he want? I don't know what to do. The guy who took us gestures out.

"Go on. Take a look," he says.

The second man lumbers down the steps, and I want to be sick because I'm starting to understand why he's here. Why we're here. Skye said it before—the clean clothes and lost bobby pins. Now...

"Stand up," he orders me.

I don't move.

"I said—stand up."

His voice is deep, but kind of shaky, like he's not sure what I might do. Don't worry, dude. I don't know what I'm going to do, either. I glance at Skye again, and she offers a slight nod. So I stand. I feel weak and I can't stop trembling, but I don't say a word. I don't look at him. I just stand there. He walks a half-circle around me, eyeing me up and down, stopping where my chains pull against the wall.

He doesn't touch me, just stares at me through his mask with the eye holes cut too wide. Then he gets closer, and I'm shaking so hard, I think my teeth might rattle. Finally, he places his hands on my arms, moving me, turning me, sizing me up.

He tilts his head at me, then looks back at our captor.

"Don't worry. She won't give you any trouble," he tells the guy. "It doesn't take much to shut her up."

I think about how I hurt him, and I want to smile because he's telling this creep that I'm no trouble. We'll see about that.

Then, he tosses a glance at Skye. "That one there...she's the one that'll draw the most."

I close my eyes. I won't cry. I won't. I know what he means, and I bet Skye does, too. We're not stupid. There's no question why we're here now.

The man backs up, climbing the steps again. "They'll do just fine." Then they both walk out and close the door, the lock clicking into place.

I drop back to the floor.

"Lexi, are you okay? What the hell was that? Who was that guy?" Skye asks questions like I'm the one with the answers.

"I'm okay. But I think it's pretty clear why we're here. Why that guy is here."

"He's selling us," she whispers, her voice cracking on that last word. "That's why he won't take off the mask. He's not going to kill us, just give us to the highest bidder."

I want to tell her no. I want to tell her it's not that, but I can't because she's right. "Yeah." And for the first time since we were taken, I know we're running out of time.

45
NATE

A vigil is happening tonight as though my daughter is already dead. The high school's Parent-Teacher board will host this show of support. The call about it came earlier, and I wanted to tell them to go fuck themselves. That my daughter is still out there, and they could take their vigil and shove it up their asses. But Ashley didn't want to raise questions about why we'd deny or not attend an event the community wished to put together for us.

Would it bring Lexi home? Of course not. It would only force us to suffer through handshakes and condolences, thoughts and prayers. I don't want any part of that. I want to find the son of a bitch who took my daughter, *that's* what I want.

As I peer through the kitchen window into our front yard, Ashley's perfume wafts in my direction. A light floral scent with a hint of vanilla. Pleasant memories arise as I inhale the fragrance, but only until I glance over at her. Wearing a flowy wrap-around dress, she puts in earrings, and her high-heeled shoes click on the tile floor as she enters.

"We really have to do this?" I ask.

"Yes." She moves toward me, gazing through the same window. "We can't look like we don't give a shit that the entire town is coming out tonight in support of finding the girls. It won't move the needle, but Nate, they can't know what's really happening."

"Yeah, I get that." I toss a nod toward the Metcalfs' house. "I don't want to ride with them, Ash. They can go on their own."

"Agreed. It's already been arranged. We'll meet them there, and you and Garrett will make a brief statement together. That's it. That's all you'll have to do," she replies.

"Except we'll have to sit through it all—the singing and the crying." I tilt my head back. "Jesus." Ashley rests her hand on my shoulder. Her touch reminds me of how we used to be. How hard we've been trying to put the past behind us, yet it refuses to stay there.

"It's a nice thing, Nate—what they're all trying to do for our families. We have to get through it and put on a united front, no matter what."

I nod, knowing there's nothing left for me to say. So, I grab my car keys. "Let's go."

We make the drive to the center of town. Montgomery Park is where the vigil is taking place. The commons are the hub of Downtown with benches and paths, shady trees, and room for throwing frisbees. We used to come here—the four of us and our kids. But that was a lifetime ago.

The parking lot is full, but it appears they've reserved spots for us and the Metcalfs. I don't see Garrett and Mara's car yet, so I pull into the spot and cut the engine. "Why aren't they here?"

"I'm sure they will be soon," Ashley replies, stepping out of the car. "Come on. We have to do this."

I climb out to join her and then lock the car. In the dusky light, I see dozens of people ahead, and more walking into the park coming from the adjacent streets. Guitars strum and people chatter. As I take it all in, a lump rises in my throat. I didn't expect to feel this way—seeing all these people here. I'm reminded that there are still good people. Many of those here now also helped in the search that first morning.

"My God. The entire town *is* here," Ashley says, taking my hand.

I want to pull it away, but I don't. And for a moment, we're one, but I know this moment won't last. "Yeah, they are."

As we make our way toward the crowd, a woman smiles and raises her hand to garner our attention. I recognize her as Councilwoman Torres.

"Mr. and Mrs. Brewer." She offers her hand to me. "Thank you for coming."

I accept her greeting. "Of course. This is really incredible. Everyone's here."

"Yes, they are." She's dressed in black. Her helmet hair and pearl necklace complete the look. For Christ's sake, she looks like she's going to a funeral.

"They want you to know that you're not alone, Mr. and Mrs. Brewer. We all support you. You and the Metcalf family, which, by the way, do you know if they're headed here?"

"They are," Ashley replies before I have the chance. "Just a few minutes behind us."

"Good. Good." The councilwoman returns a tender smile. "Well, why don't you both follow me, and I can make a few introductions for you? I assume we'll get started once Mr. and Mrs. Metcalf arrive."

I wonder if I should call Garrett. We can't afford for them to be too late. Not to mention, regardless of the outpouring of support, I don't want to be here any longer than necessary. The reminder that Lexi isn't here is overwhelming at the best of times. Seeing all these people throws it in my face.

Ashley taps on my shoulder. "They're here."

I glance back, spotting Garrett and Mara heading toward us. "It's about time." I turn back again and capture Torres's attention. "Councilwoman? The Metcalfs are here."

"Ok. Perfect," she replies. "I'll let everyone know we're about to get started."

When Garrett and Mara join us on the makeshift stage, we say nothing to each other. It's as if we all feel like frauds—maybe because we are.

I stand with Ashley at my side, though we don't touch. I wonder if the people out there, holding their candles, notice the distance between us. Between all of us.

The town commons is packed now. Hundreds of people have gathered in a semicircle. I scan the crowd, barely hearing the music. I'm not here to cry. I'm not here to pray. I'm here to see who doesn't belong.

Ashley sniffles beside me, but I don't look at her. I can't. Not with Garrett and Mara standing a few feet away, pretending we're all just four people wrapped in shared tragedy. Pretending the past didn't shatter our friendship long before our daughters vanished.

Garrett keeps his arm tightly around Mara like he's worried she'll bolt. Her face is pale, and a smudge of mascara darkens her eyes.

The mayor clears his throat and then opens the evening with a speech—something about unity, hope, community—and I tune him out. My eyes roam. Every person here is a possible answer or a dead end. Is Eric Downey here somewhere, too? Taunting us?

There's Mr. Klein, my old history teacher, holding his wife's hand. The Thompsons—both sobbing. Emma Wilson with her three kids. Just normal people.

But then, behind the tree line, just at the edge of the crowd, I catch sight of someone I don't recognize. A man in a baseball cap, hands in the pockets of his jeans, looking down. He's not holding a candle. I nudge Ashley. "You know that guy out there?"

She follows my gaze and squints. "No."

I take a step forward, but the man shifts sideways and turns away. Without another thought, I step off the stage while the mayor is still speaking and push through the crowd of people. "Sorry, excuse me, sorry."

"Nate?" Ashley calls out to me in a hushed tone.

I ignore her. By the time I reach the tree line, he's gone. Maybe he was never there at all. I stand still, listening to the murmurs of the crowd as they watch me. This isn't the kind of attention I need, so I walk back.

"Sorry for the interruption. Pardon me. Excuse me. Thank you all for coming tonight." I nod as I navigate through the crowd, returning to the stage. And when I reach Ashley, the look in her eyes reveals her disappointment. Garrett raises an eyebrow at me, and Mara doesn't look at me at all.

The mayor continues with his speech, glossing over the interruption. Instead, mentioning something to the effect that it's a difficult time and, as the parents, our stress levels are high. Really?

"I thought I saw someone," I say, more to myself than to Ashley.

"Everyone's here," Ashley whispers. "That's the point."

"Downey, too?" I turn back to the crowd. The candles keep flickering. The faces blur. And somewhere, someone out there knows what happened to our girls. Someone's watching us, gauging our reactions, wondering if we've figured out their secret yet. Is it him? Is it Eric Downey?

The vigil ends in a slow hush. The music fades, and people drift toward their cars, heads bowed. We still get pats on our shoulders, polite nods, and words of comfort. They tried to make us feel less alone. It's done the opposite.

Ashley wraps her arms together as the evening air seems to have a slight chill to it tonight. "They didn't even say anything to us."

"I picked up on that." I glance back and see Garrett and Mara fall into step behind us. They said nothing to us, and we said nothing to them. Did anyone else notice?

Then Garrett turns and comes to a stop. His whole body stiffens. I watch him stand there a moment, frozen in place, peering out into the darkness of the woods behind us. "What is it?" I ask, but he doesn't answer me. Instead, he bolts.

"Garrett—hey!" I shout, but he's already sprinting across the grass, away from the cars, away from the crowd, toward the dark sliver of woods that lines the edge of the park. I run after him.

Behind me, I hear Ashley yell my name, Mara calling for Garrett. But their voices fade the second I hit the trees. Branches whip my face. I dodge the jagged rocks that make the crossing treacherous. It's dark in here—almost pitch black, except for faint moonlight diffusing through the canopies, but I see Garrett's silhouette ahead, crashing through the undergrowth like a man possessed. "Garrett, stop!"

He does—suddenly, and I nearly slam into him. We stand there, out of breath, gasping for air like two men approaching middle age, because that's exactly what we are. There's no one else in sight. "What'd you see, man?"

"I—I don't know," Garrett says, scanning the trees. "A man. Just standing still, head down, face blocked by a baseball cap."

I look around. Only trees and shadows in my purview. "I thought I saw the same guy earlier, too." I step closer, lowering my voice. "Did you recognize him? Was it Downey?"

Garrett doesn't answer.

"Garrett."

"No." He swallows hard. "I don't know...Maybe."

I stare at him. Sweat glistens on his forehead, and his jaw is tight. There's something unhinged in his eyes. "Did you see him or not, man?"

"Fuck if I know," he replies.

The woods feel too quiet. Too still. Like the only living creatures inside it are us. Garrett and me. Anger balls in my gut. I take another step, closing the gap between us. He shifts but doesn't back away. "You know this is your fault," I say. "Everything. If you and Ashley hadn't—if you'd just kept your goddamn pants on—"

"Now isn't the—"

"No. You don't get to talk right now," I say, cutting him off. The world around me blurs and my focus is solely on him. I can almost hear his heart pounding, like he knows exactly what I can do right now. I clench my jaw. My heart rams against my ribs. I see it all—his face, broken under my fists. His body on the ground. My hands around his throat. I imagine the silence afterward—the relief. Could I do it? End him, right here, where no one can see? Plenty of people saw him running out into these woods. I came up on him this way, Officer. No, I didn't see who did this, but it has to be the man who has our daughters.

God, I could end it all so easily right now. I take another step, and now, we're inches apart. He holds my gaze and doesn't move, doesn't flinch. Maybe he wants me to come at him.

"You think you've suffered?" I whisper. "You don't know what it's like to look at your wife and see a stranger. And now all of this is because of you."

He opens his mouth, but I raise a finger. "Don't."

I could do it. God help me, I could.

But then—A sound. A branch snapping somewhere deeper in the woods. We both freeze. It's not an animal, but a footstep. I turn toward it, my rage dissolving into something else altogether —something primal. "Shit. He's still here."

46

GARRETT

What is with this guy? I come out here, sure I'd seen someone, and he's threatening me. I push deeper into the woods, straining to hear, wondering if we're being watched. Nate doesn't follow. No surprise there. He's all words and no action. Still, could Downey be out here?

But then...there's nothing. No more snapping of twigs. No rustling of bushes. "Goddam it." I head back, and my eyes land on Nate, who remains exactly where I left him. "I'm going back. Whoever it was is gone now, thanks to you."

I brush past him, managing to get several feet away when I hear him run up on me. The crunch of twigs under his feet is like a warning bell. But before he gets close enough, I spin back and thrust out my hand. "Back the hell off, Nate. Don't do something you'll regret."

"My only regret is not doing this sooner," he replies, his voice laced with a mix of desperation and resolve as he lunges at me.

He pushes me onto the ground, falling on top of me. He's all arms, flailing away, throwing punches but only landing a couple.

Each missed punch only pisses me off more. "Get off me, man. Don't do this."

His knees pin down my arms, but I manage to break free, knocking him off me with little effort. "Nate, goddam it. Knock this shit off before someone gets hurt." Now, I straddle him, balling my fist, and sending a firm strike connecting against his jaw. I hear the crack of bone. "Goddam it. I don't want to do this, all right?"

He struggles beneath me. I've got a solid twenty pounds on him and at least a couple of inches. He's not going to win this one. But before I know it, my head snaps back and stars fill my eyes as blood fills my mouth. I spit out a broken tooth. "That's it."

I ball my fist and pull back my arm. Nate shields his face. But just before I land the punch, I stop. "Jesus Christ, man. What the hell are we doing?" I climb off him and extend my hand. "Get up."

He clamps onto it, and I yank him off the ground. "We should be out there looking for Downey, not beating the living shit out of each other," I say.

We brush ourselves off, and that's when I hear the snap of twigs. Nate and I lock eyes and freeze, both of us hoping it's Downey coming back to confront us. Instead, I see Mara and Ashley. "Don't worry. We're done here."

"For God's sake," Mara begins. "And we thought you'd run out here because you saw the man who took our kids. Instead, you both look like you've been used as punching bags."

"Everyone's gone," Ashley says. "They all think you two have lost your minds or something...the way you both dashed out here. Especially after Nate interrupted the mayor's speech. We need to keep up appearances. Make it look like we're united. You both get that, right?"

"Just back off, Ashley," Mara says. "You talk as if you're not the reason they're fighting." She looks at me. "You're not over her, are you?"

"That's not what this is about," I insist. "I could've sworn I saw a man out here. Nate did too."

"So why'd you start throwing punches?" she presses.

Nate wipes blood off his lower lip. "Because I'm sick of pretending to be his friend. Putting on this so-called united front. Screw that. The only reason our daughters are gone is because of these two." He waves his finger at Ashley and me.

"I can't do this anymore," Mara says.

Ashley steps in. "What are you talking about?"

"Back off, Ash. I can't be around you or Garrett anymore. You both have taken too much from me. And now my daughter is gone."

"So is ours," Ashley snaps back.

I raise my palms in surrender. "Look, it's late. Let's just all get the hell out of here. Go back home. This whole vigil thing has been too much. We have to focus on finding Eric Downey. And it's going to take all of us to figure out how to do that." I head toward Mara; my eyes aimed at the ground. And that's when I hear it—the click of a gun.

"Oh my God. What are you doing?" Ashley says, her voice faltering.

I raise my gaze at Mara and stop cold. "Jesus Christ."

"Mara, put down the gun. Please," Nate says. "We all want the same thing here, okay? We want to find our girls."

But Mara's gaze is unyielding. She aims the gun at my head, and I see years of her pain in her steely gaze. "Where did you get that?"

"Does it matter?"

"Christ, don't you see what's happening—to all of us?" I reply. "Mara, this isn't you. We're here to find our girls. I came out here because I thought I saw someone."

"Where is he?" she asks sharply.

I shake my head. "Gone. I don't know. Maybe I was just chasing shadows. But then Nate comes at me, throwing punches, blaming me."

"Because it's your fault." Mara's gaze darts to Ashley. "Yours and hers. None of us would be here right now if you two hadn't destroyed everything. Our girls would be here."

I nod slowly, careful not to make a sudden move. "This has already gone too far, Mara. We need to stick together and see it through—all of us, whether we like it or not."

"I need my daughter back. I don't need you." Her trembling hand tightens around the gun. Tears run down her cheeks as she swallows hard.

Does she even know how to use that thing?

A deafening crack splits the silence. The muzzle flash illuminates her face. The air instantly smells of burned powder. My body reacts before my mind can catch up. I stumble back a step, ducking instinctively as the sharp ping of the bullet ricochets off a tree somewhere behind me. The sound echoes around us.

"What the hell are you doing?" I shout. "Mara! Have you lost your fucking mind?"

But she doesn't answer. Her eyes lock on me again, firm and unblinking. I throw a sideways glance at Nate, who looks like a deer in headlights. I shoot a look at Ashley. Shock masks her face. Then, without hesitation, Mara pulls the trigger again. This time, there's no ricochet.

Pain explodes in my side. Heat spreads beneath my fingers as I instinctively clutch at the wound. My knees buckle as I stagger backward against the rough trunk of a tree for support.

Ashley's scream pierces through the air—a raw, visceral sound that cuts through me almost as deeply as the bullet has. "Mara?" she shrieks. "What did you do? What did you do?"

Nate scrambles away, looking for cover. Coward. His eyes dart between me and Ashley as panic overtakes him.

I press harder against my side, trying to stem the flow of blood now soaking through my shirt. The warmth seeps between my fingers despite my efforts to hold it back. My breaths come in shallow and uneven as I look up at Mara—my wife, the woman who was supposed to be my partner in everything. The woman I vowed to love and cherish, but who I failed in every sense of the word.

"Mara..." Pain tinges every syllable I force out. "What... what have you done?"

Her expression falters for just a moment—a flicker of doubt breaking through her veneer—but it's gone almost as quickly as it appeared. She steps closer, her hands shaking now, not just from anger but from something else. Fear? Regret? Even she doesn't seem sure anymore.

"You left me no choice," she says. "You took everything from me—my dignity, my self-worth, and now, my daughter."

"Mara, please," Ashley begs, her hands raised defensively. "Please stop. Don't do this. Skye needs you—both of you. We will get her back. Her and Lexi, both. This isn't you, Mara. I'm begging you, please stop—for Skye's sake."

Mara shakes her head, tears streaming freely now, dripping off her chin. "Get away from me, Ashley. You're no better than he is."

"You're right. I'm not." She glances at Nate, who has come out from behind the tree. Her gaze shifts to the blood pooling at my feet before darting back to Mara with renewed urgency. "We need to get out of here. All of us. Garrett needs a doctor. It's over for us now, Mara. This is it. We can't hide anymore. You've just made sure of that."

For a moment, a fragile millisecond, it seems like Ashley's words might reach her. Mara's grip on the gun loosens a little; her arm wavers as though it's suddenly too heavy to hold steady any longer.

But then her gaze hardens again. "No," Mara whispers, shaking her head once more as if trying to convince herself. "No... It's too late. The kids—they're better off without any of us."

I feel myself sinking to the forest floor now, the strength draining from my legs with every passing second that blood continues pouring from my side. The bark scrapes against my back as I slide down, each movement sending fresh waves of pain through me. My vision blurs as I fight to stay conscious.

"Mara." I manage to choke out again, though my voice is barely audible now over Ashley's sobs. "I'm sorry."

Her eyes snap back to mine, sharp and accusing. For a moment, we just stare at each other, this unbridgeable chasm of betrayal and heartbreak between us.

"I trusted you," she whispers. "I gave you everything."

My chest tightens—not just from pain but from something deeper—guilt and regret. But it doesn't matter anymore. None of it matters anymore except stopping this before it spirals even farther out of control. "Yes, you did. And I'm sorry for that. But Skye and Milo need us both."

Mara doesn't respond. Instead, she simply raises the gun again, her finger tightening around the trigger. "They don't need a father like you."

The crack of the gun is the last thing I hear.

47

ASHLEY

Blood rushes through my ears, drowning out all other sounds. I don't move. I can't. My legs feel like they're rooted into the earth. I chance a look at Garrett, who's crumpled on the ground, blood all around him. He's still breathing short and shallow breaths. He's dying right in front of me.

For God's sake, how did we get here? My mind scrambles for answers, replaying the last few minutes in fragmented soundbites that make no sense. Is this really happening? It doesn't feel real, yet the smell of gunpowder saturates the air.

Nate stands several feet away, his bottom lip stained with blood, arms hanging limp at his sides. His expression mirrors mine—wide-eyed disbelief. He shifts his gaze to me, then Garrett, then back to me again, as if silently asking the same question I am —are we next?

Garrett's ragged gasps break the silence along with the faint rustle of wind through the trees. Did anyone hear the gunshots? The park isn't far from here; it's just on the other side of this wooded stretch. Someone must've heard it.

Mara still has a firm grip on the gun, though her hands tremble, and her gaze is locked on Garrett's form on the ground. She looks ready to fire again.

I force myself to look away from Garrett because if I don't, I'll know for certain this is no nightmare, but a terrible truth that's been five years in the making. My feelings for him have long since dried up, but I never wanted him to die. And now what?

"Mara." Nate's voice breaks through our deadlock.

"Don't say another word, Nate," Mara cuts him off, her tone razor-sharp and entirely certain. Her eyes flicker toward me as though she's sizing me up. "You're not innocent in this either, are you, Ashley?"

I wondered how long it would take for her to remember Garrett hadn't acted alone. My lips part to respond, but no sound comes out at first, just a shaky breath that corroborates my fear. "Please, Mara... I just want to find my daughter, same as you."

Mara scoffs. "Do you honestly think they're still alive? Are you that naïve?"

"They're alive," I say. "I believe that. They're alive, and they need us to find them. They need our help." I risk taking a step closer, lowering my tone. "Please, Mara, put down the gun."

For a moment, something flickers in her eyes—something raw and vulnerable—but it vanishes in an instant. Now, all I see is hate and rage as she raises the gun, training it on my chest. I gasp for air as I feel it rip from my lungs. Oh God. She's going to kill me.

"I should've done this a long time ago," Mara says, steadying her aim. "Maybe my daughter would still be here."

She cocks the gun, a sound that echoes in my ears. "Please don't do this, Mara. I'm begging you." I look at Nate, taking in his features, knowing this is the last time...

He charges ahead, straight toward Mara, leaves and twigs crunching beneath his feet. She spins around like she's going to shoot, but he rushes at her, knocking her to the ground. The gun slips from her hand.

I stare at it, only feet away from me. My gaze darts to Nate as he pins Mara to the ground, screaming at her to stop. I look back at Garrett. Eyes closed. I think he's gone. That could've been me. And that's enough to force me to move, to grab the gun.

"Stop!" I shout, keeping the gun at my side. "I don't know how to use this thing, but I will if I have to. That's enough. It's over."

Nate pulls off her, hurrying toward me. "Are you all right?"

I nod.

Mara slowly rises, tears filling her eyes. "They'll arrest me now. I'll spend the rest of my life in prison. Milo. My little boy... He won't have either of us now." Anguish radiates off her.

"No. It doesn't have to be that way." Out of the corner of my eye, I catch Nate watching me with a furrowed brow. "Look, we can still fix this."

Mara laughs. "Are you serious?" She wipes her tears. "I just killed my husband, and I tried to kill you. Now, you're going to help me?"

"Your kids shouldn't lose both of you," I say. "If we get Garret to a hospital... if we get him help..." I trail off a moment. Helping Mara is the last thing I want to do. But the cops won't believe us if both of them are dead. We need her alive if this is going to work. "We'll tell them it was an accident," I continue.

"Or," Nate interjects, seeming to reach the same conclusion. "We could tell them he was attacking me, and you shot him because you thought he was going to kill me."

Mara tilts her head at him, a glimmer of consideration flashing briefly across her face. "That's not what happened."

"Not entirely," I say. "But it's close enough."

"And you?" she asks, raising her chin.

"Nothing happened," I reply. "So there's nothing more to say." The sirens sound, and I keep my gaze fixed on Mara.

But can we pull this off? Can we lie about what really happened? It's not like we haven't done it before. And I'm not sure we have a choice. If they find out the truth behind Mara's actions—that she shot Garrett over his affair with me, the rest of it will come out. I can't let that happen, not while my daughter is out there somewhere, being held by someone I'm certain is out for revenge.

"Mara?" I press. "You'll lose your son and daughter."

Nate and I stare at her, willing her to agree. She closes her eyes and nods.

We hear footsteps trampling through the woods. It must be the police. I walk toward her, using my shirt to wipe off the gun. "Here, take this. Now—before they come." As I hand it to her, we lock eyes, a newfound understanding of each other emerging. "You shot him to protect Nate."

I walk back as the footsteps grow louder. There must be four or five people coming. Faint flashes of red and blue lights shine through the trees in the distance. The cops are here, and they're coming toward us. I look at Mara again, and when I'm certain we agree, I call out. "Help! Over here! Help!"

I see Officer Blackwell first, then his partner, Officer Wiley, and two other officers I recognize from the vigil.

"Drop the gun!" Blackwell shouts at Mara. "Drop the gun, now!"

She lowers it to the ground, slowly rising again with her hands up. "Garrett was trying to kill him."

Blackwell, weapon ready to fire, looks at Nate, then at Garrett. "Jesus Christ." He runs to Garrett, placing two fingers on his neck.

I pray he's dead because if he's not and he does somehow survive this, we're all going to prison. Garrett won't play along in this new game, knowing he'd be the one to pay the price for a made-up charge of attempted murder.

"I got a weak pulse!" Blackwell says. "Get an ambo over here now!"

Officer Wiley picks up Mara's gun, fixing her gaze on me while pressing the button on her radio. She suspects it's all a lie. I see it in her face. "We need an ambulance at Montgomery Park. GSW in the stomach and chest. Victim needs immediate transport." She eyes Mara. "Hands behind your back. Now."

Another officer approaches Garrett and examines him. "He's lost a lot of blood. I'm not sure he'll make it."

"I need you to keep pressure on the wounds," Blackwell replies.

"Yes, sir."

Blackwell casts a wary gaze at me, then walks to Nate. "What the hell happened here?"

"He went ballistic on me," Nate replies. "All this shit, tonight's vigil—I guess it got to him. I tried to calm him down, but he lost it."

Blackwell studies Nate's injuries. "You don't look too banged up." He then approaches Wiley, who's got a firm grip on Mara. "I'm afraid we're going to have to put you in a holding cell tonight, Mrs. Metcalf. Until we know whether your husband will pull through. And I'm going to need all of you to come in and make a statement."

"She had no choice, Officer," I say, attempting to reaffirm our position. "Mara saved my husband."

48
SKYE

It's been twelve hours since we've had food or water. That's my best guess—twelve. Lexi and I haven't said much since it became clear why we're here. And that the only way we're getting out is in the hands of someone else. Someone who could do far worse things to us than this creep has, and that's saying something.

I do my best not to lose my shit completely because it'll only scare Lexi. Both of us are walking the line between wanting to fight for our lives and losing hope we'll actually survive. "What do you think our parents are doing right now?" I ask, hoping to keep myself from spiraling.

Lexi's quiet for a moment, and I wonder if she heard me. She could be asleep but—

"Freaking out," she replies.

"Yeah, that's what I figured. Do you think this will make them friends again?"

"I don't know. Maybe." Lexi sighs. "What are we going to do, Skye? Just sit here?"

"What can we do?" I try to see her in the darkness, but she's just a faint outline behind a shadow. "He's going to hand us off, and then I don't know what will happen. I don't know where they'll take us, but if we leave here, no one will ever find us."

"So we can't leave, then, right?"

"Well… I mean, it's not like we have a choice, Lex."

"What if we do?"

I shake my head, already knowing where this is going. "We can't try another one of your escape plans. He could've killed you last time. You got lucky."

"But I hurt him, didn't I? And he did something to himself, too," she replies.

"Yeah, but it's not like it stopped him."

"I want to see my parents." Her voice falters. "Skye, I can't believe this is the end of everything. It can't be. We're only fifteen."

A lump rises in my throat. All the things I wish I hadn't said to her, rising along with it. Things I wish I hadn't said to my parents or my little brother, either. Now, all I can think about is what I'd tell them if given another chance. Like how much I love them. How sorry I am that I didn't leave practice earlier that night. How much I wish I could hug them right now.

"I know. I know, and I'm so sorry. Please don't cry, Lexi. Please. Maybe this isn't over yet, okay? There are still things we can use to help us. But you know, he's long past his usual time. Did you realize that?"

She sniffles and clears her throat. "Yeah, I guess so. But he was late last time, too. Maybe he's not on a schedule like you think he is."

I wriggle my chains, first my left hand, then my right. Then I study the metal clamp. Sort of like handcuffs, I guess. It looks kind of makeshift. "Maybe he's not here."

"What are you saying?" Lexi asks.

"I don't know…. these chains…that bobby pin might work, like we talked about before. Now could be our chance to try." I reach into my shirt and pull it out of my bra. "I could push it into the lock, see if it works like how it does on those YouTube videos."

"Yeah," Lexi replies, hope sounding in her words. "Maybe it could work. And since he hasn't been back, this could be the best time to try."

I bend the bobby pin until it's straight and pull off the little rubber tips at the ends. With my left hand, I push the metal end into the right cuff. It's a small keyhole, smaller than what's on a padlock. That has to be good, though, right?

"Is it working?" Lexi asks, eager for me to get this done.

"I'm still trying."

The cuffs dig into my wrists every time I move, but I can't stop. Sitting still means giving up, and I'm not doing that. Not yet. Soon, my fingers turn all clammy, and now the bobby pin is slick with sweat. I twist it again inside the keyhole, and the sound of metal on metal seems to get louder with each passing second. Can he hear me? Is he here?

They make it look so easy on YouTube. One little wiggle, a *click*, and they're free. But they don't show how much it hurts, how hard it is to see what you're doing, especially in the dark. I clench my jaw and push the pin in deeper, trying to remember that video I watched a year ago. It was just for fun back then. I never thought I'd need it.

I breathe in through my nose, slow and steady, like Mom always told me. 'Calm down, Skye. Focus.' That's what she'd always say when I had to do some crazy gymnastics stunt for cheerleading. How I wish that's what I was doing now.

"What's going on?" Lexi asks again. "Tell me it's working, Skye."

"Not yet." I try to hide my frustration. "I'm still working on it. Have some faith, Lex."

"Yeah, okay."

I feel something shift inside the cuff. My heart stutters. That was different. That was *something*. I go still, barely breathing, and ease the pin a little to the left. Come on. Just one more twist. One more second. And then—

Snap.

"No. Oh no, no, no."

"What is it? Are you okay?" Lexi asks.

My lips tremble as I realize what just happened. When I pull out the pin, I see it—broken. "Shit. Fuck. Shit!"

"Tell me what's happening," Lexi demands.

"It broke, okay? The bobby pin broke inside the lock."

"Oh, no," Lexi replies. "It's okay. It's okay, Skye. You tried. We'll figure out something else, all right?"

"Screw this." I fold my thumb into the palm of my hand and, with my other hand, grasp the clamp. "You know how people can slip out of handcuffs?"

"I guess," Lexi replies with renewed interest.

"What if I could squeeze out of them? I have small hands."

"You'll end up hurting yourself even worse. Break your thumb or something. No, you can't do it."

"But what if I can? Don't you think I should try?" I press.

"Then I should try too," she says. "If you think this might work, then we both do it, all right?"

She's not wrong. If one of us gets free, one of us could still make it out of here alive. "Okay. We both try it. And whoever succeeds, that person has to be ready when he comes down. We'll only get one shot at it."

"But how do we stop him?" Lexi asks. "Even with our hands free, like, what do we do?"

This is the hard part—convincing her she'll have to do something awful. Almost too awful to think about. "I just need you to remember that our lives are at stake here. So what I'm about to say, you can't be all weird about it, okay?"

"Yeah, okay. I get it."

"Whoever manages to slip out of the cuffs will have to wait until he comes down. When he does, and he gets close enough, you push your fingers into his eyes, like really hard. Hard enough to make him bleed."

"Oh gross. Seriously?" she asks.

"Yeah, Lex. I'm being serious. He's too big and too strong. I learned that in P.E. last year—self-defense. Didn't you?"

"I must've missed that lesson."

"Can you do it or not?" I ask, growing irritated. "Because if not, then leave this up to me. I'll try to get my hands free, and I'll do it."

"No," she replies. "No, I can do it. I swear. But we still have the garbage bag. What if we put it over his head? That should be easier than the whole eye thing, right?"

I think about it for a second. "Yeah, you could be right. It'd be quicker, too. Then we start now. Who knows how long we have before he comes back down? And it's best if we can both get free. We'll stand a better chance."

I waste no time and start tugging on the clamp around my left wrist. Pulling my thumb into my palm, I push it up, scraping my hand and pinching the lower knuckle on my thumb. It stings as the skin tears away.

I hear Lexi grunting as she works to do the same. "Come on," I whisper as I push harder, reminding myself this pain is nothing compared to what will happen if we're taken from here. Then I remember, both my hands are chained, so I'll have to pull off this miracle twice.

I twist my wrists against the metal clamps biting into my skin. They're tight—so tight that they've already left red marks—but I don't let myself dwell on the pain. Instead, I focus on what needs to be done.

I push the cuff upward again with all my strength, my skin stinging as it continues to get stripped away. A raw burn spreads across my hand, but I clench my teeth and keep going.

Lexi still grunts as she tugs at her restraints. Her breathing grows heavier with each attempt.

"Come on," I whisper as I push harder against the clamp. The skin on my knuckle continues to tear away in thin layers, leaving behind a trail of blood that trickles down my arm. It stings like a bitch—like someone dragging barbed wire across my skin—but I keep going.

I remind myself over and over again as I work against the restraints: This pain will pass; we have to survive.

Lexi suddenly lets out a sharp scream—a sound so loud that it jolts me out of my determined haze. "Lex? Hey! Are you all right?" My voice cracks with panic as I whip my head around to try to see her.

Her shadow looks small, like she's hunched over.

"I did it," she whispers in disbelief. "I got one hand free... but I think—I think I broke my thumb."

My breath catches in my throat. Relief swells inside me. "Oh my God. Oh my God! Lexi, you did it! You'll be okay," I say. "Just keep trying with your other hand if you can. And don't worry about me—I'll keep trying too."

I focus again on my restraints without waiting for her reply because every second matters when you don't know how many you have left.

The blood dripping on my skin has made the metal slippery, easier to move against. Kind of like when Mom put oil on my ring finger that one time because I put on a toy ring that wouldn't come off. But it doesn't dull the sharp, prickly burn of torn skin or the throbbing ache spreading through my swollen hand. Still... I don't stop. I refuse to give up.

Not when we're this close.

Not when survival might actually be in reach.

49
NATE

The needle burns as it's inserted into the wound under my lip. Two stitches, they said. Sitting on the edge of the bed while the nurse tends to me, I can't help but wonder what Mara is telling the cops right now.

Ashley is with her, or at least, with the cops down at the station. I insisted I didn't need a hospital, but I have a feeling Blackwell wanted to split us up—make sure our stories matched. I have no idea if Garrett is still alive. I hope not. It's shitty of me to think that, but things will be a lot easier if he isn't.

I told myself I'd forgiven him for what he'd done, but deep inside, I knew that wasn't true. I told Ashley the same thing, but that wasn't true either. I never forgave either of them. And it seems, neither did Mara.

In the middle of this self-imposed nightmare, my daughter is still missing. The search, the vigil—none of it having mattered at all. And now it's entirely possible that our lies are about to be exposed. Then what? What happens to our girls?

I still have the evidence. Will Ashley tell Blackwell about it? She'd be implicated, of course. We all would. But if Blackwell could see it, he'd know what to do to find Downey. They'd dig up the body, run forensics on it to get an ID, then confirm our suspicions—that Eric Downey is the son of the man Garrett and my wife killed. Somehow, though, I think all Blackwell would need to know is that Downey's car sits in Cash Goodell's body shop this very moment. How to give him that information without exposing everything else?

"You're all set, Mr. Brewer," the nurse says, disposing of the bloody gauze.

"I can leave?"

"Well." She glances at the door. "The doctor has discharged you, but I think you'll have to check with the police officer at the door."

"Right. Yeah, thanks."

She cleans up, placing her instruments on the metal cart. "I was there tonight—at the vigil."

I hold her gaze. "Thank you."

"I'm real sorry for those girls—for a lot of reasons." She pushes her cart and heads toward the door.

If that wasn't a dig at us, I don't know what is. The lies we've buried in this town are climbing to the surface, and our girls are paying the price. If that nurse could see it, who's to say Blackwell won't?

I slide off the bed and gather my things. As I head toward the door, the officer peers at me, blocking the exit. "I've been discharged."

"Then I'll have to take you down to the station, Mr. Brewer," the officer replies. "If you'll come with me."

I look around for a second, wondering if a nurse will come by to insist that I sit in a wheelchair and that they push me out, but I see no one, so I trail him. Blackwell took my phone, so I can't call Ashley and tell her I'm coming. "Excuse me, Officer?"

He glances over his shoulder as we near the lobby, heading toward the exit. "Yes?"

"Can you tell me if Mr. Metcalf, Garrett Metcalf, is doing all right?"

The officer stops just before the automatic glass doors open and squares up to me. "No, sir. He's not all right. He's dead."

The officer walks through the opening, and I lower my gaze. I should be happy, but then I think of Skye and Milo.

It also occurs to me I could destroy the flash drive now, tell Blackwell what Garrett did five years ago, and it'd all be over. Garrett would take the blame. Mara and Ashley could corroborate. The secret would be out without destroying the rest of us. And then Blackwell could focus on finding Eric Downey.

The officer puts me in the back of his patrol car, and now I feel like the criminal I am. I say nothing on the drive. Instead, I plot how I'll respond when Blackwell questions me over what happened. I can only hope Mara and Ashley tell the same story, or things are going to go off the rails pretty quickly.

When we arrive at the precinct, the officer ushers me inside. It takes a minute to see past the other cops and people milling around, but then I see her—Ashley, sitting in the waiting area. We lock eyes, and I don't like the look on her face. She stands from the chair and hurries toward me.

"Are you okay?"

To be honest, I'm surprised by her concern. "Yeah, I'm okay. A few stitches is all."

"Did you hear about..."

I nod. "How's Mara?" That's when I feel the officer's hand grip my upper arm.

"Let's get you back to see Officer Blackwell," he says, pulling me along.

"I'll find you," I say as he marches me into the hall. Ashley shrinks in the distance until we disappear around the corner. No doubt, talking to either my wife or Mara Metcalf without making my statement to Blackwell is the reason for the quick getaway.

"He's here," the officer says, standing in Blackwell's doorway.

"Mr. Brewer," Blackwell begins. "Glad to see you're out of the hospital. How are you feeling?"

"Fine, yeah, thanks for asking."

"Please, come in. I just need to ask you a few questions." He gestures to the chair across from his desk.

I walk inside, and the other cop closes the door as he leaves. It takes me a minute to grab a seat, my body still aching from an adrenaline rush and the few good blows Garrett got in.

Blackwell opens a file folder that rests on his desk. I glance through the window behind him, wondering what time it is. Without a phone, I have no idea, and I didn't ask the other cop. The sky is a lighter shade of black. It could be early morning, one or two a.m.

"So, Mr. Brewer, it's been quite a night for you, hasn't it?" Blackwell asks as if it's not obvious.

"Yes, sir. It has."

"And you're aware that Mr. Metcalf did not survive his injuries?"

"Yes. The other officer told me." I hesitate a moment, but soon continue. "What does that mean for Mara?"

Blackwell eyes me, narrowing his gaze. "This was, as you initially stated, a matter of self-defense in a way."

"That's right." I feel like he's leading me into a trap, that he wants me to say more, but I don't. "First, I have to ask, Officer, do you have any new information about my daughter? The man in the driver's license—Eric Downey—have you found him?"

"No, I'm afraid not," he replies, leaning back, folding his arms over his broad chest. "So, let's talk about what happened tonight after the vigil."

I go into the whole thing, telling the truth about most of it. I leave out the part where Mara, having reached the end of her rope, shot her husband and then threatened to shoot my wife.

He jots down something on a notepad, appearing laser-focused on it. I wonder whether our stories match—mine, Ashley's, and Mara's. Did Garrett live long enough to tell him anything? That's something I probably should've figured out before sitting down. Now, I feel my pulse quicken. My mouth dries while I wait for him to say something.

Finally, Blackwell raises his gaze. "Does the name Jason Legado mean anything to you, Mr. Brewer?"

I rummage through my memories, but come up blank. "No, sir. Should it?"

He tilts his head like he knows something I don't. "He works for Cash Goodell."

"Okay," I reply, playing cool because I can't let on that we all have our suspicions about Cash's involvement. And I don't dare mention that Garrett and Cash have already had a couple of recent run-ins.

"Apparently, Mr. Legado had some concerns he'd brought to Mr. Goodell's attention a while back."

Fuck.

"How about this, Mr. Brewer? Why don't you tell me what you know about the damage Garrett Metcalf's car suffered a few years ago?"

"Why would I know anything about that? If it was Garrett's car, maybe you should ask Mara. And I have to wonder what any of this has to do with Mara saving my life earlier tonight. Garrett blamed me for our girls going missing. I don't know why, but he did. He took out his anger on me, and would've killed me if it wasn't for her."

"Yes, sir. I believe that to be true," Blackwell replies. "All right. I think that's all I have for you right now." He rises to his feet. "You and your wife are free to go home."

"And Mara? She has a young son."

"I'm well aware. The boy is being taken care of by his grandparents. Mrs. Metcalf is currently being processed on manslaughter charges. But I suspect she'll be out on bail by morning, given the current situation and the fact she has no priors."

The news hits me like a punch to the gut. Manslaughter? That could be a fifteen-year sentence. "But she did it to save me." Does he already know I'm lying? I can't read his face.

"That will have to be proven in a court of law," he replies.

"I see. Thank you, Officer Blackwell."

He walks me to the door. "And in the meantime, of course, we'll continue our search for Eric Downey and your daughter."

"Thank you." I walk out, pissed Blackwell mentions Lexi as a sort of last-minute thought. And when I reach the lobby, I see Ashley is still waiting for me. "Hi."

She stands. "Hi. What'd he say?"

I look around. "Not here. Let's go home." We walk outside, heading toward our car in the parking lot. "Blackwell asked me about Garrett's accident. How someone named Jason Legado, who works for Cash, raised concerns a while back. Did you tell him? I don't think Cash would have."

"No, absolutely not. It must have been Mara. I don't know anyone with that name."

I stop as we reach our car and turn to her. "Maybe she's laying the groundwork to blame Garrett for all of it. I can't say the idea hasn't crossed my mind."

"Well, then, I don't understand," Ashley says. "How would she know this man? She's never said a word about him."

I open the driver's side door. "Maybe she knows more than we think."

50

MARA

Garrett's dead. My lawyer told me he didn't survive his injuries. He says I'll be out on bond by morning, in all likelihood. The lawyer is a friend of Garrett's—*was*. And he knows what Garrett's business is worth. I won't be getting any life insurance payout since I killed him. But the kids and I will be okay. I say this as though it's going to happen. As though they'll find Skye, and both she and Milo will forgive me for what I've done.

As I gaze up at the small window in my cell, squinting through the grit and grime covering it, I see a hint of gray light. Could morning be on the way?

Thank God I'm alone in here. Everyone knows who we are—what's happened to our girls. I don't need someone asking why I shot my husband.

What happens now is up to Nate and Ashley. I have to trust the Brewers—trust that they'll stick to the story that I tried to save Nate's life. I could've killed Ashley, too, but Nate stopped me. Then again, maybe I let him.

If I'm honest, I didn't think I had it in me to shoot my

husband. But these past few days with Skye gone, the chaos that surrounded us, Garrett was the root of it all.

The moment I saw both he and Nate with marks and bruises on their faces, it was as if the past five years' worth of anger and betrayal came out all at once. There was no kidnapper around—anywhere. All I saw was their selfishness—fighting out in the middle of the woods, for God's sake. I knew it had to be Garrett who started it. He was always selfish, a bully, of sorts.

And I thought...*what the hell is going on?* Nate didn't deserve that. He wasn't the one who blew up his marriage and mine. And I snapped. Well, no. That's an excuse. I didn't snap. I couldn't live the lie anymore. Not when Skye was paying the price for what he did.

I should feel remorseful, but honestly, I feel relieved. Whatever happens now, I won't have to pretend my husband didn't humiliate me. I won't have to pretend I'm happy with him anymore. But I'll still be living with a lie—the lie I'll tell my kids about what happened to their father.

Now, however, the Brewers have the chance to screw me over if they want. To dispute my version of events in order to put me away forever.

Would Blackwell believe me if I told him the truth? That we're certain our girls were taken as an act of revenge by the son of the man Garrett killed? Only if the Brewers agreed. But it would mean letting Ashley off the hook, too, telling him only Garrett was there. I'm not sure I can do that. I'm still going away for killing my husband. I just don't know for how long. So should she get off scot-free?

The holding cell is quiet, except for the low buzz of the overhead fluorescent lighting in the hall. It flickers occasionally, throwing uneven shadows on the gray cinderblock walls. Stale sweat and urine cling to every surface, and I'm certain the smell of it is seeping into my skin.

I stare down at my feet. They took my shoes, forcing me to wear these disgusting plastic sandals. They took my belt. Even the little gold chain I always wore under my shirt. When they reached for it, I almost said no. Almost put up a fight. But what would be the point? The officer tugged at it, his face blank, mechanical, like he was plucking a weed from a field, not taking one of the last pieces from me of something that mattered. "Can't let you keep this," he'd muttered, not even looking me in the eye. As if I'd hang myself with that.

I wouldn't. Not yet.

I lean back against the cold wall and close my eyes, letting the fluorescent hum vibrate through my skull until it drowns out everything else—the officers' footsteps echoing down the hall, the faint chatter of voices from somewhere else.

Garrett's gone—his blood on my hands. Blackwell asked me why I did it. I stuck to the story, of course, but did the Brewers?

51
LEXI

The metallic clink when the cuff dropped to the floor still echoes in my ears. My hand throbs, my thumb's all wrong. Bent, swollen, skin peeled back like a raw piece of chicken my mom's about to cook. There's blood everywhere—on the floor, my wrist, under my nails. It stings so bad I feel sick. I want to cry. I really, really want to cry. But I don't. Because I did it. I got one of the cuffs off me.

"Lexi?" Skye's voice sounds tiny. "Are you feeling okay?"

I nod, then remember she can't see me. "Yeah. I'm okay. It just hurts really bad." Everything's spinning, and I feel dizzy and hot all over, like I might pass out. "I gotta try the other hand still. What about you?"

"I'm still trying," she replies, grunting with effort.

"It's okay. Just keep going."

The other cuff's still clamped around my right hand. Now, I have to use my left, which hurts crazy bad, and was already weaker to begin with. I suck in a breath like I'm going underwater, then start twisting. The metal stings, rubbing against the thin skin of my wrist. I don't know if I can do this. I feel so sick and weak. My forehead is all sweaty, too. It hurts so much. But I keep going. I can't stop. Both our lives depend on me now.

He could come down at any moment. We have no idea what's going on up there. If he's even here.

"I can't get mine off," Skye says, anger and frustration in her voice. "I've tried, Lexi. I swear."

"I know," I say, yanking hard against the stubborn metal that's turning everything raw.

"Lex...If you get out...just go. Just run."

"No."

"Lexi—"

"I'm not leaving you," I snap, louder than intended.

"You have to," she says. "One of us has to get out of here, or neither of us stands a chance."

A click sounds, and I stifle a scream. Bone—my thumb breaks. I whip around and puke on the floor—the pain is too much.

"Lexi?"

I instinctively try to wipe my mouth, but the pain in my hands is too strong. I feel like someone took a buzzsaw to them. Then I realize I'm out—I'm actually out. "Skye, oh my God. I did it. I'm free." I try hard to stop the tears, but I can't. Joy and pain fight inside me, and I'm so light-headed I know I'll pass out if I move.

"Holy shit. Lex. Okay. Okay," she says, her breaths coming out hard and fast. "I'm still trying, but it's just not working."

I stare at her in the dark. "It's fine. I can do this. I promise. You're going to really hurt yourself if you keep trying."

"You can't do this alone," she replies. "I need to be there to help."

I look at the stairs. My stomach's doing flips, wondering if he's about to walk in at any moment. I'm shaking, and sweating, and bleeding. I'm gonna have to face him. Me. Not some adult.

Not the cops. Just me. I thought the worst thing that could happen was getting kidnapped. Now I know it's what happens after. But I'm free now. And I'm not gonna screw this up.

I hear footfalls above us. "Skye?" We both go quiet, listening. "He's here."

"I just need a little more time," she says, her voice rumbling as she continues to try to break free.

"We're out of time," I reply. The stairwell creaks with footsteps. Heavy ones. I think it's just him. I don't hear anyone else. "He's coming right now, Skye."

"I know. I hear him. Pretend you're still cuffed."

"What?" I ask.

"Just do it, Lex! Put them back on, now, before he opens the door."

I can't put them back on. It'll be too hard to take them off again."

"Just pretend then. Do it now!" Her tone is hushed, but her meaning is loud and clear.

I put my hands behind me, dragging the cuffs behind my back, too, like I'm still chained. Did he hear us? Has he been here all along?

The lock clicks.

The handle turns.

The door creaks open.

He flicks on the light, and I see that awful mask. Yellow hair, white face, dots of pink blush on the cheeks. I press my body flat against the wall and try to steady my breathing. I'm positive my face is pale. My hair is damp and clings to my cheeks. He's going to notice something's not right.

I peer at Skye and see the blood around her. *Oh, shit.* Dried tears stick to her cheeks, leaving salty trails. She's got her hands behind her back, too. Will he notice the blood? Then I look down around me and see more blood. Of course he'll notice. That means I have to be ready.

He's coming down the steps now. "Hello, girls. You both must be starving. Well, we'll see if I can bring down something for you in a little while."

One step. Then another.

Each footfall is slow, like this asshole has nothing better to do than scare the shit out of us. Like he thinks we're not going anywhere. Screw that. We're getting out of here.

Behind me, my hands are covered in blood, and pain radiates through them like they're being held over a burning gas stove. But I push it into the back of my mind because I'm locked in now. Focused on what I have to do if I want us to live.

His feet hit the basement floor, and he walks toward us. That horrible mask turns in our direction. His head tilts like he's studying us, and then he stops right in front of me.

I hold my breath. He stares. Then leans in so close I can hear him breathing behind the mask, but I don't move. Shit. He has to see all this blood around me. I can't hide it.

He reaches out and lifts my chin with his index finger. My pulse screams in my ears. But I keep my face blank, like I'm still scared and helpless. Which, okay, I am, sort of.

His hand drops. Yep. He sees it—the blood. He sees the way I look, all sweaty and pale. Then he moves to Skye, inspects her the same as me. This is it. He knows what we've done.

I look at Skye. She nods.

Now.

52

ASHLEY

The noise pulls me from a restless sleep—that place where nothing makes sense, but everything feels real. I hear it again. Not loud, like a crash or shattering glass, but a quiet rattle. It could be nothing—the groan of our old house settling. But then comes another sound—a faint metallic clink. My eyes snap open, trying to absorb what faint morning light I see. It wasn't the wind or the house. It was a person.

I strain to listen as the front door groans like someone's testing it, pressing against its weight. I reach out in the dark and find Nate's shoulder. "Nate." My fingers dig into his arm as I shake him.

He grunts in response. "What?"

Even in the dim light filtering through the window blinds, I can make out his fat lip and the gash under it with tiny knots holding his skin together.

I press a finger to my lips. "Listen."

For a moment, we both lie still, our breathing shallow as we strain to pick up any sound. And then it comes again. A faint scrape—metal against metal—followed by an almost impercep-tible click.

Nate is out of bed before I can say anything else. He moves quickly despite the stiffness in his body, wincing as he grabs his shirt from the back of a chair. He pulls it over his head and glances around as if searching for something that might prove useful in our defense.

I'm up and out, too. My hands fumble under the bed until they close around the smooth wood—the bat Nate took from our garage after everything started going wrong. After Lexi and Skye disappeared. Just in case. We never said what *in case* meant out loud. Though in this moment, I wish I'd had the foresight Mara had.

The bat feels heavy in my grip as I follow Nate out of the room and onto the landing. Every step down the carpeted stairs is careful and deliberate, my bare feet sinking into the fibers.

At the base of the stairs, Nate stops and motions for me to stay back. I hand him the bat. He edges toward the front window and peeks through the curtain. The porch light is off.

"I swear I heard—" I begin, but my words are cut off by a sharp noise that makes both of us flinch.

The deadbolt clicks.

My stomach drops. For a split second, I want to believe it's her —Lexi. That she's found her way home. Maybe it's the police, telling us they found her. But these are thoughts that are likely to get us killed.

Then I see him.

He steps inside, bathed in shadow. He doesn't see us yet. Even in the darkness, I realize he's a younger man, possibly only in his twenties. His facial features are too obscured under the hoodie to identify him.

But I see the gun.

It rests steady in his hand, aimed at the darkness. And then he sees us. The gun shifts in our direction. "Don't move."

Nate drops the bat and raises his hands, palms open. "Take it easy," he says, despite the tremor in his words. "Whatever you want—money—just tell us—"

"Shut up."

The man steps farther inside now, pulling down his hood to reveal himself. I'm all but certain I know who he is. I try to breathe, glancing down at the bat, but knowing it's useless against a gun anyway.

"You don't know me," the man says. "Do you?"

Surely, Nate can put two and two together. While the features aren't exactly the same as in the driver's license, I know this man.

Nate blinks. "No."

He takes a step closer, the gun still aimed ahead. "You knew my father."

I close my eyes. "Oh God."

"She knows who I am." He smiles at me. "Don't you?"

What can I say except the only thing that I'm desperate to know? "Where's my daughter?" He tilts his head slightly, like my question caught him off guard. "I know who you are, Eric. And I know you have my daughter. Where the hell is she?"

Nate's voice hitches. "Downey. It was Cash, wasn't it? He told you where to find us." Nate says this as though he's the last to catch onto the plot.

"Doesn't matter who told me what." He shifts the gun between us. "What matters is what you did."

Nate steps forward, hands still raised. "Eric, listen. We—we didn't mean—"

Downey flicks off the safety.

He's not going to give us a chance to explain, but I try anyway. "Don't," I beg. "Please believe me when I tell you he was gone in an instant. He didn't suffer."

"Is that supposed to help ease my pain?" He takes a step closer, eyes locking onto mine. "You want to know how I found you? My mom got a call from the DMV. Out of the fucking blue. She couldn't believe it. Neither could I. We'd been waiting for answers for five years about what happened to my dad. He'd been away on a business trip. And then it was like he dropped off the face of the planet."

All this time, the Downeys never knew what happened. I can't imagine what that must've done to their family. I knew all this, of course, when we'd made the decision, but hearing this man now...maybe we do deserve to die.

"They told us his car was found here in Grant, Idaho. Half-rusted out, lying at the bottom of some ravine," he continues, eyes darkening with rage. "A good Samaritan had come across it and made the call. Of course, we thought Dad would've been found inside, certain he must've had an accident. But the caller said it was empty. No sign of a body anywhere."

I don't understand who could've found the car. Who was this good Samaritan? The same person who left the license plate near the body, that much is certain. Was it Cash? He didn't know where the body was or the car. No one did, except the four of us. But Cash suspected. Maybe he had come across the car by some twist of fate and finally connected the dots.

Nate shakes his head as if in denial of the truth. "Where's our daughter? We'll do whatever you want. Just let the girls go. They had no part in any of this. They're just children."

"You must've tracked down our family, I assume, through Cash Goodell," I say. "But why come after our daughter, Lexi? You left your driver's license for her to find; certain she'd contact you, waiting to use her to get to us. But we weren't responsible for your father's death."

Downey's brow raises behind the gun. "I'm well aware of

who's responsible for killing my dad. Don't pretend like you're innocent in all this."

I glance at Nate, who seems to realize the affair is no secret to Eric Downey. *Goddam it.* It was Cash. He knew about it. Found that damn card in Garrett's car. Doesn't prove I was there, but doesn't disprove it, either. It hardly matters now as I stare down the barrel of this man's gun. He came for us because I was with Garrett that night. Lexi was targeted because of me.

"That other girl was rarely alone, so I followed your kid. Made sure to 'accidentally' lose my license at just the right moment. Had to be sure she was yours and that I was on the right track. She's a good girl, your daughter. I could've done whatever I wanted to her. But I didn't. I got the confirmation I needed. I'm only after you and the Metcalfs." He raises the gun a little higher. "And since no one's home next door, guess I'll start with you two."

"So I'm right," I say, praying I can stall this guy for as long as possible while Nate stands frozen like a statue. "Cash told you all about us, Garrett's car, the whole thing. You didn't need to take our girls. We would've willingly paid the price for our sins."

"You think it was me?" He scoffs. "You think I took those girls?"

"You wanted revenge. I get that," I reply. "But those girls had nothing to do with any of it. They were in grade school when it happened. Please let them go, and you can do whatever you want to us."

"Someone sold you on a lie, lady." He says it so confidently that I believe him.

"Were you there last night?" Nate asks. "At the vigil?"

"Yes. I've been watching you unravel. Waiting for you to lose all hope. I don't know who took your kids and I don't care. You deserve to suffer. But it's got nothing to do with me. I'm here for my father."

"No." I shake my head, confusion swirling in my brain. "No, that's not possible. You have them."

"You have our daughter," Nate says, his voice faltering. "I know you do."

"I came here to figure out for myself what happened. My mom deserves the truth. She deserves closure. Is it a coincidence—your kids being taken? From what I've seen of this town and its people, probably not. But as I said, I couldn't give a shit."

My knees almost give out. All this time, we were so sure it was him—this man who's about to kill us. We'll never know where they are now. Lexi is forever lost to us.

Nate exhales hard and rubs both hands over his face like he's trying to wipe away the truth. "You're lying. I swear to God, if you have the girls—"

"But if it's not you," I cut in, "Then who the hell has our daughter?"

Downey aims the gun at my chest. "Not my problem."

53
LEXI

"Wait," I call out.

He stops and peers at me over his shoulder. I swallow the giant lump in my throat, knowing this has to be done, or the only way Skye and me are getting out of here is in the hands of someone who's probably a lot worse than this freak.

I see his eyes blink behind the mask as he slowly turns toward me.

"What?"

"I need water," I reply. "We both do. Isn't—isn't there something I can do—for you, I mean, so that we can have water?" Now I'm really going to puke, knowing he'll understand exactly what I mean. But I don't know how else to keep his attention.

I feel Skye's gaze on me. She's afraid, but I'm definitely more afraid right now. I shrug. "Please. I'll do anything." My eyes burn with tears, but I do my best to blink them away.

Then he steps toward me. "Looks like I've trained you well. Already willing to trade favors for a sip of water."

"Please. I'll die without it," I add, trying to convince him and doing my best to leave Skye out of it. The thing is, I see his hesitation, like he suspects I'm putting on an act. Maybe I've already screwed this up because I can't figure out why he hasn't said anything about all the blood. Meanwhile, my hands burn, and my head grows lighter with each passing second. Even if he gets close enough for me to jump at him, will I have the strength?

I'm losing my nerve. It's slipping away. My body trembles as he comes closer. Can I even do this? I'm not strong enough. Then I shift my gaze to Skye, seeing the sheer determination in her face. She's telling me I can do this. Both our lives depend on it, so now I know that I have to.

He squats low, inches from me. He must see it—the blood, but still says nothing about it. Not yet. Maybe he's waiting for me to crack.

What do I do? What do I do? I need his guard down. I need him to believe me, to come closer and offer me water. The garbage bag is behind me, within reach. If I can slip it over his head, maybe...

My breath echoes in my ears. I feel like I'm dead, no matter what I do. But then an unexpected guttural roar climbs from my throat. I grip the plastic garbage bag behind me, pain bursting in my fingers. I'm not even sure I can hold onto it, but I launch toward him. *Holy shit. This is happening.*

I knock him off his heels. His head hits the concrete floor with a thump. Oh God. If only Skye was free, too. We could both take him on, but it's just me.

I throw myself on top of him before he has a chance to get up, the bag twisting in my throbbing hands. I have only seconds before he tosses me aside like a rag doll. How the hell am I going to do this? *Forget the pain. Forget it, or you and Skye are dead.*

He yells and writhes beneath me, his hands clutching my shoulders, trying to push me off. I can feel his hot breath seeping out from under the mask. I want to rip it off to see who he is, but there's no time.

I swing my right arm around, clutching the bag's opening. With my left hand, I grip the other side and try to put it around his head.

He's laughing. It isn't how I imagined this going. *Shit.*

I lean down, heart pounding in my throat. I fight off every instinct to rip off that mask. Instead, I shove the bag down over his head.

He jerks, almost in surprise that I actually did it. Now, he's twisting harder, using his hands to grip the bag and try to pull it off.

I pull it down to his neck, gathering the ends. Geez, this bag is huge. Is this even going to work? But then it collapses with his first gasp. He twists to the side, and I fall off him. My grip remains firm. My hands feel like they're on fire, but I bite down on the pain. He bucks hard against me. I don't know how much longer I can hold my ground.

"Stop," I yell, breathless, wild-eyed. "Stop moving."

"Keep going, Lexi!" Skye yells. "Kill him! Kill him!"

Her words hit me like a lightning bolt, sending shockwaves through my body. I don't stop. I keep pulling on the bag as he tries to tear a hole in it.

My breath comes in short, ragged bursts; tears blur my vision; every muscle in my arms burns, and pain shoots through my hands.

"Skye!" I shout. "I—I can't—he's too strong—"

"You can!" she cries back.

Every ounce of anger, fear, and pain he put on us, I throw right back on him. A scream rips from my throat as I pull down harder on the bag, pouring every last bit of strength into this moment.

The world narrows to just the two of us. My only advantage

—he can't see me with the bag over his head. He's clutching it, ready to tear it off. His grunts mingle with mine until I can't tell who they're coming from. I don't stop.

Until he stops me.

With his one hard shove, I let go, sliding away from him. He rips the bag off his head. My vision clears in an instant, and I see the mask fly off. He crawls over, reaching out for it. Can Skye see his face? He's on his knees, stretching his hand until he clutches the mask again.

No.

He slips it back over his face, breathing hard. Still crouched low, he turns back to me, and I know what's going to happen. So, I lie there, defeated. It didn't work. I couldn't hold on long enough. He's going to kill me now. Then Skye. We're going to die down here. But then I see her—Skye—she's stretching as far as the chains will let her. Wait...what is she....

She tosses one of her chains over his head before he has a chance to get to his feet. Then, she yanks it hard, and I watch it tighten around his neck. "Run, Lexi! Run!"

I don't want to leave her. But I have to if I want to save her. With only seconds before he flings her away, just as he did me, my survival instincts kick in. I run up the stairs and through the door. I'm in the house, but I stand frozen, shocked I made it out. I remember where the living room is and run in my bare feet, leaving a trail of blood on the old wood floors.

The front door is within reach. But he's coming. I hear him coming. My heart races. The door. The door. It's almost... I press down on the lever and use my forearm to pull it open. It's dark outside, but I hear birds chirping. I don't know what time it is, and right now, I don't care. I just run.

He yells at me, his voice echoing into the night air as I make it outside.

I'm in a neighborhood. The houses are far apart, but I run

toward one of them, praying someone is home. "Help! Help!" I scream at the top of my lungs.

I practically dive toward the walkway, racing up as fast as I can. When I reach the house, I pound on the door with my elbow. "Help me. Please, I need help!" I wait, checking behind me, wondering if he's coming after me or if he's gone back into the basement to kill Skye.

No answer.

"Shit."

I run through the yard and back down toward the sidewalk. I keep running until I see headlights. Someone's coming. Oh God. I raise my hands, blood still spilling down my arms. My clothes are ripped, my feet bare, blood all over me. Will they stop?

"Stop. Please, I need help." I stand in the road, waving my bloody arms.

The car screeches to a halt. The driver's door swings open, and a man jumps out. "Jesus Christ." He runs toward me. "Are you okay?"

I peer over my shoulder. "He's coming to kill me."

"Get in."

We rush back to his car, and I jump onto the passenger seat. Can I trust him? I don't know, but I can't stay out here.

He slips behind the wheel.

"My friend. She's still inside. He's going to kill her. We need the police."

The man grabs his phone and dials 911.

"Hello, yeah, I just found a girl on my street. She's hurt—bad. Says someone's after her, and her friend is still inside a house somewhere."

I peer through the windshield, searching for him to come into the headlights. Will he risk it? Or will he just take Skye somewhere else, somewhere I'll never find her?

"Yes. But she needs a hospital," the man says into his phone.

I turn to him. "He's going to kill her, please tell them to hurry!"

"Look, you gotta get here fast. Someone else is in danger," he pleads. "I'll stay here. Just hurry." He lowers his phone. "They're coming. Okay? They're coming. What's your name?"

"Alexis Brewer. Where am I? Where is this place?"

"You're Alexis?" he asks like he already knows me. "Oh my God. And the other girl? Is she Skye Metcalf?"

I nod. "He's going to kill her."

"Jesus. You're the missing girls."

54
NATE

This kid's going to kill us. Ashley and I are staring down the barrel of a nine millimeter handgun with a laser sight that shifts between my chest and hers. I don't want to say it's karma, but it's starting to feel that way, especially with Garrett dead and Mara in jail. It's just the two of us now. Our daughter is still missing. This guy claims to know nothing about it. I don't believe him. It's just too coincidental.

But for now, I have to figure out how we're going to survive this, if at all. "Look, it was an accident. You have to know that."

"I don't have to know anything." He sets his sights on me. "You could've called the police. Got him to a hospital, even. Instead, you said nothing. You *did* nothing. Five years, we've been searching. Now, you're going to tell me where his body is so I can take him home."

I close my eyes, images of that night flashing through my head like a slideshow. All the therapy we'd been through, all the talks, and the begging for forgiveness...I'd accepted it—or so I thought. And in all that forgiveness, I ignored the real victim. Pretended it hadn't really happened. But it did. And the one who suffered for it is standing in front of us now, ready to end our lives as a result.

But what I can't shake is that the person we thought took our children for reasons we thought we understood, doesn't seem to be the case. And if I don't find a way out of this, we'll never see Lexi again.

"The person who was driving the car that hit your father is dead," I say, feeling Ashley's gaze on me. "He was at fault and now, he's paid the price with his life."

"But you kept it a secret," Downey replies. "Tell me where his body is."

I know the moment I tell him, he'll have no more reason to keep us alive. So, I stall. The room is silent except for our breathing, sharp and shallow. Then, my phone rings. The jarring sound slices through the room. I flinch. Ashley does too.

The kid jerks the gun toward me. "Don't answer it."

I raise both hands again. "Okay. I won't." But my eyes flick to the screen anyway. It's face-up on the coffee table. Unknown number. I let it ring. It stops. A second later, a text notification pings. I glance at the screen, and a single line flashes across it.

We found Lexi.

Time freezes. My heart stops, then restarts like it's a jumped car battery. My mouth goes dry. I feel Ashley lean toward me, her breath hitching as she sees it too.

Lexi. Our daughter. Alive.

"Please," I say, my voice raw with emotion. "Just—listen. We'll tell you where he is. We'll confess to everything. You were right. We buried the truth, and we'll pay for it. Just let us go. They found her. Let us go *see* our daughter. Let us hold her one more time. Then, we'll turn ourselves in."

For a moment, I think he might crack. His jaw clenches, and the gun wavers a little.

But then he shakes his head. "No. No, you don't get to walk away from this. You don't get redemption. Your daughter may be alive, but that doesn't change what you did. I want to hold my dad one more time, too. So, I guess neither of us is going to get what we want."

He's too far gone. Eyes filled with hate, words dripping with vengeance. And now I know there's no talking him down. No bargain, no confession, no plea that will change his mind. He didn't come here for justice. He came for an ending.

But so did I.

Not the kind he wants, though. Because now I have something he doesn't. Hope. Lexi's alive. And nothing—not guilt, not grief, not this kid with a gun—is going to keep me from getting to her. I look at Ashley, then back at Downey. "Okay."

His face twists. "What?"

"You're right. We don't deserve to walk away. But we're going to because I'm not letting you stop me from seeing my daughter again."

I lunge sideways, grabbing the edge of the coffee table and flipping it toward him with everything I've got. He fires off a round, and it cuts right through the flimsy wood. But then the table crashes against his legs, buying me some time—a few precious seconds.

Ashley screams.

The gun goes off again in a flash. Fire ignites across my side. White-hot pain slices through me, but I don't stop. I ram him, and we collide, hard, both of us crashing to the floor.

The gun slips out of his hand, skipping along the wooden floor planks until stopping under the couch. He punches wildly, catching me in the jaw, the temple. My vision blurs. Blood pours out of me, and I'm growing weak. I hear Ashley in the background, still screaming. "Go, Ash! Run!" But I can't see her. Only him.

I grab a lamp from the end table and swing it down on him. Once. Twice. The base shatters, ceramic exploding in my hands.

He claws at my shirt, blood now spilling from his head, and he reaches for my wound, trying to make it worse.

I slam my forearm into his throat, pinning him down, adrenaline driving every inch of me forward because I will see my girl again. He grabs a shard of the broken lamp, slicing across my arm. Blood pours from the gash, but I keep going.

Ashley is screaming my name, pleading. Why the hell is she still here?

The kid grabs a throw pillow and tries to smother me. I headbutt him. My vision goes black for a second, then clears. His face is above mine—twisted, panicked, bleeding.

And then—the gun. I see the handle peeking out from under the couch as we roll across the floor. I reach under and grab it. He sees. He knows.

"Don't—" he breathes, hand raised.

But I do. I pull the trigger once. And again. The shots echo through the house. Downey collapses and goes still. Silence settles around us.

Ashley drops to her knees beside me, hands pressed against my side, getting soaked in my blood.

"Nate, oh God, please don't die."

My ears ring. My side is on fire, and I can't catch my breath. But I'm alive. And I killed him. I had no choice. I look at the phone, still on the table, screen now cracked in the melee, but glowing.

We found Lexi.

"Call them," I whisper. "Tell them we're coming for her."

55
SKYE

She did it. She actually got out.

I repeat the words in my head so that I'll believe them because it doesn't feel real. But then, I wonder when I'll hear the sound of his boots thudding back down the stairs. What will he do to me because Lexi is free?

Moments pass, and there's nothing. Just this terrible, heavy silence all around me. The kind of silence that makes me feel like I'm the last person on earth.

Lexi got out. I *saw* her run through that door. She was hurt—bleeding and shaking—but she got out. I know she'll come back with help. That was the plan.

But what if he caught her? What if she didn't make it, and he drags her back down here?

My stomach twists so hard it's making me nauseous. I close my eyes and try to hear something—anything—but all I get is a faint buzzing sound from upstairs, like a fridge or something. No footsteps. No yelling. No Lexi.

I'm still chained to the wall like a freaking animal. My wrists are raw, and the skin's all torn up from trying to break free, but I don't even care. I've been yanking and twisting these stupid cuffs and still can't get them off. Not like Lexi. She got out. I smile. "She made it."

I press my back against the wall and pull my knees to my chest. My teeth won't stop chattering, and not from the cold, just the fear.

I whisper again, "She made it out. I know she did." Because the other option—I can't even think about that. Lexi said we'd fight if we got the chance. That if either of us got out, we'd come back for the other. She didn't kill him, but I bought her time to escape.

"She actually did it."

The way she fought back. The look in her eyes. I've never seen her like that before—like she wasn't scared of him anymore. Like she wasn't going to take it anymore.

Even now, thinking about it gives me hope. "I know you'll come back, Lexi. You're not gonna leave me here." But I can't just sit and wait. I don't have that luxury, not if he returns.

I look down at my hands again. That stupid bobby pin broke inside the lock on my left hand. But if I can just twist my wrist again like before, like Lexi did, I can break free. If she did it, so can I. It'll just take a little more effort. Who knows how long it'll be before help comes? If I don't want to die down here, then it's up to me.

I take a deep breath and wrap my hand around the cuff. "Okay," I whisper. "One more try." I clench down, my face screwed up tight, and pull. Hard. Pain rips up my arm, searing and awful, and I scream without meaning to—but I don't let go. Not this time. I can't. I have to force it off because if Lexi's out there, then I have to be out there, too.

Maybe I deserve this. The way I've treated her. Yeah, okay, maybe that's too harsh. No one deserves this. But I made Lexi feel like she was nothing—less than nothing. And she's the one who fought to break free, to save both of us. I have to make it right, and I will. Just as soon as I get the hell out of here.

I tug and pull, harder each time. My head feels dizzy, and then I look at my hand, bloody and mangled, my skin hanging from it. Now I'm queasy. "Don't pass out, Skye. Don't do it. You gotta stay alert. You're almost there."

And just as I try again, I hear a sound above me. I look up, fixing my gaze on the ceiling. "No," I whisper. "Please don't be him. Please don't be him."

I look down at my hand. "Just do it. Just fucking do it!" I pull one more time, harder than ever, because if I don't, he's going to kill me. I feel my flesh tear away from the bone. The stinging and burning, like someone pressing a fiery poker against me, is too much. Tears stream, my nose runs. I'm gonna be sick. The pain— it's too much. I'm desperate to scream out, but I don't. Instead, I feel the cuff moving up my bloody hand.

Snap!

A bolt of pain shoots up my arm as my thumb breaks. Nausea turns my gut. Jesus, I can't...*Keep going.* It's almost past my broken thumb. *Come on. Please.* I scream inside my own head.

Then I suck in all the air my lungs can take and.... the cuff—it lands on the floor with a clink. My eyes blink fast, not truly believing what I've done. I still have my other hand to free, but I can't stop crying.

The sound upstairs grows louder.

He's coming.

I'm out of time.

I rise to my feet, unsteady at first because I'm weak from the pain. I lift my free arm, bracing myself against the wall with my elbow. Now, I wait. Wait for him to come. And even though one hand is still chained, I'll do everything I can to make him regret ever taking us.

A thud sounds upstairs. Oh no. This is it. But you can do this.

Lexi did it, and so can you. Footfalls come closer. *I'm scared.* I swallow down my fear, firming my stance. The basement door is open, but I can't see him yet. If I had gotten off the chains a few minutes sooner, I could've run out. Now, I have to face him. "I love you, Mom and Dad. Milo, too."

A figure steps into view, and a roar climbs in my throat. I'm ready...

"Skye?"

A man in a police uniform appears, one hand resting on his gun, the other outstretched. "It's okay. You're okay. I'm here to help."

I sink to the ground, tears flooding my eyes.

"Skye, it's me."

That's not the voice of a man. I look up. "Lexi? Oh my God. You're okay."

She rushes toward me, dropping down, and wrapping her arms around my neck.

"I'm okay," Lexi says. "We're both going to be okay now."

56

LEXI

We're in the living room, Skye and me, sitting next to each other on the old couch. I don't want to remember what happened on this couch. Voices sound around us, cops come and go, but we just sit here, shoulders pressed against each other, wondering if this is real, and if we did make it out alive. I'm still not sure.

The morning sun shines through the front window inside this crappy place. For the first time, I get a good glimpse. I wish I hadn't.

"We're going to get you two into the ambulance, okay?"

I don't know who's talking, my gaze somewhere off in the distance. Then I feel a hand on my shoulder. "Huh?"

An officer smiles, but it's the kind of smile you give a person when you don't know how they'll react. It's cautious. "We're going to take you both to the hospital now."

I look at Skye, who hasn't said a word since we came up here. "Hey, we're leaving. Can you walk?"

She blinks hard a few times, then turns her head toward me. "Yeah."

People come toward us. Moving us, helping us along. Eventually, we're outside. I raise my gaze and squint at the morning sun. Only hours ago, I was out here, running for my life, the sun nowhere in sight. But someone stopped. Someone helped me.

"Let me give you a hand."

I turn to see a woman. I think she's an EMT. She clutches my shoulders. "I can't use my hands."

"I know," she says. "It's okay. I'll do most of the work."

She helps me inside, and then someone else helps Skye. It's the first time I get a good look at my injuries. It's freakin' gross, and I don't know if my hands will ever look the same again, or if I'll be able to use them properly.

"Hey, we're going to get you bandaged up, all right? And I'll give you something for the pain."

The EMT must've noticed the look on my face. I nod.

As they start to fix up our bandages and stuff, me and Skye stare at each other. It's like we never thought we'd see each other again. We're both crying and smiling, then crying again. We don't say as much, but I know neither of us thought we'd survive this. And I know there must've been other girls who didn't.

The pain meds are kicking in. I'm feeling a little better. As the lady wraps my hands, I look at her. "He's still out there, isn't he?"

We're at the hospital. They took Skye to some other room; I don't know where. So here I am, alone in a room, not fully remembering how I got here. The drugs they gave me must've been pretty good. They said they called my parents. I don't know if anyone's told Skye's parents yet. They must have.

They told us not to worry about the man who took us. That they'd find him and that we'd be safe in the hospital. They don't even know who he is. I'm supposed to meet with some police sketch artist soon. But what do I know? I saw black eyes behind an insane plastic doll mask.

The last thing I said to Skye before they wheeled us in here was that they'd find him. After everything he did, they have to.

She wore this strange, broken smile. "I hope so, Lex," she'd said. "But you're the reason we're here. You got out. You saved us."

"I wasn't going to leave you. I couldn't. No matter what—I'm always coming back for you." The words still ring in my head now as I stare out the hospital room window.

She was barely holding it together and kept whispering to herself like she was the one who messed everything up. Like she was the reason we ended up in that hell.

It wasn't her fault. The only one to blame was *him*—the monster who took us. And okay, yeah, I watch too many cop shows or whatever, but seriously—his DNA has to be all over me —us. Under my nails, on my clothes. They'll use that. They'll figure out who he is. And they'll catch him. I *know* they will.

But for now, it's not over. Not really. Skye and me—we're safe here at the hospital for the time being. We're alive. And we're not his anymore.

57

ASHLEY

Nate's going to be okay, according to the paramedics. The bullet went straight through his side, missing his organs, and exited out of his back. We're headed to the hospital now. They said Lexi's been taken there. And Nate needs to be stitched up, regardless. But all I care about is seeing my daughter.

An officer is staying at our home until the coroner shows up to take away the body of Eric Downey, the son of the man we killed. So now, only three other people know the truth about what happened that night. Nate, Mara, and Cash Goodell. I'm certain Cash brought Eric Downey to our door. The kid wanted us dead. So now it's on Cash. There's no one left. With Lexi free, this nightmare is almost over.

They say Lexi is doing all right, but I won't believe it until I see her with my own eyes. She'd managed to escape a house where she and Skye were being held captive. My God—what those girls must've gone through. I can't think about it right now. It hurts too much knowing all they suffered was because of us.

I look at Nate, eyeing the bandaged wound that's still bleeding through. "You need to get that taken care of."

He darts his gaze at me. "I'm not doing anything until I see my daughter."

"What about Cash?" I press. "We know he's behind this. It's the only thing that makes sense."

He scoffs, shaking his head. "What the hell difference does it make now? Garrett's dead. Mara's in jail. I just want my daughter."

"But if we get to him first." I shoot a glance at the EMT, who appears busy checking Nate's IV and whatever else it is that they do. And then I lean closer to Nate. "Cash sent that man to kill us. I know he must've been the one to find the car. He has to be the one who took the girls."

"Jesus, Ashley. Are you serious right now? Our daughter has been missing for days, we were almost killed. Not to mention all that happened with the Metcalfs. And your answer is to..." he checks his tone, lowering it. "Is to get Cash Goodell?"

I shrug, not wanting to risk being overheard. "I won't let him get away with this. So, unless you have a better idea—"

Nate turns away. "I just want to see Lexi. She'll have answers. She'll know who took her. Whatever happens after that—none of it matters as long as our daughter is safe."

We arrive at the hospital. They wheel Nate on a gurney toward the entrance while I step out of the ambulance. The sun is trying to burn through the morning clouds. Inside, the hospital is quieter than I expected. The smell of freshly brewed coffee and disinfectant lingers. I see an officer standing near some chairs, like he's been waiting for us.

"Mr. and Mrs. Brewer." He eyes Nate. "Officer Wiley is looking for you."

"My husband is injured, as you can see. He needs to be admitted."

"Where's our daughter?" Nate asks.

Before the officer can respond, Wiley approaches from the hallway. She notices Nate lying on the gurney. "I heard about the break-in at your house."

"Yeah, well, he got the worst of it," Nate replies.

"I'm aware." Wiley licks her lips, appearing to study us for a moment. "Seems to me you two have been through hell and back lately."

I don't like her tone or the way she's looking at us, like she suspects something. "We got the message about Lexi, and by the grace of God, it served as a distraction for the man who broke in. It gave us a chance to stop him."

Wiley nods and turns to the officer. "Send another unit out to the Brewers' home and get an update on the coroner's arrival."

"On it." He leaves.

I regard Wiley for a moment, and then ask the question that burns my tongue. "Where's our daughter?"

58

SKYE

The sound of my mom's voice floats through my head, distant, warped. My eyelids flutter open, and everything's blurry, like I'm underwater. Where... where am I?

Then I see the IV in my arm, the machines blinking beside me. The sterile, too-white walls. A hospital.

"Skye?"

I turn toward the voice. My vision sharpens just enough to see her. "Mom?"

She's already leaning in, and I feel her brush the damp hair off my face. Her hand trembles as it touches me.

"Oh my God... you're awake. You're safe now, sweetheart. You're safe."

She presses her face to mine, and her tears feel warm on my skin. But she's shaking with the sobs she's trying to hold back, and now I'm not sure if I'm still dreaming. A few hours ago, I didn't think I'd ever hear her voice again.

"Where's Dad? And Milo?" I ask, the words catching in my dry throat.

She pulls back, her eyes scanning me like she still doesn't believe I'm real. Honestly? I'm not sure I am either. The last thing I remember is looking at Lexi in the ambulance. Both of us were crying, filled with disbelief that we made it out alive. Now I'm wrapped in white sheets, with my mom beside me. "Is Lexi okay? Where is she?"

"Shhh," Mom says gently. "Don't push yourself. You just came out of surgery."

I glance down at my hands and gasp. Metal rods jut out of my left hand. The skin looks wrong. Purple and swollen. Not mine. My right is bandaged. "What... what happened to me? Why do I look like this?"

Her eyes fill with fresh tears. "They had to insert pins to stabilize the bones, honey. And... they had to do a skin graft." Her voice cracks. "There wasn't much left for them to work with."

I stare at her, trying to breathe through the rising panic.

Mom must sense it as she smooths my hair. "I haven't seen Lexi, but her parents are here. I'll ask a nurse how she's doing."

"And Dad? Milo?" My voice is barely a whisper. "Why aren't they here? I want to see them. I didn't think I'd ever get to again. I thought I was going to—"

"I know," she says. "We were all so scared, baby."

But there's something in her eyes. A tightness. A weight. And suddenly I feel cold all over. "Mom, where are they?"

She hesitates. Smiles a little. "Milo's with Grandma and Grandpa. He's okay. He'll be here soon. He doesn't know the full story yet, and it's going to be hard for him to understand." She swallows. "And your dad..."

"Skye." A deep voice booms, and a doctor walks in, clipboard in hand. "I'm Dr. Keyes," he says, giving me a quick smile. "How are you feeling?"

I shrug. Everything hurts. "Okay, I guess. How long are my hands going to look like this?"

"The pins will come out in six to eight weeks. You'll probably need another graft, maybe two. But with physical therapy, I expect you'll regain most of your range of motion. Right now, we're just making sure to rehydrate you. Soon, we'll see if you're able to eat anything."

He pauses. "You're very lucky, Skye, but I don't think it was luck alone. I think you were incredibly brave."

His words are kind. But all I can think about is what I had to survive to hear them. "Thank you," I reply.

He nods and leaves, and Mom moves closer again. But I can feel it—the tension in the air, like I'm waiting for this huge shoe to drop.

"Mom," I whisper. "Where is Dad? What are you not telling me?"

Her lips tremble. Her eyes go red. And that cold feeling starts creeping into my bones again. "Mom? Please. Just tell me. You're scaring me."

"Ma'am?"

It's a man's voice, and I turn to see a police officer at the door. He steps inside and places a hand on my mom's shoulder.

"It's time to go, Mrs. Metcalf."

"What?" My pulse spikes. "What's going on?" I ask, looking between them. "Mom, what is this? What's happening?"

The cop gently ushers her away from my side.

"No. No, wait—Mom, don't go!" I try to sit up, pain flaring like fire in my arms. "You can't leave! I need you!"

"I'm so sorry, baby," she whispers, her voice breaking.

And then she's gone. They just freaking took my mom. They took her.

<h1 style="text-align:center">59
LEXI</h1>

The world comes back to me in fragments. Soft beeping. White sheets on a comfortable bed. The muted rumble of voices.

Then—my mom's face. Blurred at first, but then she comes into focus, and she's real. She's here. Her eyes are puffy, but she's smiling like she can't believe it. I can't either.

"Lexi," she breathes out. Her hand rests on my shoulder.

Dad's behind her. He steps closer, his eyes full of something heavier—something that looks like grief. He tries to smile, but it's like he can't, like all he wants to do is cry.

"You're okay," Mom says. "You're safe now."

Safe. They all keep saying that. "Where is she?" My voice comes out dry and cracked. "Skye—Is she okay?"

Mom nods quickly. "Yes. She had surgery, and she's going to be okay. She's asking about you, too."

"Thank God." But everything inside me is still buzzing. "I need to talk to the police. They need to test me. My clothes, my skin, my nails. There's DNA. There has to be."

Mom winces, her eyes filling again. "Lexi—"

"They have to find him," I press. "He can't get away with this. You have to tell them. And the place—where we were—it was this crappy old house in some crappy neighborhood. The floors creaked, and the wallpaper was peeling. It stunk. Did they stay there and wait for him?"

Dad's face goes still. Mom looks down.

They don't answer. And then I get a good look at my arms and hands. An IV sticks in the crook of my left arm. I'm wrapped in bandages from my forearms down. My hands are covered in so much gauze, I look like I'm wearing oversized winter mittens.

"Mom?"

Dad steps in, laying a hand on my forehead. That's when I notice him wince, like he's hurt or something.

"What happened to you?" I ask.

He shakes his head. "It's nothing. Just an accident."

But then I see it—the look that flashes between them. Something they don't want me to know. My throat tightens. "You're lying."

"Lexi…" Mom tries to soothe me, brushing my hair back. "Right now, you just need to rest."

"No. I need answers. I need to know what the police are doing. If they have found anything at that house where he kept us. I need to know if Skye's okay. I need to know we're not just sitting here, waiting for him to come back. He took us. He hurt us. He could do it again to someone else."

I'm out of breath. Too many words, questions I have no answers for, it all comes out in a flurry. "I'm not asking to be protected," I whisper. "I'm asking you to help me stop him before someone else ends up where we were."

Mom wipes her eyes, biting her trembling lip. Dad just nods slowly, like he's finally hearing me. "I'll tell them everything," I say. "Everything I remember. But please… don't keep things from me."

"Okay. We won't." Dad clears the emotion from his throat. "We found something in your bedroom, Lexi. It was a driver's license for a man who lives in Utah. Can you tell me how it ended up in your room?"

I close my eyes, forgetting the significance of it. "It was nothing. A guy dropped it. I found him online, and we were supposed to meet up so I could give it to him. Was it him? Do they think it was him?" Guilt presses down on me, and I want to cry.

"You were going to meet a strange man?" Mom asks. "Why would you do that, Lexi? Why wouldn't you just come to us and tell us you'd found it?"

"I didn't think...Mom, was it him? Did he take us?"

They exchange that look again.

"The police don't know who did this yet, sweetheart," she replies. "But they will—very soon. What you did was nothing short of heroic. You saved not only yourself, but Skye, too."

"So I just sit here?"

"You need to heal," Mom says, wearing a gentle smile. "You've been through a lot, too much, sweetheart. But I need you to know that you're safe here, okay? Your dad and me? We're going to work with the police to help them find whoever did this."

My lips quiver. "And if it has something to do with the guy who lost his driver's license? If this is all my fault—"

"It isn't," Dad cuts in. "It's not your fault. None of this is."

60

ASHLEY

The hallway outside Lexi's hospital room feels colder than the room itself. I rub my arms, but the chill won't leave. Nate's beside me, quiet, jaw tight. I want to say something—anything—but I'm afraid if I open my mouth, I'll just fall apart.

We make it to the waiting area. The light in here is too bright, too sterile. My body's still vibrating from Lexi's questions, her pain, the way her voice cracked when she begged us not to keep anything from her. I hate how helpless I feel. I hate that I don't have answers.

That's when I see him—Officer Blackwell.

He's standing near the double doors, arms folded, eyes scanning the hallway like he's absorbing every detail. When his gaze lands on me, he straightens and walks over.

"Mr. and Mrs. Brewer." He nods. "I was just coming to find you."

Nate steps forward. "Did you find the son of a bitch who took my girl?"

I notice he leaves out the part that we suspect Cash Goodell.

Blackwell shakes his head. "No. Not yet. We've got a forensics team sweeping the house where the girls were held. It's remote, old. Appears to have been abandoned off and on for years. They're collecting everything—hair, fibers, prints, blood. If he left anything behind, we'll find it."

My stomach turns. *Blood*. I press a hand against my chest, trying to slow my heartbeat.

He hesitates as his gaze drifts between us. "But we're close to getting answers. I promise you. The local police there contacted me just as soon as they received the nine-one-one call from the man who found Lexi. She led them to the house, and then my officers headed that way. I'll be joining them soon. They've already lifted boot prints. We'll, of course, need Lexi to let us check her for foreign DNA. It'll all be processed."

I nod, but it feels like my body is moving on delay, like I'm not quite attached to it anymore.

"I also came to talk to Lexi and Skye," he continues. "We've got a sketch artist standing at the ready, even if the guy wore the mask the whole time, it could still help. Maybe something in his voice or movements will also trigger a memory. And..." He looks at Nate, then back at me. "Mara's going to be released on bail soon."

My head snaps up. "She made bail?"

He nods. "Yes. They let her come here to see Skye earlier, then took her back, and the judge lowered the amount, given the situation. We're taking her version of events seriously."

"She was protecting Nate from Garrett," I say, knowing that keeping up the lie is the only way we get out of this nightmare. With Downey gone, it's only Cash Goodell we need to worry about.

"And based on preliminary evidence," Blackwell continues, "we have to consider that possibility. If Garrett did attack you, Mr. Brewer, and Mara intervened as you say... well, it's likely the manslaughter charges will be dropped. The case would be deemed a justifiable homicide."

I glance at Nate, who shifts uncomfortably. His eyes are locked on the floor. "Nate was attacked, and Mara saved his life, Officer Blackwell."

He exhales slowly like he's done with the topic. "I'd like to speak to Lexi now, with your consent. I will tread lightly, fully aware of what she's been through."

"Please do," I reply. "But I think we should be there to help her through it. She's trying so hard to be strong, but she's..." My voice breaks. "She's still just a young girl."

Blackwell's eyes soften. "Of course. And we're going to do everything we can to make sure the man who did this never gets the chance to hurt anyone else." He turns and walks down the corridor toward her room.

I feel Nate's hand brush mine, and I take it. For a second, we wait there in silence, the situation growing more and more suffocating by the moment. But whatever has happened to us, Lexi is who we'll focus on now. So, we follow Blackwell into the hall.

61

MARA

The fluorescent lights in the corridor flicker overhead, making my headache worse. I don't know how long I've been sitting here, waiting to be processed.

A female officer arrives. "Time to go back, Mrs. Metcalf."

I stand, and she leads me back toward the cells. I try not to look at the others locked up inside. I just want to close my eyes and vanish. That's when I see her—Officer Wiley. She's waiting near the entrance of the holding area, arms crossed, face unreadable. Something about the way she's standing makes my stomach twist.

"Mrs. Metcalf," she says, nodding to the other officer. "I'll take it from here."

The officer hands me off without a word and walks away.

Wiley gestures toward a bench just outside the holding cells. "Sit down."

I do, though I'm bracing for the worst.

"The judge granted bail," she says. "The DA may dismiss the case altogether, pending a thorough review."

My breath catches, and I realize Nate and Ashley kept their end of the bargain. "Thank God."

"Paperwork's already in motion. You'll be out of here in an hour or less," Wiley replies.

I stare at her, waiting for the catch.

"But before you go," she continues, "there's something I need to ask you."

And there it is. I tense. "Okay."

"This morning, before Lexi and Skye were found, there was a break-in at the Brewers' house."

My gaze narrows. "What kind of break-in?"

"Forced entry. Early hours. They were still asleep, apparently, but were awakened by a noise. Mr. Brewer was shot. And in the ensuing tussle, he killed the intruder."

"Oh my God." I glance down the hall, staring at nothing, while my mind spins. Was it Cash? That man—Eric Downey?

"We're not sure yet if it's connected to the abduction," Wiley adds. "But whoever it was—seems the timing was unusual at best."

I feel cold all over, not wanting to admit that all of this was our fault. "You don't appear to believe it was a coincidence. So, why are you telling me this?"

She fixes her gaze on me. "Because I want to know if there's anything you've left out about the incident with your husband."

"I already told you everything that happened."

"Did you?" Her gaze sharpens, and her tone rises an octave. "Because someone showed up at the Brewers' house not long before the girls were found. And if the kidnapper was trying to tie up loose ends...loose ends that might involve the Brewers, we need to know exactly who we're dealing with."

I get that shaky feeling again, the one that reminds me of what I've done. "I'm sorry, I don't know anything about this intruder. I tried to save Nate from my husband. That's it." I swallow hard.

"I'm not protecting anyone over anything." She doesn't believe me. I see it in her face.

"I sure would hate for things to go south now," Wiley replies, shaking her head. "Now that you've got your daughter back, she's going to need you, and so is your son."

Of course I know more. Cash and Eric Downey were probably working together. If Downey took the girls, then maybe he came back to kill Ashley and Nate. Probably looked for me too. For all I know, he could've tried to go after Cash as well. Tying up all the loose ends because Lexi broke free. I want to smile at the thought, but I don't. No need to give Wiley any more reason to doubt me. "I need to get back to my daughter. Please."

"You'll see her soon," Wiley replies. "But if you think of anything—*anything*—that can shed light on why this man came for the Brewers, you come to me. Directly. Understood?"

I nod slowly. She stands up, signaling the other officer to come and escort me. And as I'm led down the hallway again, Wiley catches up to us.

"One more thing, Mrs. Metcalf."

I pause.

She steps closer, her voice low. "Cash Goodell's on his way in. He volunteered to make a statement."

So she does know more. She was just waiting for me to make a mistake—to catch me in a lie. "A statement? About what?"

"He said he wanted to clear up a few things. Said it had to do with your husband's car."

My knees nearly give way, and I do my best to hide it. "Cash—he—he doesn't know anything."

"He claims to have repaired Mr. Metcalf's car after a run-in with a deer a few years back." Wiley tilts her head. "Maybe he's been holding onto something for a while now."

I stare at the floor, my pulse hammering. Now that Garrett's gone, Cash wants to talk. Get ahead of the situation because he knows damn well he had a hand in our daughter's kidnapping. With me being accused of murder, the Brewers being attacked, now's his chance to make up whatever the hell story he wants.

Wiley crouches a little to catch my eye. "If there's something else I need to know about, now's your chance. I can work with the truth, Mrs. Metcalf. Is Cash Goodell going to tell me the truth?"

"I don't know, Officer," I reply flatly. "You'll have to ask him."

Wiley nods, a tight smile on her lips, then she straightens. "Bail paperwork's still moving. You'll be out soon. But if I were you?" She pauses at the end of the hall. "I'd start thinking real hard about which side of this you want to be on. Because the truth will come out eventually, Mara."

62

NATE

I have to tell Blackwell. Cash Goodell has to be the one responsible for sending Eric Downey to our home this morning. The two were working together, I don't know how yet. But Cash will pay for his part in all this. Just as we're about to enter Lexi's hospital room, I clear my throat. "Excuse me, Officer Blackwell?"

He stops and turns to me, his hand on the door to her room. Ashley's face masks in confusion as her eyes search mine.

"Can I talk to you for a moment?" I ask him, and when I glance at Ashley, her expression falls, like she knows what I'm about to do. But will she try to stop me?

"Of course," Blackwell replies.

"Honey," I say to Ashley. "Why don't you tell Lexi that Officer Blackwell will be in soon to speak to her? I'll only be a minute." We lock eyes. She hesitates. Her chest rises and falls faster with each breath. "It's okay. This will only take a minute." My gaze wills her to leave. "Please, honey." If she doesn't leave, Blackwell will get concerned. She knows this. I can see it in her eyes—eyes that flicker with doubt. But she has to trust me if we still have such a thing left in our marriage.

Ashley says nothing more and opens the door to Lexi's room, disappearing inside.

I shift my gaze to Blackwell.

"What is it you wanted to discuss, Mr. Brewer?" he asks, "Because I'd really like to get the girls' statements. The sooner, the better."

"I understand." I lead him out of the corridor and toward a corner of the waiting area. With a widened stance, I raise my chin and try to muster an ounce of courage. "I think I might know who was involved in the girls' kidnapping."

Blackwell narrows his gaze, skepticism etched into his features. "Is that a fact? And why have you waited until now to say something?"

"I'll be honest, I wasn't sure. In fact, I'm still not entirely, but after what happened this morning—the man who broke into my home—I'm confident all this ties back to Cash Goodell."

"That's a serious allegation. What makes you say that?" he presses.

"He confronted Garrett the other night at the grocery store. And I think the only reason he helped in the search that first day was to figure out where the investigation was heading."

Blackwell eyes me for a moment, his expression unreadable. "I'm gonna need something a little more concrete than that, Mr. Brewer."

"I'm fairly certain it was him in the woods," I say. "During the vigil, I'd walked out past the crowd, sure I'd seen someone looking and acting suspiciously. Later, Garrett did too, before he came at me. By the time we walked around the area, whoever it was, was gone." I already know it was Downey, he admitted as much. But I need to give Blackwell something. I hope this is enough.

"And what about this suspicious person made you think it was Mr. Goodell?" Blackwell asks.

"I'm not one hundred percent sure, as I said, I couldn't fully identify him. But that driver's license we found in Lexi's room?"

"Eric Downey," he replies.

"Yes. Downey's car is sitting in Cash's yard right now. I believe he and Downey were working together to abduct the girls. And Downey now lies dead in my living room. He knew where we lived because Cash told him—told him to get rid of us because Cash knew Lexi had escaped. We knew the car was there, so we could put two and two together. Cash didn't want that. How else could you explain the timing?" I'm actually starting to believe the words coming out of my mouth.

"How do you know this—about the car, I mean?" he asks.

Well, Garrett isn't here to defend himself, so there's no point in trying to spin this away from him. "Garrett broke into the yard after his initial confrontation with Cash. Told us something seemed off about him. We all tried to tell him to let you handle it. But that's not who Garrett was."

"I see. So Mr. Metcalf saw a car, believed it belonged to Eric Downey without evidence, and then, what...just decides to keep that information from me?"

"I couldn't tell you what was going on in Garrett's head, Officer Blackwell. He'd become unhinged, as you already know." I wonder now if I'm getting through to him. Does he believe me? "I think he noticed the out-of-state plates—Utah plates, just like on the driver's license. And figured it out."

Blackwell cocks his brow. "Hell of a leap."

"But now, after everything that's happened, I think Garrett must've been right. Look, before you talk to Lexi, please question Goodell. I know the doctors are going to test Lexi and Skye for foreign DNA, so the answer will hopefully become clear soon enough. And if you get those answers before you question Goodell, he'll disappear. Gone. And at some point down the road, he might just come back for my daughter."

Blackwell nods. "All right, Mr. Brewer. All of this should've been brought to my attention. The confrontation, the suspicion about Downey's car." He shakes his head. "How could you expect me to help when you kept me in the dark like that?" He draws in a deep breath, like he's exhausted by me. "I will decide whether to question Cash Goodell. But I can't hold off on speaking to Lexi for too long."

"I understand."

"There is something else," Blackwell says, his tone shifting. "Based on conversations with your daughter here at the hospital, do you suspect there's a possibility she could ID her captor—Mr. Goodell, as you believe?"

I shrug, forgetting for a moment the pain in my side. "I don't think so. At least, that's not the impression she left me with. They both say he wore a mask, which makes it all the more likely that if it was Cash Goodell, he didn't want to be identified."

"So you believe he intended to let them go? That this was something else. Maybe an attempt at a ransom?" Blackwell presses further, his eyes narrowing slightly.

"I wish I knew." Guilt weighs down my words because, of course, I know the truth. "It would make sense if the kidnapper was looking for a ransom. Suppose it's a good reason to wear a mask to conceal his identity."

Blackwell presses his lips into a thin line. "I'll keep that in mind, Mr. Brewer." His gaze softens once more as he adds, "You should go see your daughter. I'll be in touch soon."

"Thank you." Blackwell leaves, and I enter Lexi's room to find Ashley at our daughter's side, resting her hand on her shoulder. "Hey, kiddo," I say to her.

"Hi, Dad," Lexi replies. "Has anyone checked on Skye? Can I go see her?"

I glance at Ashley, and we seem to agree. "Not just yet, honey. But I'll see if I can find her doctor and get an update."

Lexi nods, disappointment masking her face.

"I've been asking her if she can remember any more details about the man who took her," Ashley says.

I round the bed, approaching the other side. "I see. We don't want to put too much pressure on you, sweetheart. We know this is an impossible situation."

"No, it's okay. It's just that I didn't really see him, you know? I mean, like, he was kind of big." Her eyes redden.

"Hey, hey, it's okay." I brush my hand against her cheek. "You don't have to do this right now. The police will test for DNA, and that'll go a long way to identifying the man who did this." I choke up. "And when they do, I'll make sure he pays."

Lexi narrows her gaze. "I guess I do remember one thing..."

Ashley and I trade glances when I look back at Lexi. "If you want to tell us..."

"Yeah. Um. He sort of limped like he'd been injured." She closes her eyes. "I think it was his right leg."

I freeze. "His right leg."

"Yes."

My chest tightens, and red clouds my vision. "Okay. I'll be sure to let the police know."

63

MARA

I'm out. Free to go home, they tell me. But I'm not going home. I'm going to the hospital to see my daughter, to tell her why her father isn't there. I see Officer Wiley at the end of the hall, like she's been waiting for me—again.

"They said I could go."

"Yes, ma'am, you're free to leave," she replies.

The way she says it—like it's only temporary.

"Wiley?"

Before she can answer, I see Blackwell appear behind her, calling her name. He walks like a man carrying something sharp in his pocket. His eyes flick to me and then back to her.

"Figured you'd be at the hospital," Wiley says to him.

"Just got back," he replies, then eyes me again. "What do you know about Cash Goodell, Mrs. Metcalf?"

Everything in me goes still. *Cash. Shit. I was so close.* "I know he owns a body shop in town."

Blackwell tilts his head. "Hmm. Mr. Brewer seems hell-bent on my bringing the man in for questioning. You sure you don't

277

know anything about that? Anything about confrontations with your husband in the days leading up to his death?"

"Officer Blackwell, I just got my daughter back after losing my husband, so you'll forgive me if Nate Brewer's crusade means nothing to me. I was told I could leave, and I intend to." I glance between them, but they don't move. They don't blink. They already know I'm lying.

"You can go, Mrs. Metcalf," Wiley says.

I turn and walk. The hallway stretches out like I might never reach the end, but when I finally do, I stop because I have to. Their voices trail down the corridor, so I listen.

"Brewer insists Eric Downey's car is sitting in Goodell's body shop," Blackwell says. "He claims Mr. Metcalf's suspicions about Goodell are worth a second look. That Goodell likely sent Downey to the Brewer house to kill them this morning."

The blood drains from my face. What the fuck is he talking about? My knees wobble. What did Nate do? Getting Cash involved will expose everything. Goddam it. I knew they'd screw me over. I don't know how yet, but that's what's going to happen.

"Maybe we should look into it," Wiley says. "I understood Mr. Goodell was wishing to make a statement anyway. Sounds like we might have some conflicting information here. Currently, we have no motive for why Eric Downey would come for the Brewers unless he was responsible for kidnapping those girls."

"And why not go after the Metcalfs, too, then, if Mr. Metcalf held suspicions?" Blackwell adds.

"Garrett Metcalf's murder isn't sitting so good with me, all of a sudden," Wiley says.

I drop back against the wall for a moment. Goddam it. If they question Cash, he'll spill all of it. Why would Nate do this? Cash is the only other one who knows—or at least suspects what happened years ago. Unless he believes Cash was behind the abduction. Shit. I need answers. I need Cash before Blackwell gets to him. Before my daughter learns the truth about her parents.

64

NATE

I know I saw it. When Garrett and I went to Cash's home the other night—the limp. Jesus Christ, it was him. I fucking knew it. I was right to warn Blackwell. It makes all the sense in the world. He had Downey's car. He told Downey where to find us. And he's still walking around like he did nothing wrong. I'm going to kill him for what he's done. I'm going to get to him before the cops do and kill him. He could've just come after the four of us—make us pay for what we did. Instead, he came after our kids. Why? And how the hell did he find Downey in the first place?

"I—uh—I need to go back to the station and talk to Blackwell."

"Why?" Ashley asks.

I don't want to tell her what I suspect. Not until I know more. "I need to make sure the mess in the house is taken care of," I reply. "Stay here with Lex, and maybe you can get some answers about Skye, too." I look at Lexi, who has drifted off to sleep. "I won't be long."

"But you've just been shot, Nate. You're barely stitched up.

You can't go running off..." Ashley stops and regards me for a long moment. She suspects I'm lying. I was never good at it—lying was her thing.

"I'll take it easy, I promise. Doc said I'll be fine, but I gotta go." Then I remember that I didn't drive here. "Shit."

"What is it?" she asks.

"Our car isn't here." I shake my head. "Screw it. I'll take an Uber home. I head outside, and as I stand under the awning, I order the car. While I'm waiting, I notice the sun is high in the sky, heat waves rising from the asphalt parking lot. Is it midday already?

There's no more time to waste. The driver picks me up and takes me home. When he pulls up onto the driveway, I see the cops are still here, yellow tape plastered around my front porch. What must the neighbors think of all this?

Just as I step out, I catch sight of an officer sitting in his patrol car along the curb, shaded by our tall oak tree. He jumps out, hurrying toward me. "Excuse me, sir?"

I stop in the middle of my front yard and turn around. "Hello, Officer. I'm Nate Brewer. I live here."

"I'm aware of who you are, Mr. Brewer. But you can't go in there. We haven't cleared it."

My shoulders sink. "Officer, I just need to get my car keys. I'm not staying."

"I'm sorry, sir. I can't let you in." He hooks his thumbs into his duty belt, almost daring me to challenge him.

It's clear I'm not getting inside, but maybe not all is lost. "Could you go in for me, then? I just need my car keys. That's it."

He shifts his gaze between me and the front door.

"Please, Officer. I need to get back to the hospital to see my daughter." That should do it.

Finally, he nods, giving in. "All right. Stay here. Tell me where your keys are."

"The foyer table, inside the bowl. Thank you, sir. Thank you."

He raises his hand at me, issuing a silent warning before he goes in.

I peer out over the street as pain shoots through my side, reminding me I killed a man only hours ago. Did our neighbors hear the gunshots? The fighting? I imagine they never suspected their neighborhood pharmacist could be embroiled in such a horrific scandal. Or that it would result in the kidnapping of his daughter. It would be almost impossible for me to imagine, were I not living it.

The officer returns outside, dangling my keys from his index finger. "Here you go, sir."

I take them. "I appreciate it, Officer. Oh, do you know when we might get back into our house?" Never mind the bloodstains on the living room rug.

"I'd suggest you and your wife stay in a hotel tonight. We should be all clear tomorrow."

"Of course, thank you again." I step into my car and head straight toward Cash's body shop.

On the drive over, I run through the events as I see them unfolding. Corner him. Confirm my suspicions that he took my daughter, and then... Do I want to kill him? Hell yes, I do. Am I going to? Depends on whether I can make it appear accidental. He took my daughter. He sent Downey to kill us. Who's to say a skirmish doesn't erupt inside his shop? Lots of equipment and machinery around there. Cash knows a lot—too much—so we'll see how this plays out.

I arrive at the body shop and stop the car, realizing I'm about to confront the man who took my daughter, and I have no weapon. So, I get out and open the trunk to retrieve the only thing that could pass for one—a tire iron.

Clutching it in my hand, I push through the entrance, the

glass door rattling on its hinges. Three gray plastic chairs line the back wall—empty. A man sits behind the front counter, his gaze rising to me. "Where's Cash?"

He eyes the tire iron and then me, wiping his hand on his grease-stained overalls. No doubt, I appear unhinged, beaten, and shot at. He thumbs back. "In his office."

Wow. He's not even trying to stop me. Then again, with the way I look, I don't blame him.

I march through the hall, the tire iron swinging in my hand. As I reach the last office at the end, there he is, on the phone like today is just another day. "Cash?"

He sets his sights on me, eyes widening, then slowly hangs up. I see him swallow hard as he gets to his feet and rounds his desk. "Jesus, what the hell happened to you?"

I study him, just to be sure, and yep, he's limping. Son of a bitch. My eyes darken, narrowing solely on him. "You sent that kid to kill us. Eric Downey. You told him where we were."

"Look, Nate, I have no idea what you're talking about. Don't you think enough has happened—what—with Garrett Metcalf, your daughter? You want to make things worse for yourself? You got your girl back. Take the fucking win."

"She's why I'm here. You took them—the girls. I know you did."

"This bullshit again?" He waves me off.

I raise the iron, making sure he sees every inch of the thick metal with its curved end that could carve out a nice chunk of his skull. "You're limping. You get injured recently?" I eyeball him. "How'd you find the car in the ravine? Was your plan to blackmail us? Take the girls for ransom?"

"Jesus, Nate. I have a bad hip. This is how I walk. And blackmail?" He shakes his head. "The hell you talking about?"

That's when I hear a voice coming from down the hall. A woman's voice I recognize.

"Nate, what are you doing?"

Mara appears in the doorway. We stare at each other a moment—Cash, darting his gaze between us. "How did you know I was here?" I ask.

"I didn't. I'm here because of what you told the police," she replies. "That you were sure Cash was responsible for taking the girls."

"You told the cops?" Cash's eyes widen. "Guess you want to end up in prison, huh, Nate? You think I don't know about the accident?"

"Oh, I'm aware you knew all about that. But you're a kidnapper. I don't give a shit what happens to me so long as you pay for what you've done." I give Mara a sideways glance. "Go home, Mara, or better yet, go see your daughter. I'll handle this."

She locks eyes with Cash. "Was Garrett right about you?"

"You people are fucking crazy and if you don't leave, I'm calling the cops," he replies.

A crooked grin tugs at my lips. "Good. I'm sure they'll be interested to know that Lexi can ID you as her abductor."

"The fuck?" He rocks back on his heels. "That's not possible."

I feel Mara's gaze on me, but I press on. "She said the man who held them in that basement had a limp, like he'd been injured. Seems to me, you're favoring your right leg."

"Jesus Christ. I just told you..." Cash runs his hand through his curly hair.

"This was all part of your plan to get us to turn on each other," I say. "The four of us. You found the car, tracked down Eric Downey. And you thought, 'Why not make a few bucks on these assholes?'"

"You've lost it, you know that, Nate?" Cash replies.

"What I know is that my daughter identified you. That's all I need."

"Why in the hell would I take those girls?" he presses.

"You tell me. Money is my best guess. Blackmail. I just don't get why you waited until now. How the hell did you find that man's car?"

"Wait. Stop."

The voice comes from behind me. I glance back and see the man from the front desk. "Who are you?"

"Jason Legado," Cash replies. "He's my shop foreman."

Legado. Where have I heard that name? Someone said that name before—who the hell...

"You're the father of one of the girls," Legado says, raising his hands in surrender. "One of the girls who was kidnapped."

"That's right," I reply. "This doesn't involve you, so I suggest you leave."

"You should know something, sir. I've worked here for seven years. I worked on Garrett Metcalf's Mercedes. Cash said the damage was done by a deer that Metcalf struck on the road. I knew almost from the moment I saw the car that wasn't the case. I've been around this business my whole life. That kind of damage didn't come from a deer."

"Get to the point," I insist, wondering if he's already called the cops and this is a stall tactic.

"I told Cash that Metcalf wasn't being honest. That it looked more like he'd hit a person. Cash insisted I was mistaken."

"So," I reply. "Still doesn't explain why Eric Downey's car is in the yard."

"Let me finish, Mr. Brewer," Legado continues. "I went to the police without telling Cash a few months after we'd fixed the Mercedes. I raised my suspicions about what I thought caused the damage to Metcalf's car. The officer said he'd check it out, but I don't know if that ever happened. I never followed up." He shrugs. "Guess I figured I did my part."

"So, the police never said anything more to you?" Mara asks.

"No, ma'am."

"Obviously, Cash knew the truth," I reply. "He tracked down the man's family. Brought his son here to kill us and took the girls for ransom."

"I told you—I didn't fucking do it!" Cash yells. "What would be the goddam point when I could've blackmailed you five years ago?"

And then it hits me. I remember now, and shift my gaze to Legado. "Blackwell. He asked me about you earlier. Why?" I peer at him, desperate for an answer. "You'd better start talking."

65

LEXI

The door clicks shut behind Mom as she steps out of my room. She's been with me for hours, and I insisted she take a break to get herself some food or whatever. Dad's still not back. I know I'm supposed to talk to the police soon, but when?

My forearm itches under these bandages. It's annoying. I want to scratch it so bad, just to do something, but I don't move. I just lie here like a broken thing in a bed that smells like bleach. At least it's not a concrete floor, wet with pee and vomit.

I stare up at the ceiling. There's this cracked tile right above me. Just a tiny crack, barely anything, but I focus on it. I trace it with my eyes and count. One... two... three... Anything to keep my brain from spiraling. To not think about all that happened to us. I'm focused on not losing my shit while Mom's getting something from the cafeteria.

I hear her voice just on the other side of the door. It's muffled through the wall, like a TV in another room. "Thank you. I'll be back in just a minute. Going for a coffee." She says it like it's no big deal. But then—then she adds. "*Officer.*" She was talking to a cop.

My whole body goes still. God, I'm not ready for the questions. I can't think about it again. Not right now.

I stare at the door, willing it to stay closed. The hair on my arms stands on end, like someone rubbed a balloon on them. That word—*officer*. It means this was all real, no matter how hard I try to wish it away. It was real, and it happened. Now, I have to tell people about it. About what he did to us—to me.

The door opens again real slow. No clatter. Just this kind of quiet. Footsteps follow, then I see him.

He's tall, broad, and dressed in a dark blue uniform with a shiny badge pinned to his chest. The scary-looking gun seems to weigh him down on one side. He smiles at me, all nice and friendly. "Lexi," he says in a smooth, low voice that's sort of familiar, like he's an uncle or a friend's dad. "I'm Officer Blackwell. I saw your mom outside. She said I could come in and that she'd just be a moment. I wanted to check in. See how you're feeling."

I don't answer. Not right away. My mouth's too dry. My throat, too sore.

He waits and pretends he's patient. But I know what he wants to ask me. And I want to be okay with it, but I'm not...not right now...I can't face it yet. "I'm feeling okay, I guess," I manage. The words barely come out. They don't even sound like me. "Just tired."

He nods, then steps a little closer. Not a lot, but enough that I feel it. "I wanted to meet with you earlier, but I think your folks thought it best if you got some sleep. However, I'm afraid this can't wait any longer, as I'm sure you understand." He pulls a little notepad from his pocket. "I know this is hard. What you've been through. But you're safe now."

That word again.

"What you did—escaping and running to get help." He sighs

as if this was the craziest thing he'd ever heard. "You know, I've been investigating your case. Organized the search and followed whatever leads we had. Turned out, you didn't need me. You managed all on your own."

Does he want me to respond? Because it's not like I'm looking for compliments. "Yeah, sure."

"You also did great making sure you got help for Skye, too. Showing those officers where the house was. It was amazing for a girl your age to show that kind of bravery."

I look away, out the window, praying I don't have to relive all this right now. "I guess so."

"Do you remember anything specific about the man who took you? Any tattoos or scars? Did he have an accent? Anything you can think of that can help us identify him?"

"He wore a creepy doll mask," I reply, still peering through the window.

And then the door opens. Both of us look. It's Mom. She's wearing that tight expression she gets when she's pretending not to be scared, holding that cup of coffee like her life depends on drinking it.

She glances at him, and then at me. "Everything okay?"

"Just easing my way into trying to get some specifics," Blackwell replies. "I understand Lexi's been through a lot and needs her rest."

"Yes," Mom says, approaching me. "Maybe it's best if this waits until tomorrow. It is getting late in the day."

"Maybe you're right. I might've jumped the gun, here, eager to keep the momentum, but I don't want to push." Officer Blackwell drops the notebook into his pocket. "I'll come back in the morning. Let you get a good night's rest." He glances at me, a thin smile on his face.

As he's walking away, I zero in on him. Something about

how...I shake my head. No. I thought it was because of his gun... but... Am I seeing this? Is he—limping?

I'm suddenly thrown back into that basement. Hearing his voice. Seeing his eyes blink behind the mask. And the way he favors his right leg after what he did to me...

The air rips from my lungs.

I look at Mom. She doesn't see. She's looking at her phone.

Oh my God. I know you.

Blackwell turns back to me. His face falls for a split second, then he fakes a smile. "You get some rest now, Lexi."

66

NATE

I don't know how long it'll be before I hear sirens come racing up to Cash's shop, feeling pretty confident this Jason Legado has already called them. Mara is standing only feet away from me. Neither of us seems to have thought this far in advance. I came here for Cash, and yet I'm listening to this guy Blackwell mentioned—still waiting to hear why.

"I'm guessing that the police did nothing to look into my concerns," Legado says. "It made me wonder if Cash was trying to cover it up—paying off the cops or something."

Cash scoffs. "What the hell are you doing, man?"

"What I should've done a long time ago," Legado replies, turning to me. "A few weeks ago, we get this guy who shows up. Has this late model dark blue Ford Taurus. I overhear him asking Cash if he can keep it in our yard for a while. I thought it was a strange request. The car didn't need any work done. But I shrugged it off...until your girls were taken."

I swallow the lump in my throat and glance at Mara, whose attention is glued to this man.

"Just seemed like a strange coincidence, right? Anyway, I felt

291

weird about it, so I called the police, asked for the name of the officer I filed the original report with. They told me he didn't work there anymore." Lagado shakes his head. "So, I'm not sure what to do, but then I see the guy again. He comes in to talk to Cash. I overhear a few things. Money, an old car that got run off the road, or something. Says he's looking for his dad. Anyway, I wait. And when I think the coast is clear, I go into Cash's office and find the invoice. Has the guy's name and number on it, the car's make and model, but there's no estimate, only a charge for storage. A hefty charge, I might add. I write down the guy's name and go straight to Officer Blackwell with the information. Something just wasn't sitting right with me...those girls being taken and all. I knew Blackwell had been assigned to the case because Cash had volunteered for the search."

"What'd he say? Blackwell?" I press.

"That he'd look into it."

Cash is quiet for a few moments. His chest heaves, and I hear him breathing hard. "You think I wanted any of this? Blackwell came to me a month ago, asking about the Mercedes, asking what I knew about Garrett Metcalf. Course, I told him nothing of what I suspected. But he knew I was hiding something." Cash shoots a look at Legado. "Now, I know why. But then Downey shows up, offering me money to keep his car here a while. I don't know who the hell he is, so who am I to turn him down?"

"You didn't tell Downey where we lived?" I press.

"No, man. I'm telling you. Whatever he figured out, he figured out on his own."

"Or he had someone else's help," I add. It's starting to make sense now. Downey seemed surprised that we thought he had the girls. The way he confessed to following Lexi because Skye was never alone. If he already knew where we were, he wouldn't have gone through the effort. "How did Downey know to come to you?" I ask.

Cash shrugs. "I'm the only body shop in town. He asked if I remembered working on a car five years ago that had extensive front-end damage."

"Jesus," I reply, rubbing my temple.

"I swear to God, Nate, I didn't say a word. I took his money. That's it. And I had nothing to do with your girl being taken. Maybe I should've come forward with what I suspected long ago. Metcalf paid a fair sum to convince me to keep quiet. But I'll tell you, it's not me you should be looking at. It's..."

"Blackwell." Mara's already moving. "Nate, let's go. We need to find Wiley."

67

SKYE

The walls of the hospital room are too white, too quiet. I wish I could turn on the TV. I wish I had my phone. Anything to drown out the thoughts in my head. I want my mom. Where's my family? Where's Lexi?

I try to move my arms, but they're too heavy. The pins in my hand make me look like Frankenstein or something. How will I ever be able to go back to cheerleading?

Did I really just think that? I laugh out loud. "Cheerleading? That's what I'm thinking about after everything that's happened. I am selfish."

I lean back, letting my head sink into the pillows. It still smells like antiseptic in here. I've been here for... I don't know how long. No one will tell me anything. Not really. Not about Lexi. Not about my mom. They just keep saying rest, sweetie, and you're safe now, like that means anything. I don't feel safe. I feel like I'm in some alternate universe, waiting for someone to pull me out of it.

Why did they take Mom away? She wanted to tell me something, but then they took her. Where's my brother? My dad? I'm completely fucking alone in here and no one will help me.

And Lexi... I keep asking to see her, but the nurses won't let me. They just pat my head and say things like 'soon' or that 'the doctors are still checking on her', but what if that's a lie? What if something's wrong? She came back for me. She saved me. I have to see her.

The door creaks open.

I shift my gaze, waiting to see who's coming. For a second, I think maybe it's Mom or Dad. Maybe even Lexi. But it's not. It's a man I haven't seen before. He's a cop, and I see the name on his uniform. Blackwell. His smile is polite, but he's stiff.

"Hey, there, Skye," he says, stepping inside and closing the door behind him. "I'm Officer Blackwell. I've been working on your case. Listen, I've had a chance to speak to Lexi, so do you mind if I ask you a few questions?"

I look at the door, willing my mom to come through because I don't want to do this alone. But I am—alone. "I guess...Wait. You talked to Lexi? Is she okay?"

"Yes, she is. She's doing great." He pulls the chair closer to my bed and sits down. "You've been through a lot, so I won't keep you. I just wanted to ask what you remember about the man who held you both captive? Lexi mentioned he wore a plastic doll mask, so I know you didn't see his face, but what about something else? Tattoos or scars. What about his height and weight? Any of those things come to mind?"

I glance away, not wanting to remember any of it, but I know I have to try. "I—I don't remember much. Just that Lexi got out. She hurt him, I know that."

"Hurt him how?" Blackwell asks.

"Well, for starters, she bit his shoulder. Then, I got close enough to..." Tears well in my eyes as I think back to all of it. "I helped her get away."

He jots down some notes as if what I'm saying is perfectly normal. As if tears aren't streaming down my face, horrified that he's forcing me to relive it. "Do you know where my mom and dad are?"

"I don't, but I can find out." He smiles at me, tilting his head a little like that's the only way he knows how to express compassion. "I'm sorry. One of your parents probably should be here. It's just—well, I really want to find this person. What he did..." He shakes his head. "It's very upsetting. And you and Lexi were so brave."

"Thanks." I glance away for a moment. "I don't think we were the only ones."

He leans in a little. "What do you mean?"

"I mean, I found a bobby pin down there. Girls wear bobby pins, and this one didn't belong to me or Lexi. I also saw what I'm pretty sure were blood stains. We were covered in blood, but these stains didn't come from us."

"I see." He jots down more notes. "Do you happen to recall any of his facial features?"

"It was dark, and when he did turn on the light, it took a while for my eyes to adjust," I reply. "I couldn't see that much, and especially not behind his stupid mask. You said you talked to Lexi. Did she see anything more?"

"No, not really. So, we're going to have to wait for DNA testing to come back. But I want you to know, Skye." He grabs the side of my bed. "He won't hurt you or Lexi again. I promise you." He rises to his feet. "Thank you for this. You did great. I'll go see what I can find out about your folks." When he reaches the door, he glances back. "If you remember anything more, even a little thing... I hope you'll tell me first. I'm here to help."

68

LEXI

My heart races, and I don't know what to do. Do I tell Mom? Will she believe me? And most importantly, am I totally sure of what I saw and heard? I mean, I'm on a lot of meds right now. What if I'm wrong?

I shift in the bed, desperate for someone to tell me what I should do.

"Are you okay, sweetheart?" Mom looks at me, placing her hand on my head. "You look pale. Should I call the nurse?"

I want to cry, scream, or throw something. "No. No, I'm— I'm okay. It's just—"

Just what? That I might've seen the man who took me? That I might've looked straight into his face and couldn't even be sure?

I close my eyes, instinctively trying to ball my hands into fists, but that's not going to happen. So, I try to remember it all. The limp. The way he walked. His voice. The way his breath smelled like hot metal. I know I hurt his shoulder. That would prove it. But what am I going to do? Ask Mom to bring him in and demand that he show me his shoulder? He's a cop.

"Can I see Skye?" My voice breaks. "Please, Mom. We've been

here for hours, and no one's let me see her. I just... I need to know she's okay."

More than anything, I need Skye. She was there. She'll remember. Maybe she saw what I saw. Maybe together we can figure this out. Figure out if it's him.

Mom brushes back my hair, worry etched on her face. Her palm is warm. It reminds me I'm still a kid and she's still my mom. But so much has happened. I don't think I'll ever be the same again.

"Let me go ask," she says. "I think you should see her. You're both going to need each other right now."

You have no idea. Because if I'm right—if that man is who I think he is—Skye might already be in danger. If he's here in this hospital and no one knows who he is but us, we won't make it out of here alive.

Mom gives me a final, lingering look, and then she's gone. And I'm alone again. Just me and the machines and the afternoon sun that shines through the window. The room feels colder the second the door clicks shut.

If I could wrap my arms around myself for comfort, I would. He's not coming back. I keep telling myself that. Over and over. *He's not coming back.*

But what if I'm wrong? What if he's just waiting for my parents to leave?

The heart monitor beeps faster. I glance at it—my heart rate's spiking like I'm running a race even though I'm completely still. Great. *Calm down, Lex. Take a breath, or you'll have every nurse on this floor rushing in like you flatlined.*

But I can't stop thinking. What if that was him? What if he came here to see if we remembered? To make sure we wouldn't talk? What if Skye saw him too, but she's too scared to say anything? Fear wraps around me, suffocating me. I need her. I need Skye. She'll know. She'll remember. And if we're right... We're not safe.

The door opens again. It's Mom, thank God.

Behind her is a nurse pushing a wheelchair. This is it. They're going to let me see Skye. I look at Mom, eyes wide, waiting for her to tell me what I've already figured out.

"You can see her now," Mom says, wearing a smile.

"Let's get you out of that bed and into the chair," the nurse says.

I'm numb from the medication, and my body feels too heavy to move, but the nurse helps me.

She wheels me out of my room and down the hallway so slowly I want to scream. I glance back at her, expectantly, but she gives me a tight-lipped smile, like this is just a regular hospital visit. Like I haven't been missing for days, and I haven't just figured out who took us.

When she finally pushes open the door to Skye's room, I almost launch out of the wheelchair. The surge of adrenaline overpowers the pain meds.

"Whoa, hang on," the nurse says. "Take it easy."

"Lexi?" Skye's eyes light up. She tries to pull herself up, but the pain must be too much.

"Oh my God. You're okay," I say as the nurse pushes me closer. I look back at Mom. "Do you think we could talk a minute? I mean, we've been through a lot..."

She glances at the nurse, who nods her approval. "Of course. I'll be right outside if you need me."

"Mrs. Brewer?" Skye asks.

"Yes, honey?"

"Do you think you could find out where my parents are? I haven't seen my mom in a while, and I don't know where my dad is."

Mom swallows hard. "Of course. I'll see what I can find out."

When they leave, all I can do is stare at Skye. Her eyes are wide, and her mouth is open like she forgot how to speak.

She looks at my hands, and then raises hers a little. "They look about as good as mine."

"Guess we won't be playing tennis anytime soon," I reply.

"Or cheerleading," she says, smirking.

Suddenly, I feel bad for saying anything. "Yeah, right. But you're okay. I didn't know for sure. I thought—"

"I'm okay, I guess," she replies, even though I can tell that's not true. Nothing about this is okay. She pulls back to look at me, her face pale and bruised. I probably look the same.

"I think I saw him," I say. "Skye... I think he was *here*." And when I look at her reaction, I know she's seen him, too.

"Blackwell?" She closes her eyes, forcing down fresh tears. "That cop."

"So you think it's him, too? Jesus." I shake my head. "He came to my room. Asked me questions. Wanted to know if I remembered anything. I—I think he was trying to find out if I recognized him."

"He came to see me too," she whispers. "He acted all nice, but... I felt weird about it, you know? I didn't recognize him, though. Not until you said something just now. Now, I don't know how I could've missed it. Maybe I didn't want to believe a cop could do something like that." Her lips quiver. "How could it be him?"

"Maybe I'm wrong." I shake my head, panic rising in my throat. "I wasn't totally sure. I'm still not."

"Did you see his shoulder?" she asks.

"No."

"But you felt something familiar?" she continues.

I nod. "I did. His voice, I sort of recognized. But Skye, I'm sure he was limping."

"His right leg?" she asks.

"Yeah. Did you notice?"

She turns away, like she's thinking about it. "Not really. I didn't pay that close attention." She looks back at me. "What are we going to do, Lex? We have to be sure it's him."

I take a deep breath. "When he was leaving my room, he glanced back at me, smiling or whatever. Like, after I noticed his leg. And there was something in his eyes. I think he knew I'd figured it out." I reach for Skye's shoulder. "I think we're right, which means we aren't safe here. We aren't safe anywhere."

69

NATE

We pull into the precinct just after dusk, the sun now merely a stroke of orange in the rearview. Mara's knuckles are white around her seatbelt, and neither of us has spoken since we left Cash's body shop. Not really. Just enough to decide we had to come here.

As we step out of the car and head toward the entrance, my mind spins with unanswered questions. Did Blackwell find the car in the ravine? Does he know where the body is, too? Because someone does. That's where Ashley found the car's plates. And the biggest question of them all—why the fuck did he kidnap our girls?

Inside, the station's fluorescent lights buzz, and the lobby smells like coffee that's been burnt and reheated too many times. It's all I can do not to march straight through to Blackwell's office and confront him. But we have to be smart. We need to be certain.

A young officer behind the desk eyes us. He knows exactly who we are.

I approach him. "We need to speak with Officer Wiley. It's urgent."

The way he picks up the phone, keeping his eyes on me, proves I've gotten my point across. He makes the call and then returns a solemn expression. "She's on her way up."

Soon, Wiley appears, hair pulled back tightly, hand instinctively hovering near her sidearm. "Mr. Brewer. Mrs. Metcalf. What are you two doing here? Why aren't you at the hospital with your kids?"

"We need to talk. Privately," I reply.

Wiley hesitates—but only for a moment. She thumbs back and then starts walking without another word.

We follow until she stands at a doorway and nods for us to enter. I let Mara go in ahead, then trail her inside.

"What's this about?" Wiley asks, closing the door behind her. "Are your daughters okay?"

We're in an interview room. I don't like the way it feels in here—claustrophobic, foreboding, even. The steely gray walls surround us. A metal table sits in the center, flanked by chairs. "That depends on how you answer my next question," I reply.

Mara leans forward, her voice low. "We need to know we can trust you."

Wiley raises her brow. "You insist on speaking privately because you don't trust me?"

"You're partners with Blackwell," I say. "So we have to be sure."

Wiley stiffens, the lines around her mouth tightening. "Yeah. What about him?"

"How well do you know him?" I press.

"Well enough." Her eyes narrow, and she folds her arms. "Why are you asking me this?"

I glance at Mara, and she nods, understanding that this could be it for us, and the truth will come out. But if that's what it takes to know for certain Blackwell is the man behind the mask, then so be it. Like Ashley said, we're all on borrowed time. "We think Blackwell kidnapped our daughters."

Wiley doesn't flinch. She just stares at me, dead-eyed, like she's waiting to hear more before deciding if we're insane.

"Best guess is he wanted to use us," I continue. "Exploit a situation in order to shield himself from blame. Point the investigation elsewhere. Seems he dragged Cash Goodell into it, too."

"I don't know how he figured it out, but he did," Mara says. "He must've hoped to blackmail us and hold the girls for ransom if we didn't pay up."

"No ransom demand was made, as far as I know." Wiley glances at the camera tucked in the ceiling's corner. It doesn't appear to be recording. I see no lights on. Is that what she wants—to make sure no one else is watching? Suddenly, my trust in her falters, and I wonder if Mara and I have just made a colossal error in judgment.

"Blackwell was certain the man you killed in your home this morning was the kidnapper," Wiley replies, still poker-faced. "Eric Downey."

"Sounds about right," I say. "That's exactly what we thought, too."

"And now?" Wiley shifts her gaze between Mara and me.

There's no way I can do this without exposing us all. She's going to want to know Downey's connection to us. The report Cash's foreman filed years ago is where I have to start. So, that's what I do.

"A police report was filed almost five years ago, give or take," I begin. "A man named Jason Legado, who works for Cash Goodell, had filed it."

Right away, Wiley types on her laptop. She's searching for it. I regard Mara, and she seems to be holding her breath. We both are. It takes a minute or two before Wiley stops. That's when I realize she must've found the report. Her eyes narrow as she leans closer to her laptop. Either Blackwell was too arrogant to think anyone would come across it again, or too stupid to try harder to bury it. Somehow, though, I don't think he's a stupid man.

"An officer who's no longer here handled this," she says. "I don't know why he wouldn't have followed up on it at the time."

"Maybe he did," I cut in. "Maybe he went to Cash and asked him about it, and Cash said Legado was mistaken, figuring he'd use the information to hold over Garrett's head for money or whatever." I shrug. "Given what I know about Cash now? I'd say that's a very real possibility."

"Still doesn't explain how Blackwell would've come across the report years later," Mara adds.

"He took over for this officer," Wiley replies. "He must've come across it while cleaning up the old files."

There must be more to it than that. A cop doesn't just decide to kidnap two girls for ransom. So what am I missing? "This all goes back to the car accident," I say.

Wiley tilts her head. "What car accident?"

Mara clasps her hands together as if to keep them steady. "Garrett accidentally hit a man on the highway five years ago, killing him. We got rid of his car. Dumped it into a ravine a couple miles from where the accident occurred. Blackwell must've found it and started digging around."

"Whoa, whoa, wait a second." Wiley holds up her hands. "We need to back up, here."

I reach into my pocket and find the flash drive I've been carrying around, wondering what the hell to do with it. Now, I know. "You'll find the answers on here. This is where you should start. Mara and I can fill in the blanks."

Mara creases her brow as she peers at me.

"Dashcam video," I say. "I turned it on when we arrived that night." I watch her breaths coming faster and faster, panic setting in at the realization that after five years, and the death of her husband, this is it. "I'm sorry, Mara."

Karma has come for us. But I'm damn well going to make sure we don't go down alone.

70
MARA

All I can do is stare at Nate. How could he have kept this from me? *Me?* I was there with him. Both of us, trying our damnedest to keep it together in the face of what had happened.

Wiley's sitting at the table, watching the video, but I can't read her. Both of us are across from her, wondering what she's going to do. Put us in handcuffs right now? I got away with Garrett's murder, but I'm going to pay the price for keeping his secret.

"Blackwell couldn't have known any of this unless he'd found the car," Wiley finally says. She stops the video, her gaze sliding from me to Nate, and then back to me again. "I can arrest all of you now, or I can pretend I didn't see this—for the moment. I need time to understand what it is I'm dealing with."

Nate leans back against the chair. "Lexi said she thought other girls had been in that basement at some point. Skye had found a bobby pin. Someone had given both girls a change of clothes.

"Blackwell ran a search for other abduction cases across the state," Wiley says in a slow and calculating manner, like something dawning on her. "He said there was nothing to suggest a serial kidnapper or trafficking operation." She furrows her brow. "And that goddam pocketknife. Why was he searching outside the quadrants? He goes out there alone, and then just so happens to stumble on the weapon likely used on the girls?" She says all this almost to herself.

"Did he ever show you the results of the fingerprints?" Nate pulls upright again, anticipation etched on his face.

"Let's just say I took him at his word—on both counts," she replies. "He led the investigation. Led it right to Eric Downey."

Wiley's quiet for a minute. I can practically see the wheels spinning in her mind. She's beginning to doubt Blackwell. She keys in more commands on her laptop, her eyes laser-focused on the screen. A few more minutes go by.

"Jesus."

Nate and I trade glances, wondering what the hell she found. Finally, Wiley raises her hand. "None of you are off the hook, but right now, I don't like what I'm seeing."

Nate regards her with a raised brow. "There were others?"

She sighs. "Where he worked before. The last two police departments."

"He moved around a lot then," I add, attempting to validate her theory.

"In the previous two years, in each of those jurisdictions, there were five abductions, all girls, whereas there had been none in the two years prior," Wiley adds. "It's not definitive, but it's a hell of a coincidence."

"He used us—our situation," Nate says. "He stumbled on the report Legado filed…"

"Which, by the way," Wiley cuts in. "States Legado overheard Goodell and Metcalf talking, and Metcalf mentioned he'd been heading south on State Route 75 when the accident happened."

"Oh my God. He had an approximate location." I shake my

head. "It would've taken some effort, but Blackwell could've traveled the 75 heading toward the Grant exit. Eventually, coming across the car in the ravine."

Nate casts down his gaze. "He must've been pretty goddam determined to find whatever Garrett hit. He wouldn't have known there was a car to be found."

"That stretch of highway isn't far off his usual beat," Wiley says. "He could've just as easily stumbled across it by accident."

I narrow my gaze. "But how would Blackwell have found the body? He left the license plate near it for us to find."

"Wait." Wiley's expression hardens. "Where's the body?"

"Not far from the accident site," Nate replies. "And unless Garrett told Cash more than he let on, and his worker overheard it, there isn't a chance in hell anyone knew where that was."

"And why is that?" Wiley cocks her head, looking like she's figured it all out. "I just watched dashcam video of exactly where that accident occurred." She leans back. "I think you're both overlooking the obvious. All Blackwell had to do to get any of this information was to search your things, Mr. Brewer."

I stifle a gasp. She's right. And as I peer at Nate, he sees it too. "You kept that flash drive hidden for years," I say to him. "Blackwell found it." Tears prick my eyes as I realize the scope of it all. "He intended to shift the focus of the investigation onto Downey. It was his best shot at getting away with it again. He probably realized a connection to him would be made eventually. That all those missing girls wherever he went couldn't be coincidental."

"He must be trafficking the victims." Wiley covers her mouth and glances at the door as if expecting someone to enter. "Listen, I won't be able to do this alone—not without alerting Blackwell that I know something smells bad. So, I'm going to set aside what I just watched on that video—for now. And I'm going to have to trust both of you. If you want your daughters to be safe, you'll do exactly as I say." She flicks her gaze between us. "Blackwell is still here, but I don't know for how long. So I'm going to get the girls moved to another hospital ASAP." She eyes Nate. "Where's your wife?"

"At the hospital with Lexi."

"Good. I'll go there now with a couple of other officers. We'll get the girls out, but I'll need parental permission. I could do it without it, but hospital regulations would take too long to get around. Mr. Brewer, since your wife is there, she can authorize Lexi's transfer. Mrs. Metcalf, you'll need to go to the hospital with me."

"I should be there," Nate insists. "To make sure my family stays safe."

Wiley sighs. "As long as Blackwell is here, they're safe. I'm putting a hell of a lot of trust in you right now, so don't fuck me on this. You won't win. I need you to stick close to him. Question him about the house, forensics evidence, possible leads...anything you can think of to keep him here and occupied. That'll buy me time to get the girls out of that hospital and into another—far away from here."

71
ASHLEY

I'm consumed by thoughts of what comes next. I won't leave Lexi, not until they find whoever took her. And the three of us? What will happen to Nate, Mara, and me? I don't know, and at the moment, I don't care all that much.

"Ma'am?"

"Huh?" I blink out of my thoughts.

"That'll be fifteen dollars and twenty-five cents, please."

"Oh, yeah, sorry." I swipe my credit card and grab the food. "Thanks." I walk out of the hospital's cafeteria, having bought food for the girls that I know their doctors wouldn't want them to have just yet. But after what they've been through, a couple of crappy hospital cheeseburgers and some potato chips won't harm them. I threw in two chocolate chip cookies for good measure.

As I head into the corridor, toward the elevators, my phone buzzes with an incoming message. I stop, free up one of my hands, and reach for my phone.

It's a text from Mara.

On my way. Need to talk ASAP about getting the girls out of there. Wiley is with me.

"What? Get them out? Why?"

I respond with my questions and then wait near the elevator. Sure as I step into it, I'll lose my signal, so I wait here for her to reply. None arrives. Now, the girls' food is getting cold, so I head up anyway, hoping she'll get back to me and clear this up.

Wiley is with her, but what about Blackwell? And where is Nate? I ponder the questions as the elevator's digital display shows each floor until it stops on the fourth. The doors part, and for a moment, I hesitate to step out. The fact that Officer Wiley is coming with Mara gnaws at my brain because only one reason comes to mind why she would do that.

"They know who he is."

I drop the bag of food on a nearby side table and hurry back into the elevator, going down. There's an officer at the information desk, so if something's up, he'll know about it. "I need to tell Nate."

As I type a message to him, knowing he's still at the police station, I realize that if the police identified the kidnapper, and Wiley wants to move the girls, that means the kidnapper could be close. But how close? Is he already here?

72
NATE

Blackwell's office is halfway down the hall. I glance back once, hoping Wiley and Mara are already en route to the hospital. The girls need to be gone before anyone catches wind of what we know.

I reach the office. The door is closed, so I knock, fully prepared to keep this son of a bitch occupied as long as necessary. We're in this situation because of me. I saved that video for my own personal insurance, and my daughter was taken as a result.

I don't know how Blackwell found it, but it's the only answer that makes any sense. Then again, he's a cop. Would anyone think twice if he'd come to the store, selling the staff on a made-up story I authorized him to go into my office? Who's going to question that? Has he been in our home, too? "Christ."

I get no answer from inside. All the blinds are closed—on the door, on the windows—so I try the handle. The door's unlocked. Glancing over my shoulder to make sure I'm in the clear, I push it open. First thing I see is his desk and an empty chair. There's no sign of him. No jacket slung over the back, no stale cup of coffee sitting on his desk. "Shit."

Without wasting another moment, I return to the corridor. Two officers are heading toward me. "Excuse me? I'm Nate Brewer, and I'm looking for Officer Blackwell. Have you seen him?"

The cops trade glances, both shaking their heads, when one of them speaks, "Fraid not. I can call and find out where he is."

"Uh, no, thank you. I'll contact his partner, Officer Wiley." I deliver a perfunctory smile as they continue on their way. "Okay. Now what?" I reach for my phone and call Ashley. It takes two rings before she answers.

"You got my text?" she asks without so much as a hello.

"No. You texted?"

"Nate, I think the girls are in danger," she adds.

"They are." I don't question why she thinks this. There's no time. "Wiley is on her way. Look, it's Blackwell, okay? He's the one who took them."

"No. No, that's not right. He was here. He talked to Lexi already."

"What? When? Is he still there?" I raise my hand as if she can see me. "Ash, listen to me. He's the one. You have to believe me. Now, I need you to stick close to the girls until Wiley can get them out of there, okay? If he's still there, do not let him near them, you understand? Not even for a second. Wiley thought he was here, so I don't think any of us knows where he is right now."

"Yeah, okay. Mara texted to say they were on their way."

"Good. Stay with the girls until she arrives. Then help get them as far away from that hospital as possible."

"What are you going to do? Aren't you coming, too?" she asks.

"I'll confirm whether Blackwell is here. I need a few more minutes. If I can't find him, I'll head your way. Wiley should be there soon. I'll feel a lot better when she is."

"Me, too. I don't understand any of this."

I close my eyes. "I know. Wiley will explain. Please, honey, don't let him get close to those girls again. Whatever you have to do…"

"I'll do."

She ends the call, and I pocket my phone. Now, I have to find out where Blackwell is because if he's gone, then I'm gonna guess he knows we're onto him.

I return to his office, walking inside like I belong here. "Where the hell are you?" I round his desk, hands on hips, searching for anything that will shed light on his location.

I rifle through his papers. Nothing. I pull out the pencil drawer—still nothing. Then, as I yank out the second drawer down, I find a burner phone. It's definitely not police-issue. This thing is a flip phone. The only people who have those are the ones trying to keep others out of their business.

I open it and press the button to see his recent calls. Only one number. Multiple calls over multiple days. "Jesus." My finger hovers over the call button, and finally, I press it. It rings once. Twice.

A man answers. "Are the girls ready?"

My stomach drops. I feel the floor go loose beneath me, and I force myself to speak. "They're ready." Shit, do I even sound like Blackwell?

He pauses for too long. I close my eyes, praying he believes my act.

"Good. Drop them at the rest stop off Route 20 at midnight. You'll see a black van parked in the rear lot. Put them inside and leave."

I write down the location, my thoughts swirling at what the hell all of this means. But in the back of my mind—I know.

"I'll be in touch for your next pickup," he says.

My voice catches. I make a non-committal sound, like a grunt —I don't even know what I'm doing anymore.

"Same deal as before," the man adds. "Don't fuck this up. And don't sample the merch. Got it?" The line goes dead.

Sample the merch? What the hell? I stare at the phone like it's about to catch fire in my hand. The room closes in on me. Wiley was right. Blackwell's a goddam trafficker.

73
LEXI

We've been quiet for a while, Skye and me, the reality of our situation settling around us. Mom stepped out a few minutes ago to let us talk. She doesn't know any of this yet, but I know that's about to change.

I look at Skye. "We have to tell our parents that Officer Blackwell is the man who took us."

"Do you think he's here?" she asks.

"I hope not." I glance at the door. "But we need to do this now."

"Yeah, okay. Maybe your mom knows where my parents are."

"Maybe." I get up from the wheelchair and walk toward the door. "I'll be right back."

"Don't leave me alone for long, Lexi," Skye begs.

"I won't, pinky swear." I push open the door and crane left, then right down the sterile hallway. I see no carts rolling past, no one in scrubs walking around. Where *is* everyone?

"Mom?" I call out, but get no response. "*Mom!*" Still no answer. My stomach twists. "I gotta go to the nurses' station. I'll be right back."

"Lex, wait," Skye says.

"I have to find my mom. She's not out here. I'll be quick." As I walk on the cold, gray-speckled floor down the hallway, I freeze at the sound behind me. Footsteps. The only thing that's back there is a door that leads to some restricted part of the hospital. It's probably a doctor or something. So, I turn around.

My breath catches as my eyes land on him—Officer Blackwell.

We both know what's about to happen. We both know I understand exactly who he is now.

I run back into the room. "Skye!" I shout.

She's already halfway out of bed, wide-eyed, barefoot.

I don't need to say it. She sees it in my face.

"He's here?"

I nod.

Her breath hitches, but she doesn't freeze. Instead, she yanks her arm, ripping the IV right out of it, and looks me dead in the eye. "We're getting out of here."

We take off running, shooting back into the hallway. I see him still standing there like a freaking statue, so we veer left, and then round the corner toward the stairwell.

Blackwell's voice booms down the corridor. "Girls—wait! I'm here to help you."

Neither of us chance a look back. He's a liar and a monster. We need to find help. I hit the bar of the stairwell door with my shoulder, and we stumble inside, the metallic slam of the door behind us.

"Which way?" Skye yells.

"Down!"

We run, doing our best to keep our balance as we hurry down the stairs, our hands practically useless to us right now. But we don't stop. We can't. Somewhere above us, the door bangs open again. He's coming.

"Almost there," I shout, though I don't know if it's true. "We just have to hold on. Someone will help us."

We hurry to the lower floor, our steps echoing around us. The exit door is in sight. His steps sound closer now. He's coming fast. We have to get out of here. I feel blood on my left arm and realize I'm bleeding. It trickles onto my hospital gown, down my legs, and onto the steps.

"Girls," he says, his voice calm like he's about to offer us a ride. "You're scared. I get it. But I'm not going to hurt you."

Skye looks at me, sheer determination in her gaze, then she turns back. "Fuck you, asshole!" She moves in front of me like a shield. "I know it was you behind that mask, you freak! You tried to kill us!"

His gaze flickers. "You're mistaken. You're on a lot of medication right now. You don't know what you're saying."

"Liar," I shout.

He calmly walks down the few steps we have between us.

"Stay back!" Skye yells, widening her stance as she continues to block him from me. "You stay the hell away from us!"

She turns to me. "Go, Lexi! Run!"

I can't leave her. Not again. "We can make it, Skye. Both of us." I look down the stairwell. We're so close to the bottom—to the exit, where we can get help.

"I mean it!" she shouts at me. "Go!"

He closes the distance between us. I feel myself growing weaker, still losing blood. "We can still make it, Skye. Come on!"

Too late. He lunges at her, and she rams her shoulder into him, knocking him off-balance.

"Run, Lexi!" she screams.

"Screw that." I step in front of her while Blackwell leans against the railing, trying to regain his footing. This is it. He's reaching for his gun. I drop down to the steps and grab his leg, wrapping my arms around it, then I pull. Hard.

Blackwell's foot skids out from under him. He loses balance and grasps for the railing, but misses. Instead, he slips down the stairs, knocking his head along the way.

I watch him fall, his gaze locked onto mine. But I break away to find Skye. She's pressed against the wall, out of breath, bleeding. Then I turn back to him.

He lands on the bottom with a resounding thud. Soft moans escape him as he shifts his body. We have seconds, at best, to get out of here before he rises again—or reaches for his gun.

Skye moves next to me, looking down at him. "We have to go. Lex. Now."

We hurry toward the landing, our eyes fixed on Blackwell. And when we reach the exit, only feet away from him, the overwhelming urge to stomp on his face consumes me. I want to make him hurt the way he made us hurt.

But then I feel it—a hand. I look down, and he's grasping at me, trying to clamp down around my ankle. I scream. "Skye!"

She kicks at him, hard, but he won't go. He's pulling me down. I wrap my arm around the rail, using the crook of my elbow to keep myself in place. "Go! Get help, now!" I tell Skye. But she just keeps kicking him.

His free hand moves toward the gun at his side. He's going to shoot us. "Skye, please go. Go get help!"

"I'm not leaving you!"

"He's going to kill us!" His fingers dig into my ankle, pulling me down. My arm feels like it's going to snap off, but I hold on for dear life.

Skye keeps kicking him, harder and harder. Her heel crashes hard against his temple, and finally...his grip on me slips away.

"Now, Lexi! Run!"

We dart off, making it to the landing. I burst through the door, and both of us spill out onto the floor of the lobby. My legs are trembling, and I can't tell if it's the meds or the adrenaline or the fact that we escaped him again. I don't care. I just want—

"Lexi!" a voice cries out.

I raise my sights. "Mom?"

Two nurses rush toward us. One of them picks me up, then Skye. That's when I hear another voice.

"Oh my God—Skye!" It's her mom, and she pushes past mine, pulling Skye into her arms, half sobbing, half checking every inch of her. "You're okay. You're okay."

She's not. Those pins in her hand...they're all messed up.

Tears flood my eyes as Mom takes hold of me. "He came for us—Officer Blackwell. He chased us and—"

"Where is he now?" Mom demands.

"In the stairwell," I reply. "We did what we could to get away from him. He slipped and fell. He's hurt."

Mom turns back to a woman in a police uniform. "You have to stop him."

But before Mom can even get out the words, the officer rushes by us, heading straight for the stairwell. She waves over another officer. "Get them away from here." She yanks out her gun, aims it ahead, and opens the stairwell door.

The other cop ushers us away. Me and Mom just watch as the woman stands there, the stairwell door wide open. "What's she doing?"

Mom squeezes me tight. "Her job. Officer Wiley will take care of this."

The officer picks up her radio. "Requesting backup at Grant General. Wounded suspect on the loose—Suspect is Officer Dennis Blackwell. I repeat, suspect is Officer Dennis Blackwell."

"What?" I pull away from Mom and run to the stairwell door. "What's going on?"

Wiley raises her hand to keep me from getting any closer. Then she shoots a look at our moms. "Blackwell's gone."

74
NATE

When I enter the hospital, I see my wife and daughter standing in the lobby. "Oh, thank God." I jog toward them, but then I notice Officer Wiley and other cops huddled nearby. "What's going on?"

Ashley looks at Mara, then at me. "They're searching for Blackwell. He's here, they think...somewhere. But he's hurt."

"He came after us," Lexi says. "We tried to stop him."

"Hey, hey. It's okay, honey." I pull in close to her. "They'll find him. I promise." But when I see Mara and Ashley's faces, they don't appear certain.

Wiley calls out orders and signals to the officers with a sharp nod. "Get this place locked down. Block every exit! Do not let him leave!"

One officer stays with us. The others move fast. Wiley doesn't wait either—she's already moving.

The officer's radio flares, and a voice cuts in. "We've got eyes. Second floor. East wing. Pediatrics."

"On my way," Wiley's voice sounds. "You get a clear shot—take it!"

Chaos surrounds us. Nurses, doctors, visitors—they all huddle nearby while the police run in every direction.

I notice blood dripping down Lexi's arm. "Oh my God. Sweetheart, you're bleeding. Someone needs to come look at you."

"I'm okay, Dad."

"No, you're not." I step away, back toward the nurses' station. "Excuse me?" Only two people are here, and they're both crouched low. "Hey, I need some help over here. My daughter's..."

A scream pierces my ears. I whip around, eyes wide, desperate to make sense of what I'm seeing. "Lexi!" I yell.

Everything moves in slow motion. Ashley reaches for our daughter. Mara moves to block Skye. An officer grabs his gun.

I look left. "No." The single word is barely audible to my own ears.

Blackwell stands firm, gun aimed at Lexi. There's no way out. He sees it. "No!" I run toward my daughter. A gun fires, stopping me in my tracks. I search for the source. Who fired? Who's hit? Another round goes off. I instinctively duck, shielding my head with my arms.

Lexi screams. Ashley pulls her back. I stand again, my feet trying to gain traction on the tile floor as I rush toward my family. An officer falls—hit by the gunfire. I turn to Blackwell. He stumbles back, clutching his chest.

Another shot. I snap back to see Wiley, weapon trained on Blackwell, a whiff of gunpowder drifting toward me.

Blackwell collapses to the ground.

All I hear is the sound of my own breathing. I see Ashley holding onto Lexi. Mara is still shielding Skye. No one moves. An officer lies on the ground, blood pooling from under him. Wiley passes in front of me, running toward the injured cop. Doctors and nurses crowd in, tending to the victims. Tending to Blackwell.

"Are you all right?"

I feel a hand grip my arm and see Wiley. She helps me to my feet. "I'm okay." I walk to my family. Ashley and Lexi run into my arms. I hold onto them for dear life.

Doctors whisk away the injured officer on a gurney while Blackwell remains on the ground. I don't see him breathing. I look at Wiley. "Is he dead?"

She eyes the girls, then me. "He's dead."

I nod, tears filling my eyes. "Come on, girls. Let's go sit down." I usher my family toward the far corner. Mara and Skye follow. We all stare at each other, not knowing what to say.

I look at Mara and Skye, having no idea if Skye knows what happened to her father, though now isn't the time to tell her. And as I look at my family again, I realize how close I was to losing them both. But I know that punishment still awaits us all. We aren't going to escape justice, Mara, Ashley, and me.

The worst of it is over. The man who took our girls is dead. But I know more girls are out there, and I know where Blackwell's partners will be at midnight.

"Excuse me." I stand, and Ashley grabs onto me. "It's okay. I'm just going to talk to Officer Wiley for a minute." I chance a look at Mara, and it seems she knows this isn't over for the three of us, either. But there is still something I can do to help make things right.

I make my way toward the officers. "Sorry for the interruption. Officer Wiley? May I have a word?"

She nods to her colleagues and then follows me as I walk toward the exit. "I know we have unfinished business, Mr. Brewer, but it'll have to wait a little while. I assumed you'd be all right with that."

"Yes, of course. But it's not that."

Wiley folds her arms. "Then what is it?"

"When I was searching for Blackwell back at the station." I reach into my pocket. "I found this."

She eyes the flip phone in my hand.

"I called the most recent number, thinking it would lead me to finding him. Instead, a man answered. He told me to drop off the girls at a rest stop at midnight tonight. Put them inside a black van and then leave."

Wiley lowers her gaze, half in relief, and half in disgust. "Do you know which rest stop?"

"I do. I wrote it down. But I didn't get the man's name."

She looks past me. "So, he was trafficking girls."

"Seems like it." I take a breath. "You have a chance to stop it, Officer Wiley. Hopefully, for good, so other girls don't have to go through what my daughter and Skye Metcalf went through."

She takes the phone from me. "Thank you, Mr. Brewer. I imagine you've just saved a lot of young girls. Rest assured, we will act on this."

"Good." I turn to walk away.

"I'm afraid it won't change anything for you," she adds.

I stop and turn back. "I know. What we did—it was inexcusable. You know, I believed Cash Goodell was at the heart of all our troubles."

"You no longer believe that?"

I purse my lips. "I think he turned a blind eye to something he suspected. And when Eric Downey showed up, well, I guess he figured we were going to get what we deserved."

"I'm not sure if he'll face charges," Wiley says. "Technically, he did nothing wrong. He suspected something, but he didn't know for sure."

"No, I understand. And I think Eric Downey was made aware of what we did because of Blackwell. The two of them—Blackwell probably knew what Downey intended to do, and it would've solved his problem. The girls would've been trafficked, and we would've been dead—Mara, probably imprisoned."

She nods. "Seems he had it all planned out. But you stopped him."

"No." I shake my head. "I didn't stop him. If anything, I gave him ammunition by hanging onto that video. The girls stopped him. Lexi and Skye. They saved themselves. I can only hope one day, Lexi will find a way to forgive her mother and me."

EPILOGUE

My mom always said that time heals. But she never said how much time, or what it's supposed to heal exactly.

It's been two months since we were taken—Lexi and me. The whole twisted truth about what our parents did came spilling out after it happened. The affair that started it all—destroying my friendship with Lexi.

My phone buzzes next to me as I sit propped up against my headboard, pillows surrounding me. I smile as I answer the FaceTime call. "Hey, Lex."

"Hey, Skye. Oh my gosh, you cut your hair."

I shrug. "Just did it today. Only a few inches. Summer's here, and it's super hot in this place."

"But your grandma and grandpa, they have a pool, right?" she asks.

"Yep. Me and Milo went swimming just before dinner. It was fun. I wish you could've been here. I haven't met any other kids yet. But I think I might try to find a summer job around town, so maybe I'll start to make some friends. How's your grandparents? Is your room all ready for you yet?"

"Yeah, it's finished. They painted it purple. I'm so over the whole pink thing," she replies, glancing around. "I like it. A summer job would be cool. Maybe I should get one too? It's hard—not knowing anyone around here. I get what you mean. At least you have Milo."

I swat my hand. "Eh, he's just my annoying little brother."

We laugh, pretending our worlds weren't torn apart. Pretending we didn't have to move out of Grant and move in with our grandparents in different cities. Lexi lives in Boise now. I live in Missoula.

"Maybe we'll get to hang out sometime soon," Lexi says. "I bet we could talk our grandparents into letting us spend a week together, either here or where you're at."

"That would be so lit," I reply. "But you know, I'm always here for you, Lex. We can talk whenever."

"Yeah, I know. Same..." She smiles. "Well, I guess I should go."

"Sure. Talk to you tomorrow?" I ask.

"You know it!"

I end the call. Me and Lex talk every day, even if it's only for a few minutes. But we don't mention all that happened. Not the basement. Not our parents. Maybe someday we'll be ready to talk about it again, but not anytime soon.

My dad is dead. My mom killed him. I don't hate her for it. I wish I did, but I can't. They said he attacked Lexi's dad. Did Mom need to shoot him? I don't know. Maybe not, but it happened anyway.

I found out Dad had accidentally killed a man who'd been walking along the side of the road, and that Lexi's mom was with him. But instead of calling for help, our parents—all of them—buried the man, keeping the truth from everyone.

Then came Officer Dennis Blackwell. The man who took us.

They told us he'd been part of a trafficking ring, going to different towns, using whatever contacts he'd had in the police force to keep his side hustle quiet.

He used our parents' secret as a weapon. Distracted them. Let them tear themselves apart while he took us, pointing blame at a son who was only searching for what happened to his dad.

I still wake up some nights with his voice in my ear, with the feel of him on top of me, the smell of his breath under the doll's mask.

Mom's in jail now. So are Lexi's parents. For concealing a dead body. For obstruction of justice. And for being an accessory after the fact. I shouldn't know these things, but I do, thanks to them.

I don't think I'll ever fully understand how they convinced themselves it was better to keep their secret. Would it have made Dennis Blackwell look somewhere else for his next victims? Maybe. Then again, I wouldn't wish what me and Lexi went through on anyone.

We were taken. He tried to break us. But we got free all on our own. We're tough as shit. And we're not the same girls we were before. How could we be?

Now? Me and Lex have each other. We talk about maybe going to the same college in a few years.

I hope that happens.

ABOUT THE AUTHOR

Robin Mahle has published more than 40 crime fiction novels, many of which topped the Amazon charts in the US, Canada, and the UK. And most recently, she has delved into the world of psychological thrillers.

Also a screenwriter, she has adapted some of her works into teleplays, which have gone on to place in film festivals nationwide.

From detectives to federal agents, and from killers to corruption, her page-turning tales grab hold and refuse to let go. Throw in tense action and thrilling twists, and it becomes clear why her readers come back for more.

Robin lives in Coastal Virginia with her husband and two children.

ALSO BY ROBIN MAHLE

The Kate Reid FBI Thriller Series (17 books)

The Chef (stand-alone psych thriller)

The Man in My Attic (stand-alone psych thriller)

The Compound (stand-alone psych thriller)

He's Lying About Everything (stand-alone psych thriller)

The Remy Fontaine Fugitive Hunter Thrillers (4 books)

The Det. Rebecca Ellis Thrillers (5 books)

The Allison Hart PI Thrillers (5 Books)

The Lacy Merrick Spy Thrillers (4 books)